Read ALL the CAT WHO mysteries!

THE CAT WHO COULD READ BACKWARDS: The world of modern art is a mystery to many—but for Jim Qwilleran and Koko it turns into a mystery of another sort . . .

THE CAT WHO ATE DANISH MODERN: Qwill isn't thrilled about covering the interior design beat for *The Daily Fluxion.* Little does he know that a murderer has designs on a local woman featured in one of his stories . . .

THE CAT WHO TURNED ON AND OFF: Qwill and Koko are joined by Yum Yum as they try to solve a murder in an antique shop . . .

THE CAT WHO SAW RED: Qwill starts his diet—and starts a new gourmet column for the *Fluxion.* It isn't easy—but it's not as hard as solving a shocking murder case!

THE CAT WHO PLAYED BRAHMS: While fishing at a secluded cabin, Qwill hooks on to a murder mystery—and Koko develops a strange fondness for classical music . . .

THE CAT WHO PLAYED POST OFFICE: Koko and Yum Yum turn into fat cats when Qwill inherits millions and moves into a mansion. But amid the caviar and champagne, Koko starts sniffing clues to a murder!

TURN THE PAGE FOR MORE
CAT WHODUNITS . . .

THE CAT WHO HAD 14 TALES: A delightful collection of feline mystery fiction from the creator of Koko and Yum Yum!

THE CAT WHO KNEW SHAKESPEARE: The local newspaper publisher has perished in an accident—or is it murder? That is the question . . .

THE CAT WHO SNIFFED GLUE: After a rich banker and his wife are killed, Koko develops an odd appetite for glue. To solve the murder, Qwill has to figure out why . . .

THE CAT WHO WENT UNDERGROUND: Qwill and the cats head for their Moose County log cabin for a relaxing summer—but when a handyman disappears, Koko must dig up the buried motive for a sinister crime . . .

THE CAT WHO TALKED TO GHOSTS: Qwill and Koko try to solve a haunting mystery in a historic farmhouse.

THE CAT WHO LIVED HIGH: A glamorous art dealer was killed in Qwill's high-rise apartment—and he and the cats are about to reach new heights in detection as they try to find out whodunit . . .

THE CAT WHO KNEW A CARDINAL: The director of the local Shakespeare production dies in Qwill's orchard—and the stage is set for a puzzling mystery!

THE CAT WHO MOVED A MOUNTAIN: Qwill moves to a new home in the beautiful Potato Mountains. But when a dispute between local residents and developers boils over into a murder case, he has to keep his eyes open to find the culprit!

THE CAT WHO WASN'T THERE: Qwill's on his way to Scotland—and on his way to solving another purr-plexing mystery!

THE CAT WHO WENT INTO THE CLOSET: Qwill's moved into a mansion . . . and it has fifty closets for Koko to investigate! But among the junk, Koko finds a clue—and now Qwill's unearthing some surprising skeletons . . .

THE CAT WHO CAME TO BREAKFAST: Peaceful Breakfast Island is turned upside-down by real-estate developers, controversy—and murder. It's up to Qwill and the cats to find out whodunit . . .

THE CAT WHO BLEW THE WHISTLE: An old steam locomotive has been restored, causing excitement in Moose County. But a mysterious murder brings the fun to a screeching halt—and Qwill and Koko are tracking down the culprit . . .

And turn to the back for a special excerpt from . . .

THE CAT WHO TAILED A THIEF

Available in hardcover
from G. P. Putnam's Sons

Jove titles by Lilian Jackson Braun

THE CAT WHO COULD READ BACKWARDS
THE CAT WHO ATE DANISH MODERN
THE CAT WHO TURNED ON AND OFF
THE CAT WHO SAW RED
THE CAT WHO PLAYED BRAHMS
THE CAT WHO PLAYED POST OFFICE
THE CAT WHO HAD 14 TALES
THE CAT WHO KNEW SHAKESPEARE
THE CAT WHO SNIFFED GLUE
THE CAT WHO WENT UNDERGROUND
THE CAT WHO TALKED TO GHOSTS
THE CAT WHO LIVED HIGH
THE CAT WHO KNEW A CARDINAL
THE CAT WHO MOVED A MOUNTAIN
THE CAT WHO WASN'T THERE
THE CAT WHO WENT INTO THE CLOSET
THE CAT WHO CAME TO BREAKFAST
THE CAT WHO BLEW THE WHISTLE
THE CAT WHO SAID CHEESE

THE CAT WHO TAILED A THIEF
in hardcover from G. P. Putnam's Sons

The Cat Who Said Cheese

Lilian Jackson Braun

JOVE BOOKS, NEW YORK

This Jove Book contains the complete text of the original hardcover edition.
It has been completely reset in a typeface designed for easy reading and was printed from new film.

THE CAT WHO SAID CHEESE

A Jove Book / published by arrangement with the author

PRINTING HISTORY
G. P. Putnam's Sons edition published February 1996
Jove edition / March 1997

The Putnam Berkley World Wide Web site address is
http://www.berkley.com/berkley

ISBN: 0-515-12027-8

A JOVE BOOK®
Jove Books are published by The Berkley Publishing Group,
200 Madison Avenue, New York, New York 10016.
JOVE and the "J" design are trademarks
belonging to Jove Publications, Inc.

PRINTED IN THE UNITED STATES OF AMERICA

10 9 8 7 6 5 4 3 2 1

Dedicated to Earl Bettinger,
the husband who . . .

ONE

Autumn, in that year of surprises, was particularly delicious in Moose County, 400 miles north of everywhere. Not only had most of the summer vacationers gone home, but civic-awareness groups and enthusiastic *foodies* were cooking up a savory kettle of stew called the Great Food Explo. Then, to add spice to the season, a mystery woman registered at the hotel in Pickax City, the county seat. She was not beautiful. She was not exactly young. She avoided people. And she always wore black.

The townfolk of Pickax (population 3,000) were fascinated by her enigmatic presence. "Have you seen her?" they asked each other. "She's been here over a week. Who do you think she is?"

The hotel desk clerk refused to divulge her name even

to his best friends, saying it was prohibited by law. That convinced everyone that the mystery woman had bribed him for nefarious reasons of her own, since Lenny Inchpot was not the town's most law-abiding citizen.

So they went on commenting about her olive complexion, sultry brown eyes, and lush mop of dark hair that half covered the left side of her face. Yet, the burning question remained: "Why is she staying at that firetrap of a flophouse?" That attitude was unfair. The New Pickax Hotel, though gloomy, was respectable and painfully clean, and there was a fire escape in the rear. There was even a presidential suite, although no president had ever stayed there—not even a candidate for the state legislature on an unpopular ticket. Nevertheless, no one had been known to lodge there for more than a single night, or two at the most, and travel agents around the country were influenced by an entry in their directory of lodgings:

> NEW PICKAX HOTEL, 18 miles from Moose County Airport; 20 rooms, some with private bath; presidential suite with telephone and TV; bridal suite with round bed. Three-story building with one elevator, frequently out of order. Prison-like exterior and bleak interior, circa 1935. Public areas unusually quiet, with Depression Era furnishings. Cramped lobby and dining room; no bar; small, unattractive ballroom in basement. Sleeping rooms plain but clean; mattresses fairly new; lighting dim. Metal fire escape in rear; rooms with windows have coils of rope for emergency use. Dining room offers breakfast buffet, luncheon specials, undistinguished dinner menu, beer and wine. No liquor.

No room service. No desk clerk on duty after 11
p.m. Rates: low to moderate. Hospital nearby.

Business travelers checked into the New Pickax Hotel
for a single overnight because no other lodgings were
available in town. Out-of-towners arriving to attend a funeral might be forced by awkward plane schedules to
spend two nights. In the hushed dining room the business travelers sat alone, reading technical manuals while
waiting for the chopped sirloin and boiled carrots. Forks
could be heard clicking against plates as the out-of-town
mourners silently counted the peas in the chicken pot
pie. And now, in addition, there was a woman in black
who sat in a far corner, toying with a glass of wine and
an overcooked vegetable plate.

One resident of Pickax who wondered about her was a
journalist—a tall, good-looking man with romantically
graying hair, brooding eyes, and a luxuriant pepper-and-
salt moustache. His name was Jim Qwilleran; friends
called him Qwill, and townfolk called him Mr. Q with affection and respect. He wrote a twice-weekly column for
the *Moose County Something,* but he had been a prize-
winning crime reporter Down Below—local parlance for
metropolitan areas to the south. An unexpected inheritance had brought him north and introduced him to
small-town life—a unique experience for a native of
Chicago.

Qwilleran was admired by young and old, male and
female—not only because he had turned his billion-
dollar inheritance over to charity. His admirers appreciated his down-to-earth style: He drove a small car,
pumped his own gas, cleaned his own windshield; he
walked around town; he pedaled a bike in the country.
As a journalist, he showed a sincere interest in the sub-

jects he interviewed. He responded courteously to strangers when they recognized his moustache and hailed him on the street or in the supermarket. Understandably he had made many friends in the county, and the fact that he lived alone—in a barn, with two cats—was a foible they had learned to accept.

Qwilleran's housemates were no ordinary cats, and his residence was no ordinary barn. Octagonal in shape, it was a hundred-year-old apple storage facility four stories high, perched on an impressive fieldstone foundation and topped with a cupola. To make the barn habitable, certain architectural changes had been made. Triangular windows had been cut in the walls. The interior, open to the roof, had three balconies connected by a spiraling ramp. And on the ground floor the main living areas surrounded a giant white fireplace cube with great white stacks rising to the roof. The barn would have been a showplace if the owner had not preferred privacy.

As for the cats, they were a pair of elegant Siamese whose seal-brown points were in striking contrast to their pale fawn bodies. The male, Kao K'o Kung, answered to the name of Koko; he was long, lithe, and muscular, and his fathomless blue eyes brimmed with intelligence. His female companion, Yum Yum, was small and delicate, with violet-blue eyes that could be large and heart-melting when she wanted to sit on a lap, yet that dainty creature could utter a piercing shriek when dinner was behind schedule.

One Thursday morning in September, Qwilleran was closeted in his private suite on the first balcony, the only area in the barn that was totally off-limits to cats. He was trying to write a thousand words for his Friday column, "Straight from the Qwill Pen."

Emily Dickinson, we need you!

"I'm nobody. Who are you?" said this prolific American poet.

I say, "God give us nobodies! What this country needs is fewer celebrities and more nobodies who live ordinary lives, cope bravely, do a little good in the world, enjoy a few pleasures, and never, *never* get their names in the newspaper or their faces on TV."

"Yow!" came a baritone complaint outside the door.

It was followed by a soprano shriek. "N-n-now!"

Qwilleran consulted his watch. It was twelve noon and time for their midday treat. In fact, it was three minutes past twelve, and they resented the delay.

He yanked open his studio door to face two determined petitioners. "I wouldn't say you guys were spoiled," he rebuked them. "You're only tyrannical monomaniacs about food." As they hightailed it down the ramp to the kitchen, he took the shortcut via a spiral metal staircase. Nevertheless, they reached the food station first. He dropped some crunchy morsels on two plates; separate plates had been Yum Yum's latest feline-rights demand, and he always indulged her. He stood with fists on hips to watch their enjoyment.

Today she had changed her mind, however. She helped Koko gobble his plateful; then the two of them worked on her share.

"Cats!" Qwilleran muttered in exasperation. "Is it okay with you two autocrats if I go back to work now?"

Satisfied with their repast, they ignored him completely and busied themselves with washing masks and ears. He went up to his studio and wrote another paragraph:

We crave heroes to admire and emulate, and what do we get? A parade of errant politicians, mad exhibitionists, wicked heiresses, temperamental artists, silly risk-takers, overpaid athletes, untalented entertainers, non-authors of non-books . . .

The telephone interrupted, and he grabbed it on the first ring. The caller was Junior Goodwinter, young managing editor of the *Moose County Something.* "Hey, Qwill, are you handing in your Friday copy this afternoon?"

"Only if the interruptions permit me to write a simple declarative sentence in its entirety," he snapped. "Why?"

"We'd like you to attend a meeting."

Qwilleran avoided editorial meetings whenever possible. "What's it about?"

"Dwight Somers is going to brief us on the Great Food Explo. He's spent a few days in Chicago with the masterminds of the K Fund, and he'll be flying in on the three-fifteen shuttle."

Qwilleran's petulance mellowed somewhat. The K Fund was the local nickname for the Klingenschoen Foundation that he had established to dispense his inherited billion. Dwight Somers was one of his friends, a local public relations man with credentials Down Below. "Okay. I'll be there."

"By the way, how's Polly?"

"She's improving every day. She's now allowed to walk up and down stairs—a thrill she equates with winning the Nobel Prize." Polly Duncan was a charming woman of his own age, currently on medical leave from the Pickax Public Library, where she was chief administrator.

"Tell her Jody and I were asking about her. Tell her Jody's mother had a bypass last year, and she feels great!"

"Thanks. She'll be happy to hear that."

Qwilleran returned to his typewriter and pounded out another few sentences:

> Collecting nobodies makes a satisfying hobby. Unlike diamonds, they cost nothing and are never counterfeited. Unlike first editions of Dickens, they are in plentiful supply. Unlike Chippendale antiques, they occupy no room in the house.

The telephone rang again. It was a call from the law firm of Hasselrich Bennett & Barter, and Qwilleran groaned. Calls from attorneys were always bad news.

The quavering voice of the senior partner said, "I beg forgiveness, Mr. Qwilleran, for interrupting your work. No doubt the Qwill pen is penning another quotable column."

"No apology needed," Qwilleran said courteously.

"I trust you are enjoying these fine autumn days."

"There's no better season in Moose County. And you, Mr. Hasselrich?"

"I savor every moment and dread the onslaught of winter. And how, pray, is Mrs. Duncan?"

"Progressing well, thank you. I hope Mrs. Hasselrich is feeling better."

"She recovers slowly, one day at a time. Grief is a stubborn infection of the spirit." Eventually the attorney cleared his throat and said, "I called to remind you that the annual meeting of the Klingenschoen Foundation will be held in Chicago at the end of the month. Mr. Barter will represent you as usual, but it occurred to me that you might like to accompany him, since you have never appeared at one of these functions. You would be warmly welcomed, I assure you."

To Qwilleran, corporate meetings were worse than editorial meetings. "I appreciate the suggestion, Mr. Hasselrich. Unfortunately, commitments in Pickax will prevent me from leaving town at that time."

"I understand," said the attorney, "but I would be remiss if I were to allow the invitation to go untendered."

There were a few more polite words, and then Qwilleran hung up the receiver with smug satisfaction; he had avoided one more boring meeting with the financial bigwigs. Upon first inheriting the Klingenschoen fortune, his financial savvy was so scant that he needed to consult the dictionary for the number of zeroes in a billion. Wealth had never interested him; he enjoyed working for a living, cashing a weekly paycheck, and practicing economies. When the billion descended on him, he considered it a burden, a nuisance and an embarrassment. Turning the vast holdings over to a foundation was a stroke of genius on his part, leaving him happily unencumbered. He returned to the typewriter:

> How do you recognize a nobody? You see a stranger performing an anonymous act of kindness and disappearing without a thank-you. You hear spontaneous words of wit or wisdom from an unlikely source. I remember an elderly man walking with a cane in downtown Pickax when the wind velocity was forty miles an hour, gusting to sixty. We sheltered in a doorway, and he said, "The wind knocked me down in front of the courthouse, but I don't mind because it's part of nature."

When the telephone rang for the third time, Qwilleran answered gruffly but changed his tune when he heard the musical voice of Polly Duncan. "How are you?" he asked anxiously. "I phoned earlier, but there was no answer."

"Lynette drove me to the cardiac clinic in Lockmaster," she said with animation, "and the doctor is astonished at my speedy recovery. He says it's because I've always lived right, except for insufficient exercise. I must start walking every day."

"Good! We'll walk together," he said, but he thought, That's what I've been telling her for years; she wouldn't take my advice. "I'll see you tonight at the usual time, Polly. Anything you need from the store?"

"All I need is some good conversation—just the two of us. Lynette is going out. À bientôt, dear."

"À bientôt."

Before returning to his treatise on nobodies, Qwilleran took a moment to relish Polly's good news. He still remembered her late-night call for help, her frightened eyes as the paramedics strapped her onto a stretcher, his own uneasy moments outside the Intensive Care Unit, and his long wait in the surgery wing of a Minneapolis hospital. Now she was convalescing at the home of her sister-in-law but yearning for her own apartment. After preparing a cup of coffee, he wrote:

> I began my own collection of nobodies Down
> Below, my first being a thirteen-year-old boy
> who did all the cooking for a family of eight.
> The next was a woman bus driver who set her
> brakes, flagged down another bus, and escorted
> a bewildered passenger onto the right one.

The next interruption was a call from John Bushland, the commercial photographer. "Say, Qwill, do you remember the time I tried to shoot your cats in my studio? We couldn't even get them out of their carrying coop."

"How could I forget?" Qwilleran replied. "It was the battle of the century—between two grown men and two determined cats. We lost."

"Well, I'd like to take another crack at it—at your house, if you don't mind. There's another competition for a cat calendar. They'd feel more comfortable on their own territory, and I could try for candids."

"Sure. When do you want to try it? In daylight or after dark?"

"Natural light works better for eye color. How about tomorrow morning?"

"Make it around nine o'clock," Qwilleran suggested. "Their bellies will be full, and they'll be at peace with the universe."

Eventually he was able to stretch his thesis to a thousand words, ending with:

> One word of caution to the novice collector of nobodies: Avoid mentioning your choice collectibles to the media. If you do, your best examples will become celebrities overnight, and there's no such thing as a prominent nobody.

Having worked against odds, the writer of the "Qwill Pen" finished in time for the meeting at the newspaper office. He said goodbye to the Siamese as he usually did, telling them where he was going and when he would return. The more one talks to cats, he believed, the smarter they become. His two Mensa candidates responded, however, by raising groggy heads from their afternoon nap and giving him a brief glassy stare before falling asleep again.

He walked downtown. No one in Pickax walked, except

to a vehicle in the parking lot. Qwilleran's habit of using his legs instead of his wheels was considered a quaint eccentricity—the kind of thing one could expect of a transplant from Down Below. He walked first to Lois's Luncheonette for a piece of apple pie.

The proprietor—a buxom, bossy woman with a host of devoted customers—was taking a mid-afternoon break and chattering to coffee-drinking loiterers. She talked about her son, Lenny, who worked the evening shift on the desk at the hotel and also attended classes at the new college. She talked about his girlfriend, Anna Marie, who was enrolled in the nursing program at MCCC and also worked part-time at the hotel. Students, she said, were glad to work short hours, even though the skinflint who owned the hotel paid minimum wage without benefits.

Qwilleran, always entertained by Lois's discourses, arrived at the newspaper conference in good humor.

The *Moose County Something* was a broadsheet published five days a week. Originally subsidized by the K Fund, it was now operating in the black. The office building was new. The printing plant was state-of-the-art. The staff always seemed to be having a good time.

The meeting was held in the conference room. Its plain wood-paneled walls were decorated with framed tear sheets of memorable front pages in the history of American journalism: *Titanic Meets a Mightier* . . . *War in Europe* . . . *Kennedy Assassinated.* Staffers sat around the large teakwood conference table, drinking coffee from mugs imprinted with newspaper wit: "If you can't eat it, don't print it" . . . "Deadlines are made to be missed" . . . "A little malice aforethought is fun."

"Come on in, Qwill," the managing editor said. "Dwight isn't here yet. Since we hate to waste time, we're inventing rumors about the mystery woman."

There were six staffers around the table:

Arch Riker, the paunchy publisher and editor in chief, had been Qwilleran's lifelong friend and fellow journalist Down Below. Now he was realizing his dream of running a small-town newspaper.

Junior Goodwinter's boyish countenance and slight build belied his importance; he was not only the managing editor but a direct descendent of the founders of Pickax City. In a community 400 miles north of everywhere, that mattered a great deal.

Hixie Rice, in charge of advertising and promotion, was another refugee from Down Below, and after several years in the outback she still had a certain urbane verve and chic.

Mildred Hanstable Riker, food writer and wife of the publisher, was a plump, good-hearted native of Moose County, recently retired from teaching fine and domestic arts in the public schools.

Jill Handley, the new feature editor, was pretty and eager but not yet comfortable with her fellow staffers. She came from the *Lockmaster Ledger* in the neighboring county, where the inhabitants of Moose County were considered barbarians.

Wilfred Sugbury, secretary to the publisher, was a thin, wiry, sober-faced young man, intensely serious about this job. He jumped up and filled a coffee mug for Qwilleran. It was inscribed: "First we kill all the editors."

Also present, watching from the top of a file cabinet, was William Allen, a large white cat formerly associated with the *Pickax Picayune*.

Qwilleran nodded pleasantly to each one in turn and took a chair next to the newcomer. Jill Handley turned to him adoringly. "Oh, Mr. Qwilleran, I love your column! You're a fantastic writer!"

Sternly he replied, "You're not allowed to work for the

Something unless you drink coffee, like cats, and call me Qwill."

"You have Siamese, don't you . . . Qwill?"

"Loosely speaking. It's more accurate to say that they have me. What prompted you to leave civilization for life in the wilderness?"

"Well, my kids wanted to go to Pickax High because you have a larger swimming pool, and my husband found a good business opportunity up here, and I wanted to write for a paper that carries columns like the "Qwill Pen." That's the honest truth!"

"Enough!" said the boss at the head of the table. "Any more of this and he'll be asking for a raise . . . Let's hear it for our gold-medal winner!"

Everyone applauded, and Wilfred flushed. He had come in first in the seventy-mile Labor Day Bike Race, yet no one at the newspaper knew that he even owned a bike— such was his modesty and concentration on his work.

Qwilleran said, "Congratulations! We're all proud of you. Your pedaling is on a par with your office efficiency."

"Thanks," said Wilfred. "I didn't expect to win. I just signed up for the fun of it, but I decided to give it my best shot, so I trained hard all summer. I was confident I could go the entire route, even if I came in last, but everything turned out right for me, and after the first sixty miles I suddenly thought, Hey, chump, you can win this crazy race! That was between Mudville and Kennebeck, with only a few riders ahead of me, so I gave it an extra push to the finish line. Nine bikers finished, and they all deserve credit for a great try. They were as good as I was, only I had something going for me—luck, I guess. I'm hoping to compete again next year."

This was more than the quiet young man had said in his

two years of employment, and all heads turned to listen in astonishment. Only Qwilleran could think of something to say: "We admire your spirit and determination, Wilfred."

Riker cleared his throat. "While we're waiting for the late Mr. Somers, let us resume our deliberations." Then he added in a loud, sharp voice, *"Who is the mystery woman and what is she doing here?"*

Mildred said, "She always wears black and is inclined to be reclusive. I think she's in mourning, having suffered a great loss. She's come to this quiet town to deal with her grief. We should respect her need for privacy."

Qwilleran stroked his moustache, a sign of purposeful interest. "Does she ever venture out of the hotel?"

"Sure," Junior said. "Our reporters in the field have seen her driving around in a rental car with an airport sticker, a dark blue two-door."

"And," Hixie added, signaling news of importance, "one day when I was getting an ad contract signed at the Black Bear Café, I saw her in the hotel lobby with a man! He was wearing a business suit and tie, and he was carrying a briefcase."

"The plot thickens," Riker said. "Was he checking out or checking in?"

Qwilleran said, "I haven't seen her. Is she good-looking? Is she young? Is she glamorous?"

"Why don't you have dinner at the hotel, Qwill, and see for yourself?"

"No thanks. The last time I went there, a chicken breast squirted butter all over my new sports coat. I considered it a hostile attack on the media."

Wilfred said shyly, "Lenny Inchpot told me she looks foreign."

"Very interesting," said Junior. "We have a foreign

agent in our midst, a scout for some international cartel planning to come up here and pollute our environment."

"Or she's a government undercover operator, casing the area as a possible site for a toxic waste dump," Riker suggested.

The new woman on the staff listened in bewilderment, uncertain how to react to the straight-faced conjectures.

"Or she's a visitor from outer space," Mildred said merrily. "We had a lot of UFO sightings this summer."

"You're all off-base," Hixie declared. "I say the man with a briefcase is her attorney, and she's Gustav Limburger's secret girl friend, now suing him for patrimony."

Laughter exploded from all except Qwilleran and the new editor. She asked, "What's so funny?"

"Gustav Limburger," Mildred explained, "is a short, bent-over, mean-spirited, eighty-year-old Scrooge, living in seclusion in Black Creek. He owns the New Pickax Hotel."

"Well, what's wrong with my theory?" Hixie demanded. "He's rich. He's got one foot in the grave. He has no family. It wouldn't be the first time a dirty old man made a deal with a young woman."

There was more laughter and then a knock on the door, and Dwight Somers walked into the conference room, saying, "Let me in on the joke." The PR man had looked better before he shaved off his beard, but what he lacked in handsome features he made up in enthusiasm and personality. He nodded to each one at the table and nodded twice to Hixie. "Sorry to be late, gang. The plane lost its left wing somewhere over Lockmaster. Enemy fire is suspected."

"No problem," Riker said, motioning him to a chair. "The K Fund will buy the airline a new wing."

"Welcome to the *Moose County Dumbthing!*" Junior

said, while Wilfred scurried to fill a coffee mug imprinted: "First we kill all the PR people."

The publisher asked, "Was this your first visit to Klingenschoen headquarters, Dwight? I hear it's impressive."

"Man! It's staggering! You're talking about an operation that occupies four floors of an office building in the Loop. They have a think tank of specialists in investments, real estate, economic development, and philanthropy. Their thrust is to make Moose County a great place to live and work without turning it into a megalopolis. They're for saving the beaches and forests, keeping the air and water clean, creating businesses that do more good than harm, and zoning that discourages high-density development."

"Sounds Utopian. Will it work?"

"If it works, it'll be a prototype for rural communities throughout the country—that is, if they want to thrive and still maintain their quality of life."

"What about tourism?" Junior asked.

"The K Fund soft-pedals the kind of tourism that alters the character of the community. They're bankrolling country inns that operate on a small scale, serve fine food, appeal to discriminating travelers, and get high-class publicity. For tourists on a budget they're promoting small campgrounds that don't clear-cut the woods."

Someone asked about business opportunities.

"Now we come to the point," Dwight said. "If there's one industry that's clean, indispensable, and positive in image, it's food! The county's already known for fisheries, sheep ranches, and potato farms. Now the K Fund is backing enterprises such as a turkey farm and a cherry orchard, ethnic restaurants, and food specialty shops. The Great Food Explo will be a festival of all kinds of happenings related to food." He opened his briefcase and handed out fact sheets. "The Explo opens with a bang a week from to-morrow. Any questions?"

Someone said, "It sounds like it could be fun."

"The trend is to food as entertainment," Dwight said. "There are a lot of foodies out there! People are dining out more often, talking about food, buying cookbooks, taking culinary classes, watching food videos, joining gourmet clubs. Some of the new perfumes on the market smell like vanilla, raspberry, chocolate, nutmeg, cinnamon . . ."

Riker said, "I wouldn't mind having a Scotch after-shave."

"Don't worry! They'll get around to that."

"Starting next week," Junior said, "we're expanding our food coverage to a full page."

Qwilleran asked, "I suspect the mystery woman is part of a publicity stunt for the Explo."

"No! I swear it on a stack of cookbooks," Dwight said. He closed his briefcase. "I want to thank you, gang, for this opportunity to cue you in. I hope you'll jump on the bandwagon and call me if I can help."

"It's an appetizing prospect," Riker said. "Let's send Wilfred out for burgers and malts!"

TWO

Qwilleran was a congenital foodie who needed no coaxing to participate in the Great Food Explo. He hoped it would open up new sources of material for his "Qwill Pen" column. Finding topics for the twice-weekly space was not easy, considering the boundaries of the county and the number of years he had been Qwill-penning.

From the newspaper he walked to Toodle's Market to buy food for his fussy felines. Toodle was an old respected food name, dating back to the days when grocers butchered their own hogs and sold a penny's worth of tea. Now the market had the size and parking space of a big-city supermarket, but not the hypnotic glare of overhead fluorescents. Incandescent spotlights and floodlights illuminated the meats and produce without

18

changing their color or giving Mrs. Toodle a headache. It was she who ran the business, with the assistance of sons, daughters, in-laws, and grandchildren. Qwilleran bought a few cans of red salmon, crabmeat, cocktail shrimp, and minced clams.

His next stop was Edd's Editions, the used-book store. Here there were thousands of volumes accumulated from estate sales in surrounding counties. Colorless books cluttered the shelves, tables, and floor, and Eddington Smith had a dusty, elderly appearance to match his stock. Also blending into the background was a portly longhair named Winston who dusted the premises with sweeps of his plumed tail. There was always an odor in the store, compounded of mildewed books from damp basements, the sardines that constituted Winston's diet, and the liver and onions that Eddington frequently prepared for himself in the back room. On this day the aroma was unusually strong, and Qwilleran made his visit brief.

"I want something for Mrs. Duncan, Edd. She likes to read old cookbooks. She finds them amusing."

"I hope she's feeling better?"

"She's recovered her sense of humor, so that's a good sign," Qwilleran said as he examined, hastily, three shelves of pre-owned recipe books. One was a yellowed 1899 paperback titled *Delicious Dishes for Dainty Entertaining,* compiled by the Pickax Ladies' Cultural Society. Leafing through it, he noted recipes for Bangers and Beans, Wimpy-diddles, and Mrs. Duncan's Famous Pasties. "I'll take it," he said, thinking, She may have been Polly's great-grandmother-in-law.

Meanwhile Eddington was unpacking a newly arrived carton of old books from a family of dairy farmers and cheesemakers.

Qwilleran spotted *Great Cheeses of the Western World—A Compendium.* "I'll take this, too," he said. "How much do I owe you? Don't bother to wrap them." He left in a hurry as the store odors became overwhelming.

Memories of the bookstore lingered in his nostrils as he walked home along Main Street, around Park Circle, through the theatre parking lot, then along a wooded trail to the apple barn. The theatre, a magnificent fieldstone building, had once been the Klingenschoen mansion, and the fine carriage house at the rear was now a four-car garage with an apartment upstairs. The tenant was unloading groceries from her car as Qwilleran crossed the parking lot.

"Need any help?" he called out.

"No thanks. Need any macaroni and cheese?" she replied with a hearty laugh. Her name was Celia Robinson, and she was a jolly gray-haired grandmother who supplied him with home-cooked dishes that he could keep in the freezer.

"I never say no to macaroni and cheese," he said.

"I've been meaning to ask you, Mr. Q. What do you think about the mystery woman at the hotel? I think you should investigate." Mrs. Robinson was an avid reader of spy fiction, and twice she had acted as his confidential assistant when he was snooping into situations that he considered suspicious.

"Not this time, Celia. No crime has been committed, and the gossip about the woman is absurd. We should all mind our own business . . . And how about you? Are you still in the Pals for Patients program?"

"Still doing my bit! They've started a Junior Pal Brigade now, and it's my job to train them—college students who want to earn a little money. Nice kids.

They're very good at cheering up house-bound patients." She stopped and sniffed inquiringly. "Did you just buy some rat cheese?"

"No. Only a book on the subject. It belonged to a cheesemaker and acquired a certain redolence by osmosis."

"Oh, Mr. Q! What you mean is—it stinks!" She laughed at her own forthrightness.

"If you say so, madame," he said with a stiff bow that sent her into further gales of laughter.

From there he tramped through the dense evergreen woods that screened the apple barn from the heavy traffic of Park Circle. As he approached the barn, he was aware of two pairs of eyes watching him from an upper window. As soon as he unlocked the door, they were there to meet him, hopping on their hind legs and pawing his clothing. He knew it was neither his magnetic personality nor the canned seafood that attracted them. It was the cheese book! Their noses wrinkled. They opened their mouths and showed their fangs. It was what the veterinarian called the Flehman response. Whatever it was called, it was not a flattering reaction.

Qwilleran gave the cheese book an analytical sniff himself. Celia was right; it had a definite overripe stink—like Limburger cheese. It had been many years since his introduction to Limburger in Germany, but it was memorable. *Ripe* was their word for it. *Rank* would be more descriptive.

Limburger, he recalled, was the name of the old man so uncharitably described at the editorial meeting. He sounded like a genuine character. Like most journalists, Qwilleran appreciated characters; they made good copy. He remembered his interviews with Adam Dingleberry,

Euphonia Gage, and Ozzie Penn, to name a few. He went into action.

First he relegated the cheese compendium to the tool-shed, hoping it would lose its scent in a few days. Next he consulted the Black Creek section of the phone book and called a number. There were many rings before any-one answered.

A crotchety, cracked voice shouted, "Who's this?"

"Are you Mr. Limburger?"

"If that's who you called, that's who you got. Whad-daya want?"

"I'm Jim Qwilleran from the *Moose County Some-thing.*"

"Don't wanna take the paper. Costs too much."

"That's not why I'm calling, sir. Are you the owner of the New Pickax Hotel?"

"None o' yer business."

"I'd like to write a history of the famous hotel, Mr. Limburger," Qwilleran persisted in a genial voice.

"What fer?"

"It's been a landmark for over a hundred years, and our readers would be interested in—"

"So whaddaya wanna know?"

"I'd like to visit you and ask some questions."

"When?" the old man demanded in a hostile tone.

"How about tomorrow morning around eleven o'clock?"

"Iffen I'm here. I'm eighty-two. I could kick the bucket any ol' time."

"I'll take a chance," Qwilleran said pleasantly. "You sound healthy."

"N-n-now!" came a cry not far from the mouthpiece of the phone.

"Whazzat?"

"Just a low-flying plane. See you tomorrow, Mr. Limburger." He heard the old man slam down the receiver, and he chuckled.

Before going to see Polly, Qwilleran read the fact sheet about the Great Food Explo. The opening festivities would center about a complex called Stables Row. It occupied a block-long stone building on a back street in downtown Pickax. In horse-and-buggy days it had been a ten-cent barn: all-day stabling and a bucket of oats for a dime. Later it was adapted for contemporary use, housing stores, repair shops, and offices in ever-changing variety. Now it was embarking on a bright new life. Large and small spaces had been remodeled to accommodate a pasty parlor, soup bar, bakery, wine and cheese shop, kitchen boutique, old-fashioned soda fountain, and health food store.

Special events during the Explo would include a pastry bake-off, a celebrity dinner-date auction, and a series of cooking classes for men only. Qwilleran knew his friends would coax him into enrolling, but he knew all he wanted to know about cooking: he could thaw a frozen dinner to perfection. He opened a can of minced clams for the Siamese and said, "Okay, you guys. Try to stay out of trouble while I'm gone. I'm going to visit your cousin Bootsie."

Qwilleran drove his car to Pleasant Street, a neighborhood of Victorian frame houses built by affluent Pickaxians in an era when carpenters had just discovered the jigsaw. Porches, eaves, bay windows, and gables had been lavished with fancy wood trim, to the extent that Pleasant Street had been nicknamed Gingerbread Alley. Here Polly's unmarried sister-in-law, the last Duncan-by-blood, had inherited the ancestral home, and here Polly was recuperating.

On arrival, Qwilleran went slowly up the front walk, gazing up at the architectural excesses with amazement. He was unaware that Bootsie, Polly's adored Siamese, was watching him from a front window. The two males—competitors for Polly's affection—had never been friendly but managed to observe an uneasy detente. Qwilleran turned a knob in the front door, which jangled a bell in the entrance hall, and Polly arrived in a flurry of filmy blue. She was wearing a voluminous caftan that he had given her as a get-well gift.

"Polly! You're looking wonderful!" he exclaimed. It had been painful to see her pale and listless. Now her eyes were sparkling, and her winning smile had returned.

"All it takes is a good medical report plus some blusher and eye shadow," she said gaily. "Brenda came over today to do my hair."

They clung together in a voluptuous embrace until Bootsie protested.

"Lynette has gone to her bridge club tonight, so we can have a tête-à-tête with tea and cookies. The hospital dietician gave me a cookie recipe with no sugar, no butter, no eggs, and no salt."

"They sound delectable," he said dryly.

They went into the parlor, which several generations of Duncans had maintained in the spirit of the nineteenth century, with velvet draperies, fringed lamp shades, pictures in ornate frames, and rugs on top of rugs. A round lamp table was skirted down to the floor, and as Qwilleran entered the room to take a chair, a fifteen-pound missile shout out from under the skirt and crashed into his legs.

"Naughty, naughty!" Polly scolded with more love

than rebuke. To Qwilleran she explained, "He was only playing games."

Oh, sure, he thought.

"Lynette wants me to move in permanently, and I'm tempted, because Bootsie loves the house. So many places to hide!"

"So I've noticed. Does he ambush all your visitors? It's a good thing I have a strong heart and nerves of steel."

Polly laughed softly. "How do you like the cookies?"

"Not bad. Not bad. All they need is a little sugar, butter, egg, and salt."

"Now you're teasing! But that's all right. I'm happy to be alive and well and teasable . . . Guess who visited me today and brought some gourmet mushroom soup! Elaine Fetter!"

"Do I know her?"

"You should. She's a zealous volunteer who works hard at working for nothing. She volunteers at the hospital, the historical museum, and the library. I find her very good on phones and cataloguing, but she's not well-liked, being somewhat of a snob. She lives in West Middle Hummock, and we all know that's a status address, and her late husband was an attorney with Hasselrich Bennett & Barter."

"How was the soup?"

"Delicious, but too rich for my diet. Gourmet cooks have a heavy hand with butter and cream. Incidentally, she grows her own mushrooms—shiitake, no less."

Qwilleran's interest was alerted. Here was a subject for the "Qwill Pen." There was something mysterious about mushrooms, and even more so about shiitake. "Would she agree to an interview?"

"Would she! Elaine loves having her name in the paper."

"When will you feel like restaurant dining again, Polly? I've missed you." Dining out was one of his chief pleasures, and he was a gracious host.

"Soon, dear, but I must be careful to order wisely. The dietician gave me a list of recommended substitutes, and she stressed small portions."

"I'll speak to the chef at the Old Stone Mill," Qwilleran said. "For you he'll be glad to prepare a three-ounce broiled substitute with a light substitute sauce."

She trilled her musical laugh. It was good to hear her laughter again. He realized now that her physical condition had affected her disposition, long before she felt chest pains.

"Did you have any other visitors today?" he asked, thinking about Dr. Prelligate. The president of the new college was being much too attentive to Polly, in Qwilleran's estimation, and the man's motives were open to question.

"The only one was my assistant," she said. "Mrs. Alstock brought some papers from the library for me to sign. She's doing an excellent job in my absence."

"I hope she filled you in on the latest gossip."

"Well—you probably know this—Derek Cuttlebrink is enrolled in Restaurant Management at the college. No doubt it was Elizabeth Hart's influence."

"Yes, a girlfriend with an income of a half-million can be subtly influential. Let's hope that Derek has finally found a career direction . . . What else did you hear from the library grapevine?"

"That Pickax is going to have a pickle factory. Is that good or bad?"

"Not good. We'll have to choose a Pickle Queen as

well as a Potato Queen and a Trout Queen. The whole town will smell of dill and garlic from July to October."

"I thought you liked garlic, dear." She was goading him gently.

"Not as a substitute for fresh air. Can you imagine the TV commercials for Pickax Pickles? They'd be done in animation, of course—a row of pickles wearing tutus and dancing to the Pickax Polka, with pickle-voices screaming, 'Perk up with Pickax Pickles.' . . . No, tell Mrs. Alstock there's no pickle factory on the K Fund agenda for economic development. The rumor mongers will have to go back to the drawing board."

"Well, are you ready for some gossip that's absolutely true?" Polly asked. "The mystery woman came into the library and checked out books on a temporary card!"

"Hmff! If she's a reader, she can't be all bad, can she? What kind of book? How to build a bomb? How to poison the water supply?"

"Book withdrawals are privileged information," she said with a superior smile.

"So the library knows her name and address."

"No doubt it's in the files."

Qwilleran smoothed his moustache in contemplation and looked at her conspiratorially under hooded eyelids.

She recognized the humor in his melodramatic performance and retorted sweetly, "You're plotting a Dirty Trick! The Pickax Plumbers will break into the library after hours and burglarize the files, and we'll have a Bibliogate scandal."

Before he could think of a witty comeback, the front door slammed. There were footsteps in the entrance hall. Lynette had come home early.

"I didn't stay for refreshments," she explained. "I decided I'd rather visit with you two."

"We're flattered. Sit down and have a cookie," Qwilleran said in a monotone. He was reflecting that Lynette was a decent person—pleasant, helpful, generous, well-meaning, and smart enough to play bridge and handle health insurance in a doctor's office, but . . . she didn't get it! It never occurred to her that he and Polly might like a little privacy—once in a while.

Polly said to her sister-in-law, "We were just talking about the mystery woman."

Pontifically Qwilleran announced, "I have it on good authority that she's a fugitive from a crime syndicate or a terrorist group. She knows too much. She's a threat to the mob. Her life is in danger."

Lynette's eyes grew wide until Polly assured her he was only kidding. Then Lynette asked, "Does anyone mind if I turn on the radio for the weather report? Wetherby Goode says the cutest things!"

Qwilleran listened politely to the meteorologist's inanities: "Rain, rain, go away; come again another day." Then he made an excuse to leave. Polly understood; she gave him apologetic glances. Bootsie always escorted him to the front door, as if to speed the parting guest. This evening Qwilleran was escorted by a committee of three, and there was no opportunity for a private and lingering goodnight. Polly, he decided, had to get out of that house!

Arriving at the apple barn, Qwilleran stepped from his car and was virtually bowled over by a putrid stench coming from the tool shed, a hundred feet away. He was a man who made quick decisions. The cheese book had cost him six dollars, but he knew when to cut his losses. He turned his headlights on the shed, found a spade, and dug a sizable hole in the ground. Without any obsequies he buried *Great Cheeses of the Western World*. He hoped it would not contaminate the water table.

The Siamese were glad to see him. They had been neglected most of the day. They had had no quality time with him.

"Okay, we'll have a read," he announced. "Book! Book!"

One side of the fireplace cube was covered with shelves for Qwilleran's collection of pre-owned books from Eddington's shop. They were grouped according to category: fiction, biography, drama, history, and so forth, with spaces between that were large enough for Koko to curl up and sleep. He seemed to derive comfort from the proximity of old bindings. He also liked to knock a volume off a shelf occasionally and peer over the edge to see where it landed. In fact, whenever Qwilleran shouted "Book! Book!" that was Koko's cue to dislodge a title. It was a game. Whatever the cat chose, the man was obliged to read aloud.

On this occasion the selection was *Stalking the Wild Asparagus*. Qwilleran often read about nature, and he had enjoyed Euell Gibbons's book, even though he had no desire to eat roasted acorns or boiled milkweed shoots. The chapter he now chose to read was all about wild honeybees, and he entertained his listeners with sound effects: *Bzzzzzzz*. The Siamese were fascinated. Yum Yum lounged on his lap, and Koko sat on the arm of the chair, watching the reader's moustache.

Halfway through the chapter, just as the wild bees were swarming from a hollow tree, Koko's rapt attention faltered, his ears pricked, and his tail stiffened. He looked toward the back door. It was late, Qwilleran thought, for a car to be coming through the woods without invitation. He went to investigate. Standing on the threshold he saw no headlights, heard no motor noise, but unnatural sounds came from behind the toolshed. He snapped on the exterior lights and ventured toward the woods with a high-powered flashlight and a baseball bat.

As he approached the shed, there was scrambling in the underbrush, followed by dead silence, but the putrid odor told the story. A raccoon had dug up the cheese book and left it there, muddy and disheveled. The question now arose: How to get rid of it? Using the flashlight, he scoured the tool shed for containers with airtight lids and consigned the cheese book to a plastic mop pail. O'Dell's janitorial service would know what to do with it.

There was also a metal tackle box, empty and slightly rusted—the kind a mass murderer Down Below had used to send dynamite through the mails. For one brief giddy moment, Qwilleran considered mailing the cheese book to his former in-laws in New Jersey.

THREE

Friday started with a whisper and ended with a bang! First, Qwilleran fed the cats. He watched in fascination as they groomed themselves from whisker to tail tip. They seemed to sense, Qwilleran thought, that a prize-winning professional photographer was coming and that they might become famous calendar cats. The female was dainty in her movements; the male brisk and business-like. He had extremely long, bold whiskers, and Qwilleran wondered if they accounted for his remarkable intuition. Koko was also a master of one-upmanship, and he had proved more than once that he had John Bushland's number.

Bushy, as the balding young man liked to be called, arrived without noticeable photo equipment—just a small, inconspicuous black box dangling around his neck.

Qwilleran met him at the door. "Come in quietly and make yourself at home. Avoid any sudden movements. Don't touch your camera. I'm making coffee, and we'll sit around and talk as if nothing is going to happen."

Bushy wandered into the library area and looked at titles on the shelves. "Wow!" he said softly. "You have a lot of plays. Were you ever an actor?"

"I was headed in that direction before I discovered journalism. A little acting experience, in my opinion, is good preparation for almost any career."

"Shakespeare . . . Aristophanes . . . Chekhov! Do you read this heavy stuff?"

"Heavy or light, I like to read them aloud and play all the roles myself."

"Do you realize how many plays have food in the title? *The Wild Duck, The Cherry Orchard, The Corn Is Green, Raisin in the Sun, Chicken on Sunday, A Taste of Honey . . .*"

Qwilleran brought a tray to the coffee table. "Sit down, Bushy, and have some coffee and shortbread from the new bakery on Stables Row. It'll remind you of our trip to Scotland. Ignore the cats."

They were warming themselves in a triangle of sunlight on the pale Moroccan rug. Koko had struck his leonine pose, with lower body lying down and upper body sitting up, like the fore and aft halves of two different animals.

Bushy said, "Junior wants me to pull a paparazzi stunt and get some candids of the mystery woman. He thinks they'll be useful to the paper and/or the police if she turns out to be a spy or a fugitive from the FBI or whatever. What do you think about her wig? I think it's a man in drag."

"I think everyone's overreacting," Qwilleran said.

"Tell me about the Celebrity Auction. I hear you're on the committee."

"Yeah . . . well . . . the Boosters Club is raising money to aid needy families at Christmastime. People will bid against each other to have a dinner date with a celebrity, such as the mayor. I volunteered to take someone out on my cabin cruiser for a picnic supper. I'm no celebrity, but I'll throw in a portrait sitting in my studio."

Roguishly Qwilleran asked, "Is this outing going to be chaperoned?"

"Well, now that you mention it, we expect some flak from the conservative element, but what the heck! If they can stage an auction Down Below with a few million strangers, we can have one up here, where everybody is always watching everybody."

Meanwhile the Siamese were rehearsing every pose known to calendar cats. Yum Yum lounged seductively, extending one long, elegant foreleg. Koko sat regally with his tail curled just-so and turned his head in a photogenic profile. The intense rays of the sun heightened the blue of their eyes and highlighted their fur, making every guard hair glisten.

Bushy said under his breath, "Don't speak. They're lulled into a false sense of security. It's the moment of truth . . . Say cheese, you guys." He stood up in slow motion, moved stealthily to the right vantage point, lowered himself gradually to one knee, and furtively raised his camera. Immediately Koko rolled over and started grooming the base of his tail, with one hind leg raised like a flagpole. Yum Yum rocked back on her spine and scratched her right ear, with eyes crossed and fangs showing.

The photographer groaned and stood up. "What did I do wrong?"

"It's not your fault," Qwilleran said. "Cats have a sly sense of humor. They like to make us look like fools, which we are, I guess. Sit down and have another cuppa."

Now the cats turned their backs, Yum Yum in a contented bundle of fur, while Koko crouched behind her. He was staring at her backbone and lashing his tail in slow motion. Then, with body close to the floor, he moved closer, wriggling his hindquarters. She seemed quite oblivious of his curious pantomime.

"What's that all about?" Bushy asked.

"They're just playing. It's a boy-girl thing."

"I thought they were fixed."

"It doesn't make any difference."

Suddenly, with a single swift leap, Koko pounced, but before he landed, she was gone, whizzing up the ramp with Koko in pursuit.

"Well, I've got to get back to the studio," Bushy said. "Thanks for coffee. Tell the cats I haven't given up!"

Before going to Black Creek for his interview with Gustav Limburger, Qwilleran had breakfast at Lois's Luncheonette. At that hour she was hostess, waitress, cook and cashier. "The same?" she mumbled in his direction. In a few minutes she banged down a plate of pancakes and sausages and sat down across the table with a cup of coffee.

"I hear your son won the silver in the bike race," he said.

"It ain't real silver," she said, jerking her head toward the bulletin board behind the cash register. It displayed the silverish medal, a green and white helmet, and a green and white jersey with a large "19" on the back. "You know what? He's in college now, and he's tellin' me all the things I been doin' wrong for the last thirty years. I bet those professors don't teach 'em about all the headaches in the hash-slingin' business. I should be teachin' at the college!"

"Does he plan to take over this place when he finishes his course?"

"Nah. His ambition is to be manager of the New Pickax Hotel! My God! That fleabag! He's outa his bleepin' mind."

"Do you know the old gentleman who owns it?" Qwilleran asked.

"Gentleman? Hah!" Lois made a spitting gesture. "He'd come in here for breakfast when you could get four pancakes, three sausages, and five cups o' coffee for ninety-five cents, and he'd leave a nine-cent tip! Talk about cheap! One day he had the nerve to ask if I'd like to marry him and run his mansion like a boarding house! Did I ever tell him off! I said he was too old and too tight and too smelly. All my customers heard me. He stomped out without payin' for his breakfast and never come back. I di'n't care. Who needed his nine cents?"

"I was under the impression he was well off," Qwilleran said.

"If he ain't, he should be! They built the state prison on his land! He made out like Rockefeller on that deal!"

The town of Black Creek, not far inland from Moose-ville, had been a boomtown when the river was the life-line of the county, and it flourished again when the railroad was king. After that, the mines closed and the forests were lumbered out, and it became a ghost town.

When Qwilleran drove there on Friday, it still looked like a no-man's-land. All that remained of downtown was a bar, an auto graveyard, and a weekend flea market in the old railroad depot. In the former residential area, all the frame houses had burned down or been stripped for firewood, leaving only the Limburger mansion rising grotesquely from acres of weeds. Victorian in style, with tall, narrow windows, a veranda and a turret, it had been a landmark in its day, being constructed of red brick. Local building materials were wood or stone; brick had to be shipped in by schooner and hauled overland by ox cart. The Limburgers had spared no expense, even importing Old-World craftsmen to lay the brick in artful patterns. Now one of the stately windows was boarded up; paint was peeling from the wood trim and carved entrance door; the lawn had succumbed to weeds; and the ornamental iron fence with spiked top was minus an eight-foot section.

When Qwilleran drove up, an old man was sitting on the veranda in a weathered rocking chair, smoking a cigar and rocking vigorously.

"Are you Mr. Limburger?" Qwilleran called out as he mounted the six crumbling brick steps.

"Yah," said the old man without losing a beat in his rocking. His clothes were gray with age, and his face was gray with untrimmed whiskers. He wore a shapeless gray cap.

"I'm Jim Qwilleran from the *Moose County Something*. This is an impressive house you have here."

"Wanna buy it?" the man asked in a cracked voice. "Make an offer."

Always ready to play along with a joker, Qwilleran said, "How many rooms does it have?"

"Never counted."

"How many fireplaces?"

"Don't matter. They don't work. Chimney blocked up."

"How many bathrooms?"

"How many you need?"

"Good question," Qwilleran said. "May I sit down?" He lowered himself cautiously into a splintery rocking chair with a woven seat that was partly unwoven. A dozen stones as big as baseballs were lined up on the railing. "Do you know what year this house was built, Mr. Limburger?"

The old man shook his head and rubbed his nose with a fist as if to relieve an itch. "My grandfader built it. My fader was born here, and I was born here. My grandfader come from the Old Country."

"Is he the one who built the original Pickax Hotel?"

"Yah."

"Then it's been in the family for generations. How long have you been the sole owner?"

"Long time."

"How large a family do you have now?"

"All kicked the bucket, 'cept me. I'm still here."

"Did you ever marry?"

"None o' yer business."

A blue pickup drove onto the property and disappeared around the back of the house. A truck door slammed, but no one made an appearance. Thinking of the uncounted bedrooms, Qwilleran asked, "Do you take roomers?"

"You wanna room?"

"Not for myself, but I might have friends coming from out of town——"

"Send 'em to the hotel."

"It's an interesting hotel, no doubt about it," Qwilleran said diplomatically. "Lately I've noticed a fine looking woman there, dressed in black. Is she your new manager?"

"Don't know 'er." Limburger rubbed his nose again.

Qwilleran had an underhanded way of asking questions that were seemingly innocent but actually designed to goad an uncooperative interviewee. "Do you dine at the hotel frequently? The food is said to be very good, especially since you brought in that chef from Fall River. Everyone talks about his chicken pot pie."

The old man was rocking furiously, as he lost patience with the nosy interviewer. He replied curtly, "Cook my own dinner."

"You do?" Qwilleran exclaimed with feigned admiration. "I envy any man who can cook. What sort of thing—"

"Wurst . . . schnitzel . . . suppe . . ."

"Do you mind if I ask a personal question, Mr. Limburger? Who will get the hotel and this splendid house when you . . . kick the bucket, as you say?"

"None o' yer business."

Qwilleran had trouble concealing his amusement. The whole interview resembled a comic routine from vaudeville days. As he turned away to compose his facial expression and consider another question, he saw a large reddish-brown dog coming up the brick walk. "Is that your dog?" he asked.

For answer the old man shouted in his cracked voice, "Get outa here!" At the same time he reached for a stone on the railing and hurled it at the animal. It missed. The dog looked at the stone with curiosity. Seeing that it was inedible, he came closer. "Mis'rable mutt!" Limburger seized a stick that lay ready at his feet and struggled to stand up. Brandishing the stick in one hand and clutching a stone with the other, he started down the brick steps.

"Careful!" Qwilleran called out, jumping to his feet.

The angry householder went down the steps one at a

time, left leg first, all the while yelling, "Arrrrgh! Get outa here! Filthy beast!" Halfway down the steps he stumbled and fell to the brick sidewalk.

Qwilleran rushed to his side. "Mr. Limburger! Mr. Limburger! Are you hurt? I'll call for help. Where's your phone?"

The man was groaning and flailing his arms. "Get the man! Get the man!" He was waving feebly toward the front door.

Qwilleran bounded to the veranda in two leaps, shouting "Help! Help!"

Almost immediately the door was opened by a big man in work clothes, looking surprised but not concerned.

"Call 911! He's hurt! Call 911!" Qwilleran shouted at him as if he were deaf.

The emergency medical crew responded promptly and proceeded efficiently, taking the old man away in an ambulance. Qwilleran turned to the big man. "Are you a relative?"

The answer came in a high-pitched, somewhat squeaky voice that seemed incongruous in a man of that size. He could have been a wrestler or football lineman. Also incongruous was his hair: long and prematurely white. The journalist's eye registered other details: age, about thirty . . . soft, pudgy face . . . slow-moving . . . unnaturally calm as if living in a daze. Here was a character as eccentric as Limburger.

The caretaker was saying, "I'm not a relative. I just live around here. I kinda look after the old man. He's gettin' on in years, so I keep an eye on him. Nobody else does. I go to the store and buy things he wants. He don't drive no more. They don't let him drive. That's bad, when you live way out here like this. He's got a bad temper, but he don't get mad at me. He gets mad at the dog that comes around and dirties the sidewalk. I told him he'd fall down them steps if they wasn't fixed. I could fix 'em if he'd spend some money on mortar and a few bricks. All it would take is about ten new bricks."

With rapt attention, Qwilleran listened to the rush of words that answered his simple question.

The caretaker went on. "Last Halloween some kids come around beggin' like they do, and he chased 'em away with a stick, like he does the dog. Same night, a brick come through the front window. Somebody took a brick outa the front steps and threw it right through the window. I'm not sayin' it was the kids, but . . ." He shrugged his big shoulders.

Since they were on the subject of damaged property, Qwilleran asked, "What happened to the section of fence that's missing? Did someone drive a truck through it?"

The bland face turned to the gaping space. "Some lady wanted to buy a piece of it, so the old man sold it. I dunno what she wanted it for. I hadda deliver it in my truck, and she give me five dollars. She di'n't have to do that, but it was nice. D'you think it was nice? I thought it was nice, but the old man said she shoulda give me ten." Limburger's helper never referred to his boss by name.

"By the way, I'm Jim Qwilleran from the *Moose County Something.*" He held out his hand. "I was interviewing Mr. Limburger about the hotel."

The fellow wiped his hand on his pants before shaking Qwilleran's. His eyes were riveted on the famous moustache. "I seen your picture in the paper. The old man don't take the paper, but I read it at Lois's. I go there for breakfast. It's yesterday's paper, but that don't matter. I like to read it. Do you eat at Lois's? Her flapjacks are almost as good as my mom's. D'you know my mom?"

Genially Qwilleran said, "I don't even know you. What's your name?"

"Aubrey Scotten. You know the Scotten Fisheries? My granddad started the business, and then my dad and uncles ran it. My dad died five years ago. My brothers run it now. I got four brothers. D'you know my brothers? My mom still lives on the Scotten farm on Sandpit Road. She grows flowers to sell."

"Aubrey is a good Scottish name."

"I don't like it. My brothers got pretty good names— Ross, Skye, Douglas, and Blair. I asked my mom why she give me such a dumb name, and she di'n't know. She likes it. I think it's a dumb name. People don't even spell it right. It's A-u-b-r-e-y. In school the kids called me Big Boy. That's not so bad."

"It's appropriate," Qwilleran said. "Do you work with your brothers?"

"Nah, I don't like that kinda work no more. I got me some honeybees, and I sell honey. I'm startin' a real job next week. Blair got me a job at the new turkey farm. Maintenance engineer. That's what they call it. I don't hafta be there all the time. I can take care of my bees. The hives are down by the river. D'you like bees? They're very friendly if you treat 'em right. I talk to 'em, and they give me a lot of honey. It was a good summer for honey flow. Now they're workin' on goldenrod and asters, and they're still brooding. I re-queened the hives this summer."

"I'm sure the bees appreciated that." It was a flip remark intended to conceal ignorance. Qwilleran had no idea what the man was talking about. He recognized possibilities for the "Qwill Pen," however. "This is all very interesting, and I'd like to hear more about your friendly bees. Not today, though; I have another appointment. How about tomorrow? I'd like to write about it in the paper."

The garrulous beekeeper was stunned into silence.

On the way back to Pickax, Qwilleran rejoiced in his discoveries: two more "characters" for the book he would someday find time to write. Both were worthy of further acquaintance. The good-hearted fellow who didn't like his name had the compulsive loquacity of a lonely person who yearns for a sympathetic audience. It was easy to imagine a comic dialogue between the talkative young man and the grumpy oldster who was stingy with words as well as money. It was less easy, however, to imagine Aubrey Scotten as a maintenance engineer.

Qwilleran knew about the turkey farm, underwritten by the K Fund. His friend, Nick Bamba, had been hired as manager—with option to buy in two years. They had sent him to a farm in Wisconsin to learn the ropes. At last Nick could quit his unrewarding job at the state prison near Mooseville. While the original Hanstable turkey farm would continue to supply fresh turkeys to the prison and to local markets, the new "Cold Turkey Farm" would raise birds, fast-freeze them, and ship to markets Down Below.

Meanwhile, Nick's wife, Lori, had submitted an idea to the K Fund which was accepted, and she would open a small restaurant in Stables Row. Details had not been announced.

Qwilleran admired the energy and ambition of the young couple, who were rearing a family of three as well as tackling new challenges. He questioned the wisdom, however, of hiring Aubrey Scotten as maintenance

engineer of the Cold Turkey Farm. As soon as he returned to the barn, he called directory assistance for the
number of the new enterprise and phoned the manager.

After a few pleasantries, Qwilleran said, "Nick, I just
met a man who says he's been hired as your maintenance engineer."

"Aubrey Scotten? Yeah, aren't we lucky?"

"What do you mean?"

"He's a genius at repairing things—anything! Refrig-
eration, automated machinery, automotive equipment—
anything! He has a God-given talent, that's all."

"Well!" Qwilleran said, "I'm surprised, to say the
least."

"It's a long story. I'll tell you when I see you," Nick
said. "And what do you think about Lori's venture?"

"I haven't heard any details."

"Call her! Call her at home. She'll be tickled to fill
you in."

The golden-haired Lori Bamba had been Mooseville
postmaster when Qwilleran first met her. Since then she
had started a secretarial service and, later, a bed-and-
breakfast inn on Breakfast Island, all the while parenting
three children and five cats. Now she was opening a
restaurant!

"How's it going?" he asked her on the phone.

"Super! We'll be ready to open next Friday."

"What's the name of your restaurant?"

"First, I have to ask you a question. What does spoon-
feeding mean to you, Qwill?"

"Being sick in bed when I was a kid."

"Well, smarty, the dictionary says it means pampering
and coddling. My family loves any kind of food that can
be eaten with a spoon, so I'm opening a high-class soup
kitchen called the Spoonery."

"You mean you'll serve nothing but soup?"

"Soups and stews—whatever can be eaten with a spoon. Eat in or take out. How does it sound?"

"Daring! But if it's good enough for the K Fund, it's good enough for me."

"You'll like it! I've got dozens of exciting recipes."

"Well, I wish you luck, and I'll be your first customer. Just don't serve turnip chowder or parsnip bisque!"

Koko was antsy that afternoon. First, he walked away from the feeding station when the midday treat was served; he drove Yum Yum crazy by pouncing on her and chasing her up to the rafters; he pushed several books off the library shelves. When he started rattling the handle of the broom closet, Qwilleran got the message. As soon as the door was opened, Koko bounded into the closet and sat on top of the cat-carrier.

"You rascal!" Qwilleran said. "You want to roll on the concrete!"

During the summer he had taken the Siamese to the cabin at the beach on several occasions, where their chief pleasure was rolling on the concrete floor of the screened porch. They writhed and squirmed and flipped from side to side in catly bliss that Qwilleran failed to understand. Yet, he indulged their whims. Soon they were driving to the log cabin he had inherited from the Klingenschoen estate.

It was a thirty-mile jaunt to the lake. In cat-miles it was probably perceived as a hundred and thirty, although the Siamese rode in privacy and cushioned comfort in a deluxe carrier on the backseat. Thoughtfully, Qwilleran used the Sandpit Road route to avoid heavy truck traffic; eighteen-wheelers disturbed Yum Yum's delicate digestive system. Both cats raised inquisitive noses when they passed the Cold Turkey Farm and again when they reached the lakeshore with its mingled aromas of fish, seagulls, and aquatic weeds.

At the sign of a letter K on a post, a relic of the Klingenschoen era, they turned into a narrow dirt lane that wound through several acres of woods, up and down ancient sand dunes, and between oaks and pines and wild cherry trees. That was when Koko became excited, bumping around in the confines of the carrier and rumbling internal noises that alarmed his partner.

Qwilleran recognized the performance; the cat was sensitive to abnormal situations; something unusual lay ahead. He himself noticed recent tire tracks and was annoyed when he found another car parked in the clearing adjoining the cabin. He imagined insolent trespassers, surf-fishing and building illegal fires on the beach and throwing beer cans in the beach grass. When he parked behind the unauthorized vehicle, however, he noted a local license plate and a rental car sticker in the back window of a dark blue two-door.

His reaction was a gradual buildup of dumb disbelief, then amazement, then challenge and triumph! What a coup! He was about to come face-to-face with *that woman!* And he had her trapped!

FOUR

There was no doubt in Qwilleran's mind: the dark blue two-door with airport sticker in the window had been rented to the stranger who was mystifying Pickax. He had an exclusive news break! His colleagues would be green with envy.

The doors of the cabin were still locked; she would be walking on the beach, he assumed. The cabin perched on the crest of a high sand dune overlooking the lake, and he walked to the edge. At the foot of the weathered wooden steps leading down to the beach, he saw a large straw hat. Under it, with back turned to him, was a figure dressed in black, sitting in a folding aluminum chair—the kind perennially on sale at the hardware store.

He needed only a moment to decide on a course of action. He would avoid frightening her or embarrassing her; he had everything to gain by being pleasant—even hospitable. There were comfortable chairs on the porch; there were cold drinks in the car, as well as two good-will ambassadors who had winning ways—when they felt like it.

As he started down the steps, his thudding footsteps were drowned out by the splashing waves below and the screaming seagulls above. Halfway down, he coughed loudly and called out in a comradely voice, "Hello, down there!"

The straw hat flew off, and a dark-haired woman turned to look up at him.

"Good afternoon! Beautiful day, isn't it?" he said in the mellifluous voice he used in crucial situations.

She jumped to her feet, clutching a book. "My apology! I not know someone live here."

English was not her native tongue; her accent had an otherwhereness that he considered charming. "That's all right. I live in Pickax and just stopped to check for storm damage. There was a severe wind storm a few days ago. What are you reading?" That was always a disarming question, he had learned.

"Cookbook." She held it up for proof. "I go away now." Flustered, she started to fold her chair.

"You don't need to rush off. Perhaps you'd enjoy a glass of cider on the porch. It has a magnificent view of the lake. By the way, I'm Jim Qwilleran of the *Moose County Something*."

"Ah!" she said joyfully, focusing on his moustache. "I see your picture in the paper . . . But you are too kind."

"Not at all. Let me carry your chair." He ran down the few remaining steps. "And what is your name?"

She hesitated . . . "Call me Onoosh."

"In that case, call me Qwill," he said jovially.

She smiled for the first time, and although she was not a beauty by Hollywood standards, her olive complexion glowed and her face was radiant. At the same time, a gust of wind blew her dark hair away from her left cheek, revealing a long scar in front of her ear. She stuffed books and other belongings into a tote bag, and Qwilleran reached for it.

"Allow me."

As they reached the top of the dune, she exclaimed about the log cabin and the stone chimney. "Beautiful! Is very old?" She pronounced it *be-yoo-ti-ful*.

"Probably seventy or eighty years old." He ushered her into the screened porch. "Have a chair and enjoy the view, and excuse me for a moment while I unload the car and bring in my two companions. Do you like cats?"

"All animals, I adore!" Her face again glowed with happiness.

She could be in her thirties, he guessed as he went to the car. She could be from the Middle East. She may have lived in France. Her black pantsuit, far from being mourning garb, had a Parisian smartness.

He served the cider and asked casually, "Are you vacationing up here?"

"Yes, but no," she replied cryptically. "I look for place to live. I like to cook in restaurant."

"Where are you staying?"

"Hotel in Pickax."

"Have you been there long?"

"Two weeks. People very nice. Desk clerk give me big room in front. Very good. I talk to chef. I tell him how to cook vegetables. He try, but . . . not good."

"Yes, we do have friendly people here. How did you

happen to find Moose County? It's off the beaten path, and few people know it exists."

Shyly she explained, "My honeymoon I spend here—long time ago. Was nice."

"Honeymoons are always nice," Qwilleran said. "So your husband is no longer with you?" He considered that a good way of putting a prying question.

She shook her head, and her face clouded, but it soon brightened. The Siamese, who had been rolling and squirming on the concrete of the back porch, now arrived to inspect the stranger and leave their seal of approval on her ankles. "Be-yoo-ti-ful!" she said.

"They're especially fond of people who read cookbooks."

"Ah! Cooking I learn very young, but something more is always to learn."

"What do you think of the food in our local restaurants?"

She looked at him askance, from behind her curtain of hair. "Is not too good."

"I agree with you, but we're trying to improve the situation."

Brightening, she said, "Mediterranean restaurant—very good here, I think."

"You mean, stuffed grape leaves and tabouleh and all that? When I lived Down Below I haunted Middle Eastern restaurants. We used to ask for meatballs in little green kimonos."

"Very good," she said. "I make meatballs in little green kimonos." She waved a hand toward a tangle of foliage on the dune. "Wild grapevines you have in woods. Very good fresh. In jars, not so good." She paused uncertainly. "You have kitchen? I stuff some for you."

Qwilleran's tastebuds were alerted. "I have kitchen, and I have salt and pepper, and I drive into town to buy whatever you need." Without any intention of mocking, he was imitating her cavalier way with pronouns, verbs, prepositions, and adverbs.

"Is too much trouble," she protested.

"Not so! Tell me what to buy."

She recited a list: ground lamb, rice, onion, lemon, fresh mint. "I pick small young leaves—boil five minutes—ready when you come back."

Before leaving, Qwilleran checked out the Siamese. They were asleep on the guest bed. If Koko had wanted so badly to drive to the cabin, why had he spent five minutes rolling on the concrete and the rest of the afternoon in sleep? Cats were unpredictable, unfathomable, and impossible not to like. Koko raised his head and opened one eye. "Mind the house," Qwilleran instructed him. "I'm running into town."

There were stores in Mooseville, but he would hesitate to trust their meat. Fish, yes. Lamb, no. He drove to Pickax. At Toodle's Market, where he was a regular customer for lunch meat, the butchers knew him and gladly ground some lamb, fresh. Onoosh had not specified quantity, so he asked for two pounds, to be on the safe side. At the produce counter, a Toodle daughter-in-law helped him choose a lemon and three onions but said they never had fresh mint. "Everybody has it in the backyard," she said. "It grows like wild."

At the rice shelf he was puzzled. There was long grain, short grain, white, brown, precooked, preseasoned.

Another customer, better-groomed and better-dressed than the other women shoppers, said, "Having a problem, Mr. Q? Perhaps I can help you. I'm Elaine Fetter. We've met at the library, where I volunteer."

"Yes, of course," he said emphatically, as if it were true. She was a statuesque woman with an air of authority and surely some opinions about rice. "What kind of rice would you suggest for . . . uh . . . meatballs?"

"I believe you'd be safe with white short-grain. Do you have a good recipe for meatballs?" she asked. "I'm compiling a community cookbook for the Friends of the Library, and we'd be honored if you would let us print one of your favorite recipes. I know—"

At that moment they were both startled by a loud BOOM!

"Oh, heavens!" she exclaimed. "What was that? It sounded so close!"

"I'd better go and check it out," he said. "Excuse me. Thanks for the advice." He snatched a package of white short-grain and took his purchases to the check-out counter.

"Did you hear that sonic boom?" the cashier asked. "It was loud enough to curdle the milk."

"Sounded like an explosion on Pine Street," Qwilleran said. "They're doing construction work on Stables Row and could have hit a gas main."

As he pulled out of the parking lot, scout cars were speeding toward downtown, and the flashing lights of emergency vehicles could be seen coming from the hospital and the firehall. The trouble was not on Pine Street, however. Main Street traffic was being detoured. He parked where he could and ran toward the center of town.

One irrelvant and irreverent thought crossed his mind: Whatever the blast might be, it was *not* happening on the newspaper's deadline, and Arch Riker would have a fit! It would be Monday before the *Something* could report it, while WPKX would be broadcasting it all weekend.

That was the way it always seemed to happen in Pickax. Like the Friday night toothache after the dentist's office closed for the weekend, disasters always happened after the Friday newspaper had gone to press.

A procession of pedestrians was hurrying to the scene, and the shout went up: *"It's the hotel! The hotel blew up!"*

A cordon of yellow crime-scene tape kept onlookers away from the shattered glass and debris that covered the sidewalk and pavement in front of the New Pickax Hotel. There were businessfolk standing in front of their stores and offices . . . farmers in town on business . . . shoppers carrying bundles . . . teens wearing high school athletic jackets. Many were horrified; others were there for the excitement; a few grinned and said it was about time they bombed it. Stretcher bearers hurried up the front steps. The medical examiner arrived with his ominous black bag and was escorted into the building by the police.

"Somebody's killed," the watchers said.

On the far side of the yellow tape was a gathering of persons Qwilleran knew. To reach them he ran around the block and into the back door of Amanda's Design Studio. The shop was empty. He zigzagged through the furniture displays and found everyone on the sidewalk, watching and waiting: Amanda Goodwinter herself, her assistant, the installation man, and two customers. One of the studio's large plate glass windows was cracked. No one noticed Qwilleran's arrival; they were all looking up at the second floor of the hotel.

Like all the buildings on downtown Main Street, it was solidly built of stone that had survived fire, tornado, and even a minor earthquake. The windows of all three floors were shattered, however. On the second floor, wood sash had been blown out. Fragments of draperies and clothing hung from projections on the outside of the building. The arm of an upholstered chair lay on the sidewalk.

"Lucky it's only the arm of a chair," the installer said with a sly leer.

Amanda, cranky as usual, said, "Old Gus probably bombed it himself to collect the insurance, or had that creepy helper of his do the dirty work."

"He ain't creepy! He's an all-right guy!" the installer said belligerently. He was one of the big young blond men indigenous to Moose County, and he contradicted his employer with the confidence of an indispensable muscleman in a furniture business run by two women.

"Shut up and get some tape on that cracked glass!" Amanda shouted.

"Hi, Qwill!" said Fran Brodie, her assistant. "Are you covering this for the paper, or just nosing around?" She was not only a good designer and one of the most attractive young women in town; she was the daughter of the police chief and, as such, had semiofficial status. She said, "Dad always complains that nothing big ever happens on his turf, but this should keep him quiet for a while."

The chief was swaggering about the scene, towering over the other officers, giving orders, running the show. The state police were assisting.

"I was buying groceries and heard the blast," Qwilleran said. "Does anyone know what happened?"

In a confidential tone, Fran said, "They think it was a homemade bomb. They say room 203 is really trashed. Everyone's wondering about the mystery woman."

Qwilleran thought of Onoosh; hadn't the desk clerk given her a big room at the front? "Any injuries?" he asked. "Your dad was wearing his doomsday expression when he took the coroner into the building."

"Oh, he always looks like that when he's on duty. So far, it doesn't look serious. Leonard Inchpot came out with a bandage on his head, and he and some others were hustled away in a police car—to the hospital, no doubt. Someone said a chandelier fell on his head."

Outside the yellow-tape, bystanders were making guesses; a reporter was maneuvering to get camera shots; a WPKX newswoman was thrusting a microphone in front of officials and eyewitnesses. Inside the tape, an ambulance with open doors had backed up to the front steps. Then the coroner came out, and silence fell on the crowd. He was followed by medics carrying a body bag on a stretcher. A sorrowful moan arose from onlookers, and the question was repeated: Who was it? Guest or employee? No one knew. "I can't hang around," Qwilleran told the designer. "I'm due back in Mooseville. I'll tune in my car radio to hear the rest."

He wanted to break the news to Onoosh, gently, and he wanted to observe her reaction. It would reveal whether she was really a cook looking for a job in a restaurant, or the intended victim of a murderous plot.

As he drove back to the cabin, he heard the *bleat-bleat-bleat* of a helicopter. That would be the bomb squad from the SBI—the State Bureau of Investigation. His radio was tuned in, with the volume turned down to muffle the country music favored by the locals. He turned it up when an announcer broke in with a news bulletin:

"An explosion in downtown Pickax at four-twenty this afternoon claimed the life of one victim, injured others, and caused extensive property damage. Thought to be caused by a homemade bomb, the blast wrecked several front rooms of the New Pickax Hotel. A member of the staff was killed instantly. Others were thrown to the floor and injured by falling debris. All windows facing Main Street were shattered, and those in nearby buildings were cracked. The hotel has been evacuated, and Main Street is closed to traffic between Church and Depot Streets. Police have not released the name of the victim, pending notification of relatives, nor the name of the guest registered in the room that received the brunt of the blast. Police Chief Andrew Brodie said, 'There aren't many guests around on Friday afternoon, or the casualties would have been greater.' Stay tuned for further details."

Qwilleran stepped on the accelerator. A quarter-mile from the letter K on a post, he rounded the last curve in the road in time to see a car leaving the K driveway in a cloud of dust. It turned onto the highway without stopping, heading west. As he approached from the east, it picked up speed.

All his previous surmises were thrown into confusion as he covered the winding trail to the cabin faster than usual. Her car was gone. He thought, She sent me to buy lamb so she could escape; she was headed for the airport. Then he thought, Maybe she wasn't the target of the bomb; maybe she was involved in the bombing. He tried to make sense of the disparate elements: the eccentric owner of the hotel . . . the mystery woman . . . property insurance . . . the old man's tumble down the stairs . . . the mechanical genius who worked for him . . . the possibility of a homemade bomb . . . and all the rumors he had heard in the last two weeks. Qwilleran felt his face flushing. Having fallen for her ruse, he was too embarrassed to think straight. That woman could have ransacked the cabin! She could have taken the cats!

He jumped from his car when he reached the clearing

and rushed indoors, going first to the guest room. The cats were still asleep, drugged by the lake air. Then he checked the lake porch. She had left her beach hat, the folding chair, and three books from the public library. They were all cookbooks.

In the kitchen a paper towel was spread with damp grape leaves, and the saucepan in which they had been boiled was draining in the sink; the salt and pepper shakers were standing ready; the chopping board and knife were waiting for the onion; and the countertop radio was blaring country music. He turned it off irritably.

Only then did he realize that Onoosh had been working in the kitchen and listening to the radio when the bulletin was broadcast. She had dropped everything, grabbed her tote bag, and headed for the airport. She knew the bomb was intended for her. He searched the cabin, hoping she might have left a note, but all he could find was a number on the telephone pad. It looked familiar. He called it and was connected with the airport terminal. "Did the five-thirty shuttle leave on schedule?" he asked.

"Yes, sir."

"A woman was racing to catch it. Do you remember a woman in a black pantsuit boarding the plane?"

"Yes, sir," said the attendant, who sold tickets, rented cars, and even carried luggage in the small terminal. "She turned in a rental and ran to the plane. Didn't even have any luggage. Lucky we had a seat for her. On Friday nights we're usually sold out."

Now Qwilleran thought he understood. Whether or not she was a cook, she was a fugitive—in hiding—fearing for her life. With all due respect to the PPD and SBI, he believed they would never apprehend the bomber who killed the wrong person. The Pickax mystery woman, like the Piltdown man, would remain forever the subject of debate.

FIVE

Qwilleran sat glumly on the porch overlooking the lake without seeing the infinity of the blue sky, the turquoise expanse of water, and the white ruffles of surf at the shoreline. He was organizing his reactions. He grieved over the senseless death of a hotel employee; in a small town everyone was a friend or a neighbor or a nodding acquaintance or the friend of a friend. Further, he regretted the wanton destruction of the building, no matter how substandard its rating or how disliked its owner. And personally he was disappointed by the sudden departure of the fascinating woman who had said, "Call me Onoosh." An exclusive news story had slipped through his fingers; his vision of a Mediterranean restaurant on local soil had faded away; and he had lost a potential purveyor of meatballs in little green kimonos. All of these considerations added up to a determination to solve the who and why of the bombing. It was none of his business; it was police business. Yet, his curiosity began a slow boil.

Meanwhile, he had unwanted souvenirs of the afternoon's adventure: two pounds of ground lamb, a package of rice, and three large onions. The lemon he could use in Squunk water, an innocuous beverage from a local mineral spring. The rice could be returned to the store; Mrs. Toodle would be glad to give him a refund. As for the onions, he could hurl them into the adjoining woods—to spice the diet of a wandering raccoon.

The problem was . . . the lamb. When the Siameses taggered out of the guest room, he offered them a taste; they declined even to sniff it. "You ungrateful snobs!" he scolded. "There are disadvantaged cats out there who don't know where their next mouse is coming from!" He had pointed out that fact frequently, without effecting any change in their attitude. They liked Scottish smoked salmon, oysters, lobster out of the shell, caviar (fresh, not tinned), and escargots.

His next thought—to give the lamb to Polly as a treat for Bootsie—would lead to embarrassing inquiries and awkward explanations. His friend, though a wonderful woman in every way, was inclined to be overpossessive and unnecessarily jealous. That eliminated another solution.

To donate the lamb to Lois for her ever-bubbling soup pot would create a countywide stir. There were no secrets at the Luncheonette, and two pounds of ground lamb from the richest bachelor in northeast central United States would be good for two months of delectable gossip.

There remained Celia Robinson. As his so-called secret agent, she had proved an ability to follow instructions without asking questions, and she was probably the only individual in Moose County who could keep a secret. He telephoned her from the cabin, and there was no answer. He decided to put the problematic meat in the freezer. He knew Onoosh would never return, but if she did . . .

Qwilleran and the Siamese returned to the apple barn. There was no storm damage at the cabin; in fact, there had been no storm. The county was enjoying an exceptionally pleasant September.

He fed the cats a can of red salmon and then went to Lois's for the Friday dinner special, fish and chips. One of the part-time cooks was manning the deep-fryer, and Lois was waiting on tables, taking customers' money, and venting her rage about the bombing. Only a public figure with Lois's thirty years of experience could rave, rant, and rail so histrionically while pouring coffee and making change. Qwilleran's arrival launched another tirade:

"Oh! . . . Oh! . . . Did you hear the six o'clock news? D'you know who was killed? Anna Marie! Lenny's girlfriend! Sweet girl—never hurt a soul. Why her? Why her? . . . *Sit anywhere, Mr. Q. Fish and chips special tonight* . . . Only twenty years old! She was gonna be a nurse! Lenny and her were childhood sweethearts. They were goin' to college together. She worked part-time as a housekeeper at the hotel . . . *How many pieces, hon? Two or three? Coleslaw or reg'lar?* . . . They say the cops are investigatin'. Ha! What the hell good is that? A beautiful girl with her whole life snuffed out! Somebody should sue! . . . *Are you guys through with the ketchup bottle?* . . . Lenny just called me from home. He was lyin' down and heard it on the radio. He's bein' very brave, that kid, but he's hurtin' inside—hurtin' bad. He was the one who got her the job. That makes it twice as bad . . . *Coffee, anybody? New pot.* . . . The blast dumped a light fixture on Lenny's head, but it ain't serious. They stitched him up and sent him home, but he's out of a job till they fix the damage. That'll take forever if they leave it to the ol' coot who owns the place . . . *More bread? Got enough butter? It's the real thing—not that low-cholesterol stuff."*

Qwilleran's next destination was Gingerbread Alley. Even as he reached for the doorbell at the Duncan homestead, Polly yanked the door open. She was looking painfully grieved. Lynette, sober-faced, hovered in the background. In unison they said, "Did you hear the latest?"

"Yes," he said. "It's Anna Marie Toms. Did you know her?"

"She worked as a page at the library while she was in high school," Polly said. "Lovely girl—so conscientious."

"Her family lives in Chipmunk," Lynette added, "but they're good people. They go to our church."

"It's unfair to judge one by one's address," Polly protested. "Well, let's go into the parlor."

Qwilleran kept an eye on the skirted table as he seated himself. Lynette served instant decaf and pound cake from the new bakery.

"There's a rumor," she said, "that someone in Lockmaster wanted to buy the hotel, and old Scrooge wanted too much money, so they blew it up in revenge."

Stupid rumor, Qwilleran thought, and yet it was the kind of tale that flourished in scandal-hungry Pickax. He said, "Gustav Limburger is in the hospital. He fell down his front steps this morning. I was interviewing him about the history of the hotel. I'd like to know his condition, but the hospital won't give any information on the phone."

"I can find out," Lynette said. She worked for a clinic and had connections. When she returned, she recited a litany of bad news: multiple fractures, advanced osteoporosis, hypertension, cardiac arrhythmia, and more.

"Oh, dear! I should feel sorry for him," Polly said, "and yet . . ."

"He's a character," Qwilleran said. "Did you ever meet him?"

"My only contact was by mail. Every year when the library appealed for funds, he returned our envelope with two one-dollar bills. In spite of inflation, it never changed."

"Better than nothing," Lynette said. "By the way, the Toms family are patients at our clinic, and I suppose I shouldn't tell you this—I know you won't either of you repeat it—but Anna Marie was enrolled in prenatal care."

"Oh, dear!" said Polly.

Qwilleran huffed into his moustache as possibilities invaded his mind.

Then she said with an effort to be cheerful, "Well, what did you do this afternoon? Anything interesting?"

"I took the cats for a ride. Koko has been tormenting Yum Yum lately, and that means he's restless."

"Elaine Fetter phoned a while ago and said she saw you at Toodle's, buying ingredients for meatballs, and you're going to contribute your meatball recipe to the community cookbook! Have you been keeping secrets from me, dear?" she concluded with a mischievously oblique glance.

"Mrs. Fetter is confused. You know and I know, Polly, that I'm a culinary illiterate. The day I take up cooking will be the day the sky falls."

"But you *were* buying ingredients for meatballs!" she continued with the persistence of a prosecuting attorney. She enjoyed putting him in the hot seat, knowing his ability to wiggle out of any uncomfortable situation.

Qwilleran had to think fast; he did that well, too. "I was picking up groceries for Mrs. Robinson. She makes a special meatball for her cat, and I asked her to make a batch for my two gourmands."

"What makes it so special?"

"I don't know. I had to buy lamb, rice, onion, and lemon."

"That sounds Middle Eastern," Polly said. "I'd love to have her recipe. Could you get it for me?"

The situation was becoming sticky. "I'm afraid she doesn't share recipes. She's . . . uh . . . going into catering and wants to have a repertory of exclusive dishes." He congratulated himself on that ingenious fabrication but found it advisable to cover his tracks. He left early. He said he had some writing to do. Within minutes he was phoning Celia Robinson, and there was urgency in his voice.

"What's up, Chief?" she asked eagerly.

"I have a favor to ask, Celia—nothing to do with a criminal investigation."

"Aw shucks!" she said with a merry laugh.

"First, a question: Do you ever make meatballs with rice?"

"No, I use bread crumbs."

"If you were to make meatballs with rice, would
Wrigley eat them?"

"Oh, sure, but he'd throw up. Rice is something he
can't seem to digest."

"I see," Qwilleran said. "Well . . . if anyone asks you,
would you be good enough to say that you make meatballs with rice for Wrigley? And if anyone requests your
recipe . . . *just say no!*"

"Okay, Chief. It won't be the first fib I've told for
you, and I haven't been struck by lightning yet!"

He hung up with a sense of relief. He was covered. He
knew that Polly would mention the meatballs to her assistant, Mrs. Alstock, who would mention them to her
dear friend, Celia Robinson. It was one of the complexi-
ties of living in a small town. In a way, life Down Below
was simpler, despite traffic jams, air pollution, and street
crime. There was a comfortable anonymity in a city of
millions.

His next call was to the police chief at home. "Anything good on the tube tonight, Andy?"

"Nah, I turned it off, and I'm reading your column on
Nobodies in today's paper. The trouble is, all the Nobodies in Pickax think they're Somebodies and exempt
from paying traffic fines . . . What's on your mind?"

"The explosion. Was it pretty bad?"

"Everything in a certain radius was blown to bits.
That poor girl never knew what hit her."

Qwilleran asked, "Am I correct in thinking room 203
was registered to the mystery woman?"

"Right, and she hasn't been seen since."

Qwilleran paused dramatically before saying, "I spent
the afternoon with her."

"What! How come? How did you meet her? What do
you know?"

"Why don't you put on your shoes, Andy, and come over for a Scotch?"

In five minutes the police chief drove into the barnyard. He was a tall, husky, impressive figure, even out of uniform, and he was especially impressive when he wore a full Scottish kit and played the bagpipe at weddings and funerals. He walked into the barn with a piper's swagger.

Qwilleran had a tray ready with Scotch and cheese, and Squunk water for himself. As the two men settled into big chairs in the lounge area, the Siamese walked into view with a swagger of their own. Coming close to the coffee table, they sat down with noses on a level with the cheese platter. As the guest raised his glass in a Gaelic toast, the two noses edged closer.

"No!" Qwilleran thundered. Both cats backed off a quarter of an inch and continued to contemplate the forbidden food with half-shut eyes.

"Cocky little devils," Brodie said. "Bet you spoil them rotten."

"Try this cheese, Andy. It's a kind of Swiss from the new Sip 'n' Nibble shop in Stables Row. It's run by two guys from Down Below. They like to be called Jerry Sip and Jack Nibble. Jerry's the wine expert, and Jack knows everything about cheese."

"Gimme a slice. Then tell me how you met that woman."

"It was a weird coincidence. I'd never seen her, but they were talking about her at the paper yesterday and mentioned that she drove a dark blue rental car. So, this afternoon I drove to the cabin on a routine inspection, and there was a dark blue two-door in my parking lot! My car almost reared up on its hind wheels! The woman was sitting on my beach at the foot of the dune, reading a cookbook, so I figured she wasn't dangerous."

Brodie grunted at intervals as Qwilleran told the whole story. "So she offered to make some stuffed grape leaves if I'd buy the ingredients, and that's what I was doing when the bomb went off."

The chief chuckled. "She wanted to get your car out of the drive so she could make a getaway."

"That was my first thought. For a few minutes I felt like an absolute dunce. Then I realized—correctly, I believe—that she'd heard the bulletin on the air and had to get out of town fast. Somehow she knew the bomb was intended for her. I called the airport, and they said she'd turned in the car and boarded the shuttle."

Brodie said, "She might have decamped in a hurry because she was a conspirator in the bomb plot. She was conveniently out of the building—and hiding out on your property—when the bomb exploded."

Qwilleran drew a heavy hand over his moustache, as he always did when he was getting a major hunch. A tingle on his upper lip was a signal that he was on the right track. "I maintain, Andy, that she's a fugitive trying to go underground. This neck of the woods is ordinarily as underground as you can get, but there's another clue to consider. When the wind blew her hair away from her face, I saw a long vertical scar in front of her left ear."

"Could be the result of an auto accident," Brodie suggested. "What name did she give you?"

"Only her first name: Onoosh."

"Onoosh? What kind of name is that? On the hotel register she signed Ona Dolman."

A dark brown paw stole slowly over the edge of the coffee table.

"No!" Qwilleran bellowed, and the paw was quickly withdrawn.

"I didn't know cats liked cheese," said the chief, who thought they lived on rodents and fish-heads.

"Since the new store opened, both cats are turning into cheese junkies," Qwilleran said.

"Well, I guess we'll never see Ona Dolman again, but it's no big loss. The hell of it is the murder of that innocent girl—Anna Marie Toms. I know the family—good people! Not everybody living in Chipmunk gets into trouble with the law. She was kind of engaged to Lenny Inchpot, Lois's son. I'll play the bagpipe at her funeral service, if they want me to."

"Do you know exactly how it happened, Andy?"

"It'll come out later, but I'll fill you in now—off the record." Brodie had gradually accepted this journalist from Down Below as trustworthy and useful. Qwilleran's experience as a crime reporter in major cities around the country had given him insights into investigative processes, and his natural instinct for snooping often unearthed facts of value to official investigators. In pursuing his private passion, Qwilleran was quite satisfied to remain in the background, tip off the authorities, and take no public credit. Brodie, for his part, appreciated his cooperation and occasionally leaked confidential information—through his daughter, the designer. It was a casual arrangement, unknown to other local law enforcement agencies.

"Anything you see fit to tell me is always off the record, Andy. That goes without saying."

"Okay. About four o'clock this afternoon an unidentified white male—about forty, medium build, clean-shaven—came in the front door of the hotel with a gift package and some flowers for Ona Dolman. Lenny, on duty at the desk, said she wasn't in but he'd send them up to her room as soon as the porter returned from his break. The suspect said the gift was hand-blown glass, very fragile, and he'd feel more comfortable taking it upstairs himself and putting it in a safe place. He asked for a piece of paper and wrote: OPEN WITH CARE, HONEY. So Lenny told him to ask the housekeeper on the second floor to let him into 203. When the suspect came back down, he yelled thank-you and went out the back door. The porter was having a cigarette in the parking lot and saw a blue pickup drive slowly down the back street and pick up a man in a blue jacket. So what? Blue pickups and blue jackets are a dime a dozen around here."

Qwilleran asked about witnesses on the second floor.

"The manager's office is up there. She didn't see the suspect, but the housekeeper asked where to get a vase for some flowers and later took the vacuum cleaner into 203, saying the flowers had made a mess on the rug. When she plugged in the cord or pushed the machine around, she probably tripped the bomb. Lenny feels he's responsible for her death. That boy's gonna need counseling."

"Bad scene," Qwilleran said somberly. "Can he describe the suspect?"

"Two witnesses got a close look at him—Lenny and the florist who sold him the flowers. The SBI computer is making a composite sketch from their descriptions, but I don't know how they'll find any clues in the rubble. A bomb blows up a lot of evidence."

"Yes, but the forensic people work miracles. Every year there seems to be new technology." Qwilleran poured another Scotch for Brodie and asked how he liked the cheese.

"Good stuff! I've gotta tell the wife about it. What d'you call it?"

"Gruyère. It's from Switzerland."

"Yow!" came a loud demand from the floor, and Qwilleran gave each cat a tiny crumb of it, which they gobbled and masticated and savored at great length as if it were a whole wedge.

Brodie asked, "Did Ona Dolman say anything at all that might finger the bomber?"

"No, I'm afraid I missed the boat. I intended to ask some leading questions while we were eating our grape leaves. I even picked up a bottle of good wine for her!" Qwilleran said with annoyance.

"Well, anyway, now that we know she left on a plane, we can start a search. If she was in hiding, she falsified information but there'll be prints on the car, if they haven't cleaned it." He went to the phone and called the airport; the car had been thoroughly cleaned when it was returned. Qwilleran said there would be prints on the kitchen sink at the cabin, and he turned over the key to Brodie, along with the folding chair, cookbooks, and straw hat that she had left behind.

"We'll need your prints, too, Qwill. Stop at the station tomorrow."

"I don't envy you, Andy. You don't know who she really is, where she really lives, why she's being pursued, where she went, who planted the bomb, where he lives, what's his motive, how he found her, and who drove the getaway vehicle."

"Well, we should be able to lift her prints, and just about every man, woman, and child in Pickax can describe her . . . What did you call that cheese?"

"Gruyère."

"Yow!" said Koko.

Qwilleran said, "I asked the guy at the cheese store why a cat would prefer this to Emmenthaler, which is also Swiss. He said it's creamier and saltier."

"Is it expensive?"

"It costs more than processed cheese at Toodle's, but Mildred says we should buy better food and eat less of it."

Brodie stood up. "Better be goin' home, or the wife'll call the police."

Just then a low rumble caught the attention of the two men. It came from under the coffee table. As they turned to look, Koko came slinking out, making a gutteral noise, waving his tail in low gear, sneaking up behind Yum Yum.

"Watch this!" Qwilleran whispered.

POW! Koko pounced! WHOOSH! Yum Yum got away, and they were off on a wild chase up the ramp.

"They're just showing off," Qwilleran said. "They do it to attract attention."

The chief went home carrying a wedge of Gruyère.

SIX

On Saturday morning Qwilleran fed the cats, policed their commode, brushed their coats, and combed airborne cat hair out of his moustache and eyebrows. Koko had pushed a book off the library shelf. "Not now. Later," he said. "I have a lot of calls to make. Expect me when you see me." He replaced the playscript of *A Taste of Honey* on the shelf. Then he thought, Wait a minute! Does that cat sense that I'm going to interview a beekeeper? And if he does, how can he associate my intentions with the word "honey" on a book cover? And yet, he had to admit, Koko sometimes used oblique avenues of communication.

He went to the police station to be fingerprinted and then to the library for a book on beekeeping. Rather than appear to be a complete dolt, he looked up the definitions of brooders, supers, and smokers, also swarming, hiving, and clustering. While there he heard the clerks greeting Homer Tibbitt, who arrived each day with a briefcase and brown paper bag. Although the sign on the front door specified NO FOOD OR BEVERAGES, everyone knew what was in the paper bag. He was in his late nineties, however, and allowances were made for age. With a jerky but sprightly gait, he walked to the elevator and rode to the mezzanine, where he would do research in the reading room.

Qwilleran followed, using the stairs. "Morning, Homer. What's the subject for today?"

"I'm still on the Goodwinter clan. Amanda found some family papers in an old trunk and gave them to the library—racy stuff, some of it."

"Do you know anything about the Limburger family?" Qwilleran dropped into a hard oak chair across the table; the historian always brought his own inflated seat cushion.

"Yes, indeed! I wrote a monograph on them a few years ago. As I recall, the first Limburger came over from Austria in the mid-nineteenth century to avoid conscription. He was a carpenter, and the mining companies hired him to build cottages for the workers. But he was a go-getter and ended up building his own rooming houses and travelers' inns. Exploiting the workers was considered smart business practice in those days, and he got rich."

"What happened to his housing empire?"

"One by one the buildings burned down. Some were pulled down for firewood in the Great Depression. The Hotel Booze is the only building still standing. The family itself—second generation—was wiped out in the flu epidemic of 1918. There was only one survivor, and he's still living."

"You mean Gustav?" Qwilleran asked. "He has a reputation for being quite eccentric."

"Haven't seen him for years, but I remember him as a young boy, recently orphaned. Pardon me while I refresh my memory." The old gentleman struggled to his feet and went to the restroom, carrying his paper bag. It was no secret that it contained a thermos of decaffeinated coffee laced with brandy. When he returned, he had recalled everything.

"Yes, I remember young Gustav. I was a fledgling teacher in a one-room school, and I felt sorry for him. He'd lost his folks and was sent to live with a German-speaking family. His English was poor, and to make matters worse, there was a lot of anti-German sentiment after World War One. It's no wonder he was a poor student. He played truant frequently, ran away from home a couple of times, and finally dropped out."

"Didn't he inherit the family fortune?"

"That's another story. Some said his legal guardian mismanaged his money. Some said he went to Germany to sow his wild oats and lost it all. I know he sold the Hotel Booze to the Pratts and kept the New Pickax hotel. I hear it was wrecked by a bomb yesterday."

"Apparently Gustav never married," Qwilleran remarked.

"Not to anyone's knowledge. But who knows what he did in Germany? When I was writing the Limburger history, I tried to get him to talk, but he shut up like a clam."

"He's in the hospital now, in serious condition."

"Well, he's up in years," Homer said of the man who was fifteen years his junior.

Driving north to the Limburger house, Qwilleran passed the decrepit Dimsdale Diner at the corner of Ittibittiwassee Road and noted half a dozen farm vehicles in the weedy parking lot. That meant the Men's Dimsdale Coffee and Current Events Smoker was in session. That was Qwilleran's name for the boisterous group of laughing, gossiping, cigarette-smoking coffee hounds who gathered informally in-between farm chores. He parked and joined them and was greeted by cheers.

"Here's Mr. Q! . . . Move over and make room for a big cheese from downtown! . . . Pull up a chair, man!"

Qwilleran helped himself to a mug of bad coffee and a stale doughnut and sat with the five men in feed caps and farm jackets. They went on with their quips, rumors, and prejudices:

"That explosion was an inside job. You can bet on it!"

"They should've dynamited the whole inside and then started over."

"Looks like that foreign babe was in on it."

"Old Gus was taken to the hospital when he heard the news."

"What'll happen to the hotel when he cashes in?"

"He'll leave it to that fella that does his chores."

"That's a laugh! Gus is too stingy to give a penny away—even after he's dead!"

"He won't die unless he can figger out how to take it with 'im."

"I'll bet he's got a coupla million buried in his back-yard. What d'you think, Mr. Q?"

"If you believe everything you hear, there's enough money buried in Moose County backyards to pay the national debt."

With that, they all laughed, pushed back their chairs, and trooped out to their blue pickup trucks.

En route to Black Creek, Qwilleran detoured through the town of Brrr, so named because it was the coldest spot in the county. He wanted to chat with Gary Pratt, owner of the Hotel Booze and chummy host at the Black Bear Café. Gary was a big bear of a man himself, having a shaggy black beard and a lumbering gait. He was behind the bar when Qwilleran slipped onto a bar stool.

"The usual?" he asked, plunking a mug on the bar and reaching for the coffee server.

"And a bearburger—with everything," Qwilleran said.

The noon rush had not yet started, and Gary had time to lean on the bar in front of his customer. "What are they jawboning about in Pickax today?"

"The bombing. What else?"

"Same here."

"Any brilliant theories as to motive?"

"Well, folks around Brrr think it has to do with that foreign woman. They've seen her sitting on the beach and doing the tourist shops on the boardwalk. That hair of hers is what makes them leery. She'd come in here for lunch, and I'd try to get her into conversation. No dice. Then last Saturday she had dinner with one of our registered guests—a man."

"What kind of guy?"

"Looked like a businessman—clean-cut and about her age—wore a suit and tie. In Brrr, a suit and tie look suspiciously like the FBI or IRS, so he made folks nervous. He checked into the hotel about five-thirty, which looks like he came up on the shuttle flight and she picked him up at the airport. She drives a rental; we've seen it on our parking lot. So, anyway, they had dinner together— sat in a corner booth and talked like long-lost-whatever."

"Intimately?" Qwilleran asked.

"No."

"Furtively?"

"Not that either—more like a serious business deal, but every time I took them another glass of wine or walked by with the coffee server, they were talking about the weather. The thing of it is, how much can you say about the weather? One guy around here has it figured out that the bombing was an insurance scam, and she was a plant; it was set up to look like the bomb was meant for her."

"Gary, can you honestly see that old geezer in Black Creek plotting a sophisticated insurance scam?"

"Not him. They suspect the property management sharpies in Lockmaster. They run the hotel for him. I have a theory myself. It's common knowledge at the Chamber of Commerce that Lockmaster has been trying to get him to sell. He won't. You know how the Germans are about property. Well! Now that the building is damaged, he'll be willing to sell—at their price."

Qwilleran huffed into his moustache as he reflected that everyone in Moose County considered everyone in Lockmaster to be a crook. Likewise, Lockmaster denizens thought Moose County was populated with hayseeds. Race, color, and creed had nothing to do with this absurd bigotry; it was purely a matter of geography. He said to Gary, "This man wearing a suit and tie—was he swarthy like her?"

"No, he had light skin, reddish hair. They were together the next day, too, and then I think she drove him to catch the Sunday-night shuttle. He checked out around four-thirty—paid his bill with cash. Makes you wonder what he had in his briefcase."

The bearburger arrived with all the trimmings, and Gary changed the subject to the Labor Day Bike Race. "I didn't finish—didn't expect to—but it was fun. Have you heard what's next? The Pedal Club's sponsoring a bike-a-thon called Wheels for Meals. It'll benefit the hot-meal program for shut-ins—our contribution to

Explo. Sponsors can pledge anywhere from a dime to a dollar per mile. I figure I'm good for thirty miles. After that, they'll have to cart me away in the sag wagon."

"What's the sag wagon?" Qwilleran asked.

"Just kidding. It's not an ambulance. It's a support vehicle with water, energy drinks, first aid, and racks for disabled bikes. No food. No hitchhiking."

"Okay, I'll sponsor you." Qwilleran signed a green pledge card for a dollar a mile. Then he said, "Do you happen to know Aubrey Scotten?"

"Sure. I knew him in high school. I know all the Scotten brothers. They belong to the Outdoor Club. Aubrey comes in for a burger once in a while. Have you met him?"

"Briefly. I'm supposed to interview him about beekeeping this afternoon. Do you think he'll make a good subject?"

"Oh, he'll spout off, all right. Most of the time he's laid back, but if he likes you, he won't stop yakking. I don't know how much of it you'll be able to use."

"Can you fill me in on a few things?"

"Such as . . . ?"

"Is he a reliable authority on beekeeping? Is his honey considered good? Was his hair always snow-white?"

Gary looked uncertain and then decided it was all right to talk to this particular newsman. "Well . . . about the hair: It happened while he was in the Navy. He had an accident, and his hair turned white overnight."

"What kind of accident?"

"Some kind of foul-up aboard ship, never really explained. Aubrey got clunked on the head and dumped in the ocean and nearly drowned. In fact, he was a goner when they hauled him out, but he came back to life.

Those Scottens are a tough breed. It changed his personality, though."

"In what way?"

"For one thing, he'd been a bully in high school, and now he's a kind-hearted guy who won't swat a fly! For another thing, he used to work in the Scotten fishing fleet; now he's terrified of boats, and the sight of a large body of water gives him the screaming-meemies. The Navy gave him an honorable medical discharge and sent him home . . . Don't let anyone know I told you all this stuff." Gary poured another cup of coffee for Qwilleran. "But there was a plus! Aubrey turned into some kind of genius. He can repair anything—*anything!* He was never that way before. He fixed the big refrigerator here and my stereo at home."

Qwilleran's blood pressure was rising; a near-death experience would be more newsworthy than the honeybee business.

Then Gary said, "Aubrey won't talk about his accident, and neither will his family—especially not to the media. Some scientists wanted to come up here and study his brain, but his brothers put the kibosh on that scheme in a hurry."

For the second time in two days, Qwilleran had seen a good lead turn out to be no-story, so . . . back to the honeybees!

Surrounded by the devastation of Black Creek, the Limburger mansion loomed like a haunted house. Still, Qwilleran thought as he parked at the curb, it could be renovated to make a striking country inn, given a little imagination and a few million dollars. The exterior brickwork—horizontal, vertical, diagonal and herringbone—was unique. The tall, stately windows, with the exception of the Halloween casualty, had stained-glass transoms or inserts of etched and beveled glass.

On the railing of the veranda the row of stones waited for the patient's return, and the reddish-brown mongrel that had provoked the old man's accident was still hanging around.

Qwilleran mounted the crumbling brick steps with caution and rang the doorbell. When there was no answer, he walked around the side of the house, saying, "Good dog! Good dog!" The animal nuzzled and whimpered and looked forlorn; Qwilleran wished he had brought some stale doughnuts from the Dimsdale Diner.

"Hello! Hello? Is anyone here?" he shouted in the direction of the weathered shed. The door stood open, and a bulky white-haired figure materialized from the interior gloom. Aubrey seemed bewildered.

Qwilleran said, "I was here yesterday, when Mr. Limburger fell down the steps. I'm Jim Qwilleran, remember? I told you I'd return to ask you all about beekeeping."

"I di'n't think you'd come back," the young man said. "Folks say they'll come back, and they never show up. A man ordered twelve jars of honey, and I had 'em all packed up in a box. He never showed up. I don't understand it. It's not friendly. D'you think it's a friendly thing to do?" The plaint was recited in a high whining voice.

"Some people don't have consideration for others," Qwilleran said with sympathy. "How is Mr. Limburger? Do you know?"

"I just come from the hospital. He was in bed and yellin' his head off about the food. He likes rabbit stew and pigs' feet and stuff like that. He likes lotsa fat. I seen him eat a pound of butter, once, like candy. It made me sick."

Qwilleran pointed to the shed. "Is that part of your honey operation?"

"That's where I draw the honey off."

"Do you have any for sale? I'd like to buy a couple of jars."

"Pints or quarts? I don't have no quarts. I sold 'em all to Toodle's Market. Mrs. Toodle is very friendly. She knows my mom." He disappeared into the dark shed and returned with two oval jars containing a clear, thick amber fluid.

"Why are honey jars always flat?" Qwilleran asked. Cynically he thought, Makes them look like more for the money; makes them tip over easily.

"Flat makes the honey look lighter. Most people want light honey. I don't know why. I like the dark. It has lotsa taste. This is wildflower honey. I took some to Lois, and she give me a big breakfast. Di'n't have to pay a penny. She give me prunes, turkey hash, two eggs, toast, and coffee."

Aubrey rambled on until Qwilleran suggested that they sit on the porch and turn on the tape recorder. First, Aubrey had to find something for Pete to eat. Pete was the reddish-brown dog. Qwilleran waited in Limburger's creaking rocker, which was situated on a squeaking floorboard. He rocked noisily as he thought about the poor old dog, coming every day to be fed at the back door and stoned at the front door—not that the old man ever struck his target. Still, the treatment must have confused Pete, and it was not surprising that he dirtied the brick walk.

When Aubrey appeared, he had walked through the house and come out the front door, carrying a large book which he handed to Qwilleran. It was a very old, leather-bound, gold-tooled Bible with text printed in Old German. The beekeeper explained, "It came from Austria more'n a hunerd years ago. The old man's gonna leave it to me when he kicks the bucket. The cuckoo clock, too. It di'n't work, but I fixed it. Wanna see the cuckoo clock? It's on the wall."

"Later," Qwilleran said firmly. "Sit down and let's talk about bees. Do you ever get stung?"

Aubrey shook his head gravely. "My bees ain't never stung me. They trust me. I talk to 'em. I give 'em sugar-water in winter."

"Would they sting me?"

"If you frighten 'em or act unfriendly or wear a wool cap. They don't like wool. I don't know why. Bees never sting me. I seen a swarm of wild honeybees go inside an old tree, once. I went to look, and they swarmed all over me. I think they liked me. They was all over my face and in my ears and down my neck. It was a crazy feeling."

"I'll bet!" Qwilleran said grimly.

"I went home and come back with an empty hive. I hived the whole swarm. I think they was glad to get a good home. Bees are smart. If there's an apple tree and a pear tree, they go to the apple tree. It's got more sugar. The old man don't like honey. He likes white sugar. I seen him eat a whole bowl of sugar with a spoon, once. It made me sick. Would it make you sick?"

Piecemeal, with numerous digressions, the interview filled the reel of tape: A bee hive was like a little honey factory. Every bee had a job. The workers built honeycombs. The queen laid eggs. The field workers collected nectar and pollen from flowers. They brought it back to the hive to make honey. The door keepers guarded the hives against robbers. The drones didn't make honey;

they just took care of the queen. If the hive got crowded, the drones were thrown out to die.

Qwilleran asked, "How do they get the nectar back to the hive?"

"In their bellies. They carry pollen in little bags on their legs."

Skeptically Qwilleran asked, "Are you telling me the truth, Aubrey?"

"Cross my heart," said the big man solemnly. "Wanna see the hives?"

"Only if you lend me a bee veil. They might think my moustache is made of wool."

"If a worker stings you, he dies."

"That's small comfort. Give me a bee veil and some gloves."

They walked down a rutted trail to the river, where all was quiet except for the rushing of the rapids and the cawing of crows. On the bank stood a shabby cabin with a paltry chimney and a hand pump on a wooden platform at the door. A lonely outhouse stood in a nearby field.

Aubrey said, "My family had six cabins they rented to bass fishermen. Two burned down. Three blew away in a storm. I live in this one. The walls were fulla wild bees, and I hadda smoke 'em out and take off the siding, and underneath the walls were fulla honey."

As they neared the cabin, Qwilleran became aware of a faint buzzing; he put on the gloves and the hat with a veil. On the south side of the building, exposed to the sun and protected from the north wind, was a row of wooden boxes elevated on platforms—not as picturesque as the old dome-shaped hives pictured on honey labels. The boxes were Langstroth hives, Qwilleran later learned, designed in 1851.

Aubrey said, "The bees do all the work. I take the trays of honeycomb up to the shed and draw the honey off and put it in jars. Those trays get pretty heavy."

"Sounds like sticky business," Qwilleran said.

"I hadda crazy accident, once. I di'n't put the jar right under the spout, and the honey ran all over the floor."

The busy bees paid no attention to the journalist. He spoke quietly and made no sudden moves. "What do they do in winter?"

"They cluster together in the hives and keep each other warm. I wrap the hives in straw and stuff. They can get out if they want, but the mice can't get in."

"What about snow?"

"It don't matter if the hives are buried in snow, but ice—that's bad. My whole colony was smothered by ice, once."

It was a fantastic story, if true, Qwilleran thought. He would check it against the bee book at the library. "And now I'd like to see the cuckoo clock," he said. Truthfully, it was the interior of the mansion that interested him: the carved woodwork, the staghorn chandelier, the stained glass. The furnishings were sparse. The old man had sold almost everything, Aubrey said. Only one room looked inhabited. There were two overstuffed chairs in front of a TV, a large wardrobe carved with figures of wild game, and a gun cabinet with glass doors. The pendulum of the carved clock wagged on the wall.

"Who's the hunter?" Qwilleran asked.

"The old man shoots rabbits and makes hasenpfeffer. He shoots crows, too. I used to do lotsa hunt'n' with my brothers. I was a good shot." He looked away. "I don't wanna hunt any more."

The clock sounded *cuckoo cuckoo cuckoo*, and Qwilleran said it was time to leave. He paid for his honey and left with a new respect for the thick amber fluid. How many bellyfuls of nectar would it take, he wondered, to make a pint of honey?

He propped his purchases in a safe place in his car, where they would not tip or spill. Then he drove to Toodle's Market to buy something fresh for the Siamese and something frozen for himself. On the way he thought about the industrious workers and the hapless drones . . . about nature's way of converting flowers into food without chemicals or preservatives . . . and about the mild-mannered beekeeper who talked to his bees. Not a word had been said about the hotel bombing, an incident that was on everyone's tongue.

Arriving at the market, Qwilleran opened his car door and heard a sickening sound as glass broke on concrete pavement in a puddle of amber goo. He looked down at the disaster, then up at the sky and counted to ten.

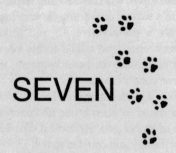

SEVEN

A jar of honey spilled on a parking lot is not as bad as a jar of spilled honey mixed with broken glass. Qwilleran, having made this profound observation, notified Mrs. Toodle, and she summoned one of her grandsons. The three of them marched single file to the scene of the accident, Qwilleran apologizing profusely and Mrs. Toodle thanking him for reporting it. The situation tickled the funny bone of the young Toodle; it was almost as funny as the time he dropped a crate of eggs.

"You'll have to get every last bit of glass," his grandmother admonished. "If a dog comes along and licks the spot, he could cut his tongue." When her back was turned, Qwilleran slipped the young man a generous tip.

"That's not necessary," she said, having developed eyes in the back of her head after years of running a supermarket.

He bought some corned beef at the deli counter—enough for the cats' dinner and a late-night snack for himself, then drove downtown to buy flowers for Polly. At five o'clock she would be venturing out of doors for her first walk since having surgery. He parked in the municipal lot and walked to the florist shop.

Downtown Pickax was a three-block stretch of heterogeneous stone buildings: large, small, impressive, quaint, ornate, and primitive. All were relics of the era when the county was famous for its quarries. Together with the stone paving, they gave the town its title: City of Stone. A Cotswold cottage, the Bastille, Stonehenge, and a Scottish castle did business side by side. To Qwilleran, Main Street was Information Highway; friends and acquaintances stopped him to report the latest scandal, rumor, or joke.

Today he bumped into Whannell MacWhannell, the accountant. Big Mac, a burly Scot, greeted Qwilleran with "Aye! There's a rumor the 'braw laird of Mackintosh' has ordered a kilt, tailor-made! You can wear it to Scottish Night at the lodge and the Highland Games in Lockmaster."

"That is, if I'm ''braw' enough to wear it at all. It's supposed to be a surprise for Polly, so don't spread the rumor." Even though his mother was a Mackintosh, and even though he had joined the clan as a tribute to her memory, Qwilleran had reservations about appearing in public in a kilt.

The two men stood on the sidewalk and gazed with dismay at the boarded windows of the hotel across the street. "A crying shame!" said the accountant. "It wasn't a good hotel, but it was all we had, and who knows what'll happen to it now? The owner's in the hospital, and the management agency will be dragging its feet. They're based in Lockmaster, you know, and couldn't care less about a little creeping blight in downtown Pickax."

Qwilleran said, "I met the owner just before he had his accident, and he's eccentric, to say the least. I hope his affairs are in order—legal and financial. I hope he has an attorney, and an estate-planner, and a will."

"The problem is that no one wants to work with the scoundrel," Big Mac said. "Our office used to do his tax work, but he was impossible. Didn't keep records. Wouldn't take advice. What does one do with a client like that? I've forgotten whether we fired him or he fired us. His local attorney bowed out in desperation, too. The Lockmaster agency probably handles all his affairs now. They have my sympathy!"

Main Street was crowded with Saturday shoppers, since there was no mall to lure them from downtown, and they were joined by quite a few sightseers, gawking at the scene of the explosion. Among them was Mitch Ogilvie, dressed more like a farmer than a museum manager.

Qwilleran grabbed him roughly by the arm. "Mitch, you dirty dog! What happened to you? I hear you left the museum. You look as if you're going to a costume party!" He was wearing grubby denims, field boots, and a feed cap. He had also grown a beard.

"Yeah, I'm working my way up the ladder," the young man said. "From hotel clerk . . . to museum manager . . . to goat farmer! I'm glad I wasn't working here when the hotel blew up."

"Yes, but what's this about goat farming?"

"Kristi started a new herd, and I helped her sell her mother's antiques. She realized enough to make some big improvements in the house and the farm, so I hired on."

"Have you learned how to milk goats?"

"Believe it or not, I'm the cheese-maker. I went to a farm in Wisconsin and took a course. The new cheese shop on Stables Row is handling our product. Maybe you've seen our label: Split Rail Farm. We got rid of the old white fence, and I built one myself out of split rails."

"I've not only seen your label, I've bought your cheese," Qwilleran said. "I've tried the feta and the pepper cheese. Great eating! I'd like to see the cheese operation; I might be able to write about it."

"Sure! Great! Anytime!"

Qwilleran suggested the next afternoon. "That is, if you don't mind working on Sunday."

"There are no days off in the goat business, Qwill." Mitch glanced at the hotel. "But it's safer than working at the Pickax Hotel . . . See ya!"

Qwilleran continued on his way to the shop called Franklin's Flowers. It was across from the hotel and next door to Exbridge & Cobb, Fine Antiques. Susan Exbridge was a handsome match for her upscale establishment. She collected Georgian silver, won bridge tournaments at the country club, received alimony from a wealthy developer, and bought her clothes in Chicago. When Qwilleran happened along, she was standing on the sidewalk, critiquing a display she had just arranged in the window.

Stealing up behind her and disguising his voice, he said, "There's a wrinkle in the rug, and the lamp shade is crooked."

She saw his reflection in the glass and turned quickly.

"Darling! Where have you been all summer? The town has been desolate without you!" As one of the more flamboyant members of the theatre club, she over dramatized.

"It's been a hectic summer in many ways," he explained.

"I know. How's Polly?" The two women were not warm friends, but they observed the civilities, as one is required to do in a small town.

"Improving daily. We have to find her a place to live. Her apartment is being swallowed up by the college campus. Temporarily she's staying with her sister-in-law."

"Why don't you and Polly—" she began.

"Our cats are incompatible," he interrupted, knowing what she was about to suggest.

They discussed the possibilities of Indian Village, a complex of apartments and condominiums on the Ittibittiwassee River. There were nature trails; the river was full of ducks; the woods were full of birds.

"The quacking and chirping sometimes drive me up the wall," Susan said, "but Polly would love it." There was a tinge of snobbery in her comment. In Indian Village, the bridge-players never went birding, and the bird-watchers never played bridge. Some day, Qwilleran thought, he would write a column on cliques in Moose County. He might lose a few friends, but it was a columnist's duty to stir things up occasionally.

Susan opened the front door. "Come in and see my new annex."

The premises always gleamed with polished mahogany and shining brass, but now an archway opened into a new space filled with antiques of a dusty, weathered, folksy sort.

"Do you recognize any of those primitives?" she asked. "They were in Iris Cobb's personal collection, and I never had a place to display them until the store next door was vacated. I rented half of it, and Franklin Pickett took the other half. Honestly, he's such a pill! He always wants to borrow antique objects for his window display, but he never offers a few flowers for my shop."

In the archway a rustic sign on an easel announced: THE IRIS COBB COLLECTION. Qwilleran noted a pine cupboard, several milking stools, benches with seats made from half-logs, wrought-iron utensils for fireplace cooking, an old school desk, some whirligigs, and a faded hand hooked rug with goofy-looking farm animals around the border. He picked up a basket with an openwork weave that left large hexagonal holes. It had straight sides and was about a foot in diameter. He questioned the size of the holes.

"That's a cheese basket," Susan explained. "They'd line it with cheesecloth, fill it with curds, and let it drip. It belonged to a French-Canadian family near Trawnto Beach. They were shipwrecked there in 1870 and decided to stay. They raised dairy cattle and made their own cheese until the farmhouse was destroyed by fire in 1911. The daughter was able to save the cheese basket and that hooked rug. She still had them when she died at the age of ninety-five."

Qwilleran gave her a stony stare. "You should be writing fiction, Susan."

"Every word is true! Iris recorded the provenance on the catalogue card."

Qwilleran shrugged a wordless apology to the memory of the late Iris Cobb. She had been an expert on antiques and a wonderful cook and a warm-hearted friend, but he had always suspected her of inventing a provenance for everything she sold. "And what is that?" he asked, pointing to a weathered wood chest with iron hardware.

"An old sea chest," Susan recited glibly, "found in an attic in Brrr. It had been washed up on the beach following an 1892 shipwreck and was thought to belong to a Scottish sailor."

"Uh huh," Qwilleran said skeptically, "and there was a wooden leg in the chest thought to belong to Long John Silver. How much are you asking for the cheese basket and the chest? And are they cheaper without the provenance?"

"Spoken like an experienced junker," she said. "Because you're an old friend of dear Iris, I'll give you a clergyman's discount, ten percent. She'd want you to have it."

Qwilleran grunted his thanks as he wrote the check, thinking that dear Iris would have given him twenty percent. He said, "I don't suppose her personal cookbook turned up, did it?"

"I wish it had! Some of my customers would mortgage their homes to buy it! The book was a mess, but the recipes she had developed were priceless. She kept it in that old school desk, but by the time I was appointed to appraise the estate, it was gone."

"It was left to me in her will, you may recall—a joke, I presume, because she knew I was no cook and never would be."

"I hate to say this," Susan said, "but I think it was taken by one of the museum volunteers. There were seventy-five of them—on maintenance, security, hosting, cataloguing, etc. Mitch Ogilvie was the manager then, and he put a notice in the volunteers' newsletter, pleading for its return—no questions asked. No one re-

sponded. . . . I'll have my man put a coat of oil on the
sea chest for you, Qwill, and deliver it to the barn."

Qwilleran left with his cheese basket and visited the
florist next door, pushing through a maze of greeting
cards, stuffed animals, balloons, chocolates, and decorated mugs to reach the fresh-cut flowers.

"Hello, Mr. Q," said a young clerk with long silky
hair and large blue eyes. "Daisies again? Or would you
like mums for a change?"

"Mrs. Duncan has an overriding passion for daisies
and unmitigated scorn for mums," he said sternly. "Why
are you pushing mums? Did your boss buy too many?
Or does he get a bigger markup on mums?"

She giggled. "Oh, Mr. Q, you're so funny. Most people like mums because they last longer, and we have a
new color." She showed him a bouquet of dark red. "It's
called vintage burgundy."

"It looks like dried blood," he said. "Just give me a
bunch of yellow daisies without that wispy stuff that
sheds all over the floor."

"You don't want any statice?" she asked in disbelief.

"No statice, no ribbon bows, no balloons." Then, having asserted himself successfully, he relented and said in
a genial tone, "You had some excitement across the
street yesterday."

She rolled her expressive blue eyes. "I was paralyzed
with fright! I thought it was an earthquake. My boss was
in the back room working on a funeral, and he was as
scared as I was." She added in a whisper, although there
was no one else in the shop, "The police have been here,
asking questions. The man that planted the bomb bought
some flowers from us."

"Did you see him?"

"No. I was in the back room working on a wedding.

Mr. Pickett waited on him. He bought mums in that new color."

"Well, tell your boss to stock up on vintage burgundy. There'll be a run on it when the public discovers it was the bomber's choice. Don't ask me why. It's some kind of wacky mass hysteria."

Somewhat behind schedule—because of the spilled honey and the unplanned meetings on Main Street and the purchase of the antiques—Qwilleran hastily chopped corned beef for the Siamese. The salty meat seemed to give them a special thrill. Then they inspected the cheese basket on the coffee table, its open weave making a crisp lineal pattern on the white surface.

"We will not chew this basket!" Qwilleran warned them. "It belonged to Mrs. Cobb. You remember Mrs. Cobb. She used to make meatloaf for you. Her basket deserves your respect."

Koko sniffed it and walked away with the bored attitude of a cat who has sniffed better baskets in his time. Yum Yum tried it on for size, however, and found it a perfect fit. She curled into it with her chin resting on the rim, a picture of contentment.

Qwilleran drove to Gingerbread Alley and found Polly dressed for her first walk but apprehensive. "I know it's silly to feel this way, but I do," she said apologetically.

"One turn around the block, and you'll be ready for another," he predicted. He gave her the flowers.

"Daisies!" she cried. "They're the smiley faces of nature! Looking at them always makes me happy. Thank you, dear." She deposited them casually into a square, squat vase of thick green glass that showed off the crisscrossed stems. "Daisies arrange themselves. One should never fuss with them."

Qwilleran noted a large pot of mums in the entrance hall. "Unusual color," he remarked.

"It's called vintage burgundy. Dr. Prelligate sent them. Wasn't that a thoughtful gesture?"

He huffed into his moustache. Previously, Polly had thought the man good-looking, charming, and intellectual; now he was thoughtful as well. Obviously he was trying to keep Polly from moving out of her on-campus apartment—all the more reason why she should relocate in Indian Village.

They walked down the street slowly, hand-in-hand. She said, "You know the neighbors will be watching and circulating rumors. In Pickax hand-holding in public is tantamount to announcing one's engagement."

"Good!" Qwilleran said. "That'll give them something else to think about besides the hotel bombing." He did most of the talking as she concentrated on her breathing and posture. He described his interview with Aubrey and the mysteries of honey production. "The poet hit the nail on the head when he wrote about *the murmuring of innumerable bees.*"

"That was Tennyson," Polly said. "Perfect example of onomatopoeia."

"I won a fourth-grade spelling bee with that word once," he said. "They gave me a dictionary as a prize. I would have preferred a book about baseball."

"How are Koko and Yum Yum?"

"They're fine. I'm reading Greek drama to them— Aristophanes right now. They like *The Birds* . . . For sport Koko and I play Blink. We stare at each other, and the first one to blink pays a forfeit. He always wins, and I give him a toothful of cheese."

"Bootsie won't look me in the eye," Polly said. "He's very loving, but eye contact disturbs him."

The excursion was more therapeutic than social, and Polly was glad to return to her chair in the Victorian parlor. Lynette was busy in the kitchen, preparing a spaghetti dinner for the new assistant pastor of their church. Qwilleran was invited to make a fourth, but he was meeting Dwight Somers at Tipsy's Tavern.

Meanwhile, he went home and read some more Aristophanes to the Siamese. "Do you realize," he said to them, "that you're two of the few cats in the Western world who are getting a classical education?" They liked the part about Cloud-Cuckoo-Land, where the birds built a city in the sky. He embellished the text with birdcalls as he read about thirty thousand whooping cranes flying from Africa with the stones; curlews shaping the stones with their beaks; mud-larks mixing the mortar; ducks with feet like little trowels doing the masonry; and woodpeckers doing the carpentry. Yum Yum purred, and Koko became quite excited.

Tipsy's Tavern in North Kennebeck was a roadhouse in a sprawling log cabin—with rustic furnishings, bustling middle-aged waitresses, noisy customers, and a reputation for good steaks. Dwight ordered a glass of red wine, while Qwilleran had his usual Squunk water from a local mineral spring.

"Do you really like that stuff?" Dwight asked. "I've never tasted it."

"It's an acquired taste." Qwilleran raised his glass to the light, then sniffed it. "The color should be crystal clear; the bouquet, a delicate suggestion of fresh earth." He sipped it. "The taste: a harmonious blend of shale and clay with overtones of quartz and an after-taste of . . . mud."

"You're losing it!" his dinner companion said.

Chiefly they talked about the plans for the Explo. The bombing had hurt morale downtown, but Dwight had jacked up the hype, and merchants were rallying around. That was the commercial aspect of Explo. There was more. He said:

"The K Fund, frankly, is afraid of being perceived as a year-round Santa Claus. That's why they're encouraging community fund-raising for charity. They're matching, dollar for dollar, all the money raised by the celebrity auction, bike-a-thon, pasty bake-off, etc. All proceeds will go to feed the needy this winter. There'll be more hardship than usual because of the financial scandal in Sawdust City."

"Who are the celebrities to be auctioned?" Qwilleran asked.

"The idea is to have five bachelors and five single women. In some cases, the dinner-date package will include a gift. Everything is being donated by restaurants, merchants, and other business firms. The public will pay an admission fee—high enough to discourage idle sight-seers—and that'll add a couple of thousand to the take."

"Who's the auctioneer?"

"Foxy Fred. Who else? He's donating his services, and you know how good he is! People will have lots of fun . . . Here's a list of the packages being offered." He handed Qwilleran a printout.

1—Dinner and dancing at the Purple Point Boat Club with Gregory Blythe, investment counselor and mayor of Pickax.

2—Transportation by limousine to Lockmaster for a

gourmet dinner at the five-star Palomino Paddock with interior designer Fran Brodie.

3—Portrait-sitting at John Bushland's photo studio and a picnic supper on his cabin cruiser, catered by the Nasty Pasty.

4—A cocktail dress from Aurora's Boutique and dinner at the Northern Lights Hotel with Wetherby Goode, WPKX meteorologist.

5—A boat ride around the off-shore islands and dinner at the exclusive Grand Island Club with Elizabeth Hart, newcomer from Chicago.

6—An afternoon of horseback riding on private bridle paths and dinner at Tipsy's with Dr. Diane Lanspeak, M.D.

7—A motorbike tour of the county and a cook-out at the State Park with Derek Cuttlebrink, former chef at the Old Stone Mill.

8—A poolside afternoon at the Country Club and dinner in the club gazebo with Hixie Rice, vice president of the *Moose County Something.*

9—An all-you-can-eat feast and acoustic rock concert at the Hot Spot with Jennifer Olsen, the theatre club's youngest leading lady.

Qwilleran read the list, nodding at the choices and chuckling a couple of times.

Dwight asked, "How does it strike you? Have we covered the bases? We included Derek and Jennifer to get the young crowd. Derek's groupies will attend en masse, screaming."

"He's not a former chef at the Old Stone Mill," Qwilleran said. "He's a former busboy, who spent two months in the kitchen mixing coleslaw. Girls like him because he's six-feet-eight—and an actor."

Dwight was making notes. "Got it! Any other comments?"

"Everything else looks good. It's well known that Elizabeth Hart has a trust fund worth millions; that'll up the bidding . . . Greg Blythe will go over big. Bidders will expect to get some hot investment tips as well as the Boat Club's famous Cajun Supreme, which is really carp."

"How does Dr. Diane's package hit you, Qwill?"

"She's a personable and intelligent young woman, and everyone likes Tipsy's steaks, but not everyone cares for riding. Are substitutions allowed?"

"You mean, like a complete set of blood tests and an EKG? I doubt it. But we're advertising the auction in Lockmaster, and their horsy crowd will be up here, bidding."

Then Qwilleran said, "Wait a minute! You have only nine packages on this list."

"Precisely why I'm buying your dinner tonight," Dwight said slyly. "Check this out for number ten: A complete makeup and hair styling at Brenda's Salon, prior to dinner at the Old Stone Mill with popular newspaper columnist, Qwill Qwilleran."

The popular columnist hemmed and hawed.

"You're an icon in these parts, Qwill—what with your talent, money, and moustache. Women will bid high to get you! Bidders would fight even to eat tuna casserole at the bombed-out hotel with the richest bachelor in northeast central United States. Fran Brodie will attract high-rollers, too. She's a professional charmer; the Paddock is self-consciously expensive; and the limousine will be driven by the president of the department store in a chauffeur's cap."

Qwilleran nodded with amusement. "That's Larry's favorite shtick. Where are you getting the limousine?"

"From the Dingleberry Brothers, provided they don't have an out-of-town funeral."

When the steaks arrived, Qwilleran had time to consider. Actually the adventure would be material for the "Qwill Pen." The twice-a-week stint was ceaselessly demanding, and readers were clamoring for three a week. Down Below, in a city of millions, it would be easy, but Moose County was a very small beat. Finally he said, "I hope we don't have to stand up in front of the audience like suspects in a police lineup."

"Nothing like that," Dwight assured him. "We've booked the high school auditorium, and there's a Green Room where the celebrities can sit and hear the proceedings on the PA. Onstage there'll be an enlarged photo of each celebrity, courtesy of Bushy. After each package is knocked down, the winner and celebrity will meet onstage and shake hands—amid applause, cheers, and screams, probably."

"I'm glad you explained all this, Dwight. It gives me time to disappear in the Peruvian mountains before auction night." He was merely goading his friend. Finally he said, "Let me congratulate you, Dwight, on your handling of Explo—and not just because you're buying my steak."

"Well, thanks, Qwill. It was a big job. Only one thing worries me. The timing of the explosion at the hotel could not have been worse; it gives 'Explo' a bad connotation. I can't help wondering if there's an element in the county that opposes our celebration of food. Nowadays we have anti-everything factions, but can you imagine anyone being anti-food?"

"The cranks are always with us," Qwilleran said, "hiding behind trees, peeking around corners, going about in disguise, and plotting their selfish little schemes."

When Qwilleran arrived home, it was dark, and the headlights of his car picked up a frantic cat in the kitchen window—leaping about wildly, clawing at the sash—his howls unheard through the glass. Qwilleran jumped from his car, rushed to the back door, and fumbled anxiously with the lock. In the kitchen, a single flick of the switch illuminated the main floor, and Koko flew to the lounge area. Qwilleran followed. There, on the carpet, Yum Yum appeared to be in convulsions, lashing out with all four legs, trying to turn herself inside out. Her tiny head was caught in one of the holes of the cheese basket. The more she fought the wicker noose, the greater her panic.

Qwilleran was in near-panic himself. He shouted her name and tried to grab her, but she was a slippery handful. Going down on his knees, he seized the basket with one hand and held it steady, at the risk of hurting her. With the other hand he captured her squirming flanks and squeezed her body between his knees. How could he withdraw her head without tearing her silky ears? It was impossible. Incredibly, she realized he was trying to help, and her body went limp. Murmuring words of assurance, he broke the strands of dry wicker with his free hand, one after the other, until her head could be freed from the trap.

She gulped a few times as he clutched her to his chest, massaged her ears, and called her his little sweetheart. "You gave us a scare," he said. After a few moments, Yum Yum wriggled out of his arms, licked a patch of fur on her breast, gave one tremendous shudder, and went to the kitchen for a drink of water.

EIGHT

On Sunday morning the church bells rang on Park Circle—the sonorous chimes of the Old Stone Church and the metallic echo of the Little Stone Church.

Earlier in the morning, Qwilleran had received a phone call from Carol Lanspeak, who lived in fashionable West Middle Hummock. She and Larry drove into town every Sunday with garden flowers for the larger, older, grander of the two places of worship. This time they were bringing a new couple to church, recently arrived from Down Below: J. Willard Carmichael and his wife, Danielle.

"He's the new president of Pickax People's Bank, a distinguished-looking man and a real live wire," Carol said. "His wife is much younger and a trifle—well—

flashy. But she's nice. It's a second marriage for him. I think you'd like to meet Willard, Qwill, and they're both dying to see your barn."

Qwilleran listened patiently, waiting for her to come to the point.

"Would you mind if we stopped at the barn after the service—for just a few minutes?"

Qwilleran could never say no to the Lanspeaks. They were a likable pair—not only owners of the department store but enthusiastic supporters of every civic endeavor. "I'll have coffee waiting for you," he said.

"Then we'll skip the coffee hour at the church and see you about twelve-fifteen. Your coffee is better, anyway. Strong, but better."

It was to her credit that she liked his coffee. Some of his best friends made uncomplimentary remarks about its potency. It was, as Carol said, *strong!*

To the Siamese, Qwilleran said, "I want you guys to be on your best behavior. Some city dudes are coming to visit. Try not to act like country bumpkins. No picking of pockets! No untying of shoelaces! No cat fights!" Both of them listened soberly, Koko looking elegantly aristocratic and Yum Yum looking sweetly incapable of crime.

When the Lanspeaks' car eventually pulled into the parking area, Qwilleran pressed the button on the automated coffee maker and gave the visitors a few minutes to admire the barn's exterior before going out to greet them. They were introduced as Willard and Danielle from Detroit.

"Grosse Point, really," she said.

They had an urban veneer, Qwilleran noticed. It was evident in the suavity of their manner, the sophistication of their dress and grooming, and the glib edge to their speech. He invited them indoors.

Carol said, "We've brought you some flowers from our garden . . . . Larry, would you bring them from the trunk?"

It was a pot of mums, blooming profusely.

"Thank you," Qwilleran said. "Unusual color."

"Vintage burgundy," Larry said.

Indoors there were the usual gasps and exclamations as the newcomers viewed the balconies, ramps, lofty rafters, and giant white fireplace cube. The Siamese were sitting on top of it, looking down on the visitors with bemused whiskers.

"Handsome creatures," said Willard. "When we're settled, I'd like to get a couple of Siamese. Is there a local source?"

"There's a breeder in Lockmaster," Qwilleran said with a lack of endorsement, referring to the friend of Polly's who had introduced the belligerent Bootsie into his peaceful life.

Danielle, who had been silently staring at the famous moustache, spoke up, "I'd rather have a kinkajou. They have sexy eyes and yummy fur." Her rather tinny voice reminded Qwilleran of the sound track of early talkies. The other members of the party looked at her wordlessly.

"Shall we have coffee in the lounge?" he suggested. As he served, he was thinking that Danielle was hardly Moose County's idea of a banker's wife—or even a Sunday churchgoer; her dress was too short, her heels too high. Everything about her was studiously seductive: her style, her glances, her semidrawl, her flirtatious earrings. Dangling discs twisted and flashed when she moved.

"And what brings you people to the north woods?" he asked.

The husband, who seemed to be in mid-life, said, "I've reached the stage of maturity where one appreciates the values of country living. Danielle is still looking back, like Lot's wife, but she'll adapt . . . Won't you, sweetheart?"

Sweetheart was pointedly silent, and Qwilleran filled the void by asking her for her first impression of Pickax.

"Well, it's *different!*" she said. "All those farmers! All those pickup trucks! And no malls! Where do people go to shop?"

He glanced at the Lanspeaks, who wore sickly smiles. "We have an excellent department store downtown," he said, "and quite an assortment of specialty shops. We're old-fashioned. We like the idea of shopping downtown."

The banker said, "I'm surprised that mall developers Down Below haven't latched on to this county. There's a lot of undeveloped land between here and the lakeshore."

Qwilleran thought, This guy's dangerous. He said, "That land was owned by the wealthy Klingenschoen family and is now held in trust by the Klingenschoen Foundation—with a mandate to preserve its natural state in perpetuity."

"I don't care. I like malls," Danielle announced. "I lived in Baltimore before I married Willard."

"Ah! Home of the Orioles! Are you a baseball fan?"

"No. Football is more exciting."

Carol said, "Danielle has stage experience, and we're hoping to get her into the theatre club."

Sure, Qwilleran thought; she could play Lola in *Damn Yankees.* "Where are you living?"

"In Indian Village until our house is ready. We

bought the Fitch house in West Middle Hummock—the modern one. I really love the neat modern stuff in this barn. It's exciting."

"Thank you, but all the credit goes to Fran Brodie, a designer at Amanda's studio on Main Street."

"I'll have to go and see her. Our house needs a lot of doing-over. Nobody lived there for three years. It's funny, but it was built for another banker—but he died."

Qwilleran thought, For your information, sweetheart, he was murdered.

The sharp edge of her voice was disturbing the Siamese on the fireplace cube; they were getting restless. Carol too may have reacted to the tension in the air and Danielle's sultry glances beamed in Qwilleran's direction. She said, "Qwill, I've been meaning to ask you: How's Polly?" She turned to the Carmichaels. "Polly Duncan is a very charming woman whom you'll meet eventually—head of the Pickax Public Library. Right now she's recovering from surgery . . . . How soon will she be back in circulation, Qwill?"

"Very soon. I'm taking her for a walk every day."

"Take her to the Scottish Bakery for afternoon tea. She'll love the scones and cucumber sandwiches."

There was increased activity on top of the fireplace cube. Koko stood up and stretched in a tall hairpin curve, then swooped down onto the Moroccan rug that defined the lounge area. Yum Yum followed, and while she checked the banker's feet for shoelaces, Koko walked slowly toward Danielle with subtle intent. She was sitting with her attractive knees crossed, and Koko started sniffing her high-heeled pumps as if she had a nasty foot disease or had stepped in something unpleasant. He wrinkled his nose and bared his fangs.

"Excuse me a moment," Qwilleran said, and grabbed

both cats, banishing them to the broom closet, the only suitable detention center on the main floor.

When he returned to the group, Larry said, "We have something we'd like to discuss with you, Qwill. The recent financial disaster in Sawdust City is going to leave hundreds of families and retirees with no hope of a Christmas, and the Country Club is undertaking to buy food, toys, and clothing for them. We're planning a benefit cheese-tasting; you've probably heard about it. Sip 'n' Nibble will supply the cheese and punch at cost, and Jerry and Jack will sort of cater the affair."

A yowl came from the broom closet as Koko heard a familiar word.

"We were wondering how much to charge for tickets, when our new financial wizard came up with an idea. You explain it, Willard."

"It doesn't take a wizard to figure it out," the banker said. "The lower the ticket price, the more tickets you sell—and the more cheese the purchasers consume. You're better off to charge a higher price and attract fewer people. Your revenue remains the same, but your costs are lower. After all, you're doing this to raise money for charity—not to serve a lot of cheese."

Another round of yowls came from the broom closet.

Larry said, "We were planning to hold the event at the community hall until my dear wife came up with another idea. Tell him, Carol."

"Okay, it's like this. We could charge even more for tickets if we had the cheese-tasting in a really glamorous place. There are people in Moose County who'd give an arm and a leg to see this barn—especially in the evening when the lights are on. It's enchanting."

"You could ask one hundred dollars a ticket," the banker suggested.

It crossed Qwilleran's mind that the K Fund could write a check to finance all the Christmas charities, but it was healthier for the community to be involved. He said, "Why not charge two hundred dollars and limit the number of guests? The higher the price and the smaller the guest list, the more exclusive the event becomes." And, he mused, the less wear and tear on the white rugs.

"In that case," said Willard, "why not make it black tie and increase the price to three hundred?"

"And in that case," Larry said, "we would have two punch bowls, one of them spiked."

There were sounds of thumping and banging in the broom closet and an attention-getting crash.

"We'd better say goodbye," Carol said, "so the delinquents can get out of jail."

Qwilleran was heartily thanked for his hospitality and his generosity in offering the use of the barn. "My pleasure," he mumbled.

Larry pulled him aside as they walked to the parking area and said, "The Chamber of Commerce has formed an ad hoc committee to inquire into the future of the hotel. We can't afford to have a major downtown building looking like a slum. Not only that, but the city needs decent lodging. The owner is in the hospital, possibly on his death bed. His management firm in Lockmaster is suspect—as to capability and, let's face it, honesty. The committee will go to Chicago to petition the K Fund to buy the hotel, either from the owner or from his estate. I hope you approve."

"Excellent idea!" Qwilleran said. "But when it comes to renovating the interior, we don't want any Chicago decorators coming up here and telling us what to do."

All his guests had parting words. Carol whispered, "Koko's shoe-sniffing act was a riot!" . . . The banker said, "Let's have lunch, Qwill." . . . The banker's wife said, "I love your moustache!"

They drove away, and Qwilleran released two poised animals from a closet cluttered with plastic bottles, brushes, and other cleaning equipment knocked off hooks and shelves. Cats, he reflected, had a simple and efficient way of communicating; they were the inventors of civil disobedience. As for Koko's impudent charade with Danielle's shoe, it might be one of his practical jokes, or it might be a sign of a personality clash.

As Qwilleran drove to the goat farm later that afternoon, he remembered only its shabbiness. Now it was registered as a historic place.

The Victorian frame building was freshly painted in two tones of mustard, set off by a neat lawn and a split rail fence. A bronze plaque gave the history of the farm built by Captain Fugtree, a Civil War hero. New barns had been added, goats browsed in the pastures, and a new pickup truck stood in the side drive.

The former hotel clerk and museum manager came out to greet him, looking like a man of the soil. "Kristi will be sorry to miss you. She's in Kansas, showing one of her prize does."

Qwilleran complimented him on the condition of the farm and asked about some shaggy dogs in the pasture with the goats.

"A Hungarian breed of guardian dog," Mitch said. "Do you notice a difference in the new herd? We're specializing in breeds that give the best milk for making the best cheese—two hundred of them now."

"Does Kristi still give them individual names?"

"Absolutely—names like Blackberry, Moonlight,

Ruby, and so on, and they answer to their names. Goats are intelligent—also very social."

They were walking toward a large, sprawling barn—new, but with a weathered rusticity that suited the landscape. One side was open like a pavilion, its floor spongy with a thick covering of straw. Several does of various breeds and colors were lounging, mingling sociably, and amusing themselves as if it were a vacation spa. Hens strutted and pecked around a patient Great Dane, and a calico cat napped on a ledge. Qwilleran took some pictures. Two members of the sisterhood nuzzled his hand and leaned against his legs; a half-grown kid tried to nibble his notebook. This was the holding pen; from here the does would go into the milking parlor, fourteen at a time.

The rest of the barn had white walls, concrete floors hosed down twice a day, stainless-steel vats and tanks, and computerized thermometers. Here the milk was cooled, then pasteurized, then inoculated with culture and enzymes; later the curds would be hand-dipped into molds. This was the French farmstead tradition of cheese-making, using milk produced on the site.

"Sounds like a lot of work," Qwilleran observed.

"It's labor-intensive, that's for sure," Mitch said. "I mean, feeding and breeding the goats, milking two hundred twice a day, plus making the cheese. But there's a lot of joy in goat-farming, and I'll tell you one thing: The does are easier to get along with than some of the volunteers at the museum. The old-timers resented a young guy with new ideas ... Want to go to the house and taste some cheese?"

They sat in the kitchen and sampled the farm's chevre—a white, semisoft, unripened cheese. Mitch said, "It's great for cooking, too. I make a sauce for fettucine that beats Alfredo's by a mile!"

"You sound like an experienced cook," Qwilleran said.

"You could say so. It's always been my hobby. I was collecting cookbooks before I owned my first saucepan. I do more cooking than Kristi does."

"Does she still have ghostly visitors during thunderstorms?"

"No, the house isn't so spooky now that the clutter's gone and the walls are painted. We're thinking of getting married, Qwill."

"Good for you!" That was Qwilleran's ambiguous response to all such announcements. "By the way, do you remember the furor over the disappearance of Iris Cobb's cookbook?"

"I sure do. I thought it was quietly lifted by one of the volunteers, and I had an idea who she was, but it would have been embarrassing to accuse her, and I didn't have proof."

Qwilleran went home with a variety of cheeses: dill, garlic, peppercorn, herb, and feta. On the way back to the barn he pondered the fate of the Cobb recipe book. If it could be recovered, he would have the K Fund publish it for sale, the proceeds going to an Iris Cobb memorial. He could envision a chef's school in conjunction with the college, drawing students from all parts of the country and sending graduates to five-star restaurants. What a tribute it would be to that modest and deserving woman! The Iris Cobb Culinary Institute!

It was pie in the sky, of course. Whoever swiped it probably destroyed it after cannibalizing the best recipes. Everyone thought the culprit was a museum volunteer; no one ever suggested that the culprit may have been the museum manager.

NINE

The electronic chimes of the Little Stone Church clanged their somber summons on Monday morning as hundreds of mourners flocked to the memorial service for Anna Marie Toms. Many were strangers. It was Moose County custom to attend funerals, for whatever reason: sympathy for the survivors, neighborly compassion, curiosity, grim sociability, or just something to talk about all week. Qwilleran walked to the Park Circle to see what was happening. The traffic jam was more than the local police could handle, and state troopers were assisting.

The crowd overflowed the church. Onlookers clustered on adjoining lawns and filled the circular park that divided Main Street into northbound and southbound lanes. Among them were persons that Qwilleran thought he identified as plainclothes detectives from the SBI. He also noticed a misplaced apostrophe in signs carried by Anna Marie's fellow students from Moose County Community College.

ANNA MARIE WE LUV YA
LENNY WER'E WITH YA

He had his camera and took snapshots to show Polly. A detective asked for his identification. Photographers from the *Moose County Something* and the *Lockmaster Ledger* were busy. The afternoon papers would carry their first coverage of the Friday bombing, and they would go all out.

From there Qwilleran walked downtown to the newspaper office and handed in his Tuesday copy. He said to Junior Goodwinter, "I saw Roger and Bushy at the memorial service. The *Ledger* was covering it, too."

"Yeah, we're giving it the works. But, do you know what? You'll never believe this, Qwill. Franklin Pickett, the florist, was in here an hour ago, trying to make a deal. He's the one who sold the flowers to the bombing suspect, and he wanted us to *buy his story!* I told him no thanks and suggested he try the *Ledger!*" The young managing editor exploded with laughter. "I even gave him the address. I told him to ask for the editor in charge of checkbook journalism. He wrote it all down."

"You have a wicked sense of humor," Qwilleran said.

"Well, the *Ledger* is always dumping their rejects on us, you know. They sent us the guy with the talking pig—right after we'd carpeted the city room! Everyone knows how pigs are!"

Qwilleran chuckled at the recollection. "So . . . what are you doing on the front page, Junior?"

"Police releases are minimal, as usual, but we've got man-on-the-street stuff, photos, and a computer sketch of the suspect based on witnesses' descriptions and supplied by the SBI. He's a white, fortyish, clean-shaven male, Qwill, so that lets you off the hook."

"Thanks. I was worried."

"Then we've got a sidebar on the history of the hotel, courtesy of good old Homer. Jill is at the memorial service right now, trying to get a sappy feature story. Roger went to the hospital, hoping to get an interview with Gustav Limburger, but the old crab threw a bedpan at him. Roger also contacted the realty firm in Lockmaster that manages the hotel, but they weren't talking to the media."

"What about the mystery woman? Wasn't her room the target?"

"Yeah. Ona Dolman, her name is. At least, that's the way she registered. She's skipped, though. Left without checking out. Didn't have any luggage to come back for, that's for sure. Owes for five nights. Ona Dolman is also the name she used at the car rental and the library and on traveler's checks. There's no evidence that she used a credit card or personal checks anywhere . . . So we've been busy! How did you spend your weekend?"

"Just scrounging material for my column. Did you talk to any hotel employees?"

"We buttonholed Lenny at the scene, but the police wouldn't let him talk. The chef was chummy with Ona Dolman, according to one of the waitresses. After the blast he picked himself up off the floor, grabbed his knives, and took off! Probably went back to Fall River, Massachusetts. Sounds as if he knows something about

Dolman that the rest of us don't know. Anyway, the police will be checking him out. Frankly, I hope he stays in Fall River."

After talking with Junior, Qwilleran made the rounds of the newspaper offices, where his twice-weekly visits were always welcomed as if he were handing out ten-dollar bills. He wanted to have words with Arch Riker, but the publisher was still at lunch. His secretary, Wilfred, said, "He's been gone a couple of hours, so he should be back soon. Are you sponsoring anybody in the bike-a-thon, Mr. Q?"

"If you're riding, I'm sponsoring. I always back a winner," Qwilleran said as he signed a green pledge card for a dollar a mile.

Next he picked up his fan mail from the office manager, who delighted in handing it to him personally. He knew her only as Sarah, a small woman with steel-gray hair and thick glasses, who had never married. Junior called her "Qwill's number one fan." She memorized chunks of the "Qwill Pen" and quoted them in the office; she knew the names of his cats; she crocheted catnip toys for them. For his part, Qwilleran treated Sarah with exaggerated courtesy and suffered good-natured ribbing in the cityroom about his "office romance."

"Would you like me to slit the envelopes for you, Mr. Q? There are quite a few today." She kept a record of his columns according to topic, plus a tally of the letters generated by each one. She was able to say that cats and baseball were his most popular topics.

"Sarah," he said sternly, "if you don't stop calling me Mr. Q, you'll lose your job. It's a condition of employment here that you call me Qwill."

"I'll try," she said with a happy smile.

"And yes, I'd appreciate it if you'd slit the envelopes."

Next, Hixie Rice beckoned to him from the promotion department. "Sit down," she said. "We have a problem to discuss. Did you see the teasers on the Food Forum in last week's editions? We haven't been getting any results—not one!"

"I remember seeing them," he said. "Show me a copy to refresh my memory." The announcement, which looked more like an ad than a news item, read:

ATTENTION! FOODIES!

Do you have questions about food, cooking, or nutrition? Are you hunting for a particular recipe? Would you like to share one of your own? Do you have any pet peeves about food, or food stores, or restaurants?

THE FOOD FORUM IS FOR YOU!

Send us your queries, quips, beefs, and suggestions. We want to hear from you. They'll be printed in the Food Forum on the food page every Thursday.

Hixie said, "Is there something wrong with our readers? Or is there something wrong with us?"

Qwilleran considered the questions briefly. "Well, first of all, our readers may not know what a foodie is. Second, they may not want to be called foodies. Third, you don't state whether their names will be used. Mostly, I would say, they don't quite get the idea, or they're waiting for someone else to start it. This is not Down Below; this is four hundred miles north of everywhere."

"What are you saying, Qwill? That we should run a dummy column on the first food page?"

"Something like that—to prime the pump . . . Why are you looking at me like that, Hixie? I see a sudden happy expression of premeditated buck-passing."

"Would you do it, Qwill? Would you write some fake letters with fake signatures? You'd be good at it."

"Are you implying that fakery is my forte? I've always left that to the advertising profession."

"Ouch! I don't care. Hit me again. Just do this one favor for me, and I'll be forever grateful. The Food Forum was my idea, and I'd hate to have a complete flop."

At that point Wilfred interrupted; the boss had returned.

"Okay, Hixie, I'll see what I can do," Qwilleran said.

"And don't let anyone on the staff know," she cautioned him.

"No problem. I'll hand in my copy disguised as a box of chocolates."

He was still in a bantering mood when he went into the publisher's office. "Were you having another power lunch?" he asked. "Or was it a three-Scotch goof-off?"

Riker rebuked him with a frown. "I was having an important luncheon with the editor in chief of the *Lockmaster Ledger.*"

"At the Palomino Paddock? Who paid?"

There was another scowl. "The *Ledger* is giving full coverage to the bombing, and we both think it's a two-county story. We're sharing sources. We also discussed the hostility and prejudice that exists between the two counties. We should be working for the same goals instead of sniping at each other at every opportunity."

"Let's not get too brotherly," Qwilleran said. "Sniping is the spice of life."

"Since you're feeling so good," Riker said, "how'd you like to take on an extra assignment—in a pinch?"

Qwilleran's flippancy switched to wariness. "Like what?"

"Wednesday night's the opening session of Mildred's series of cooking classes for men only, and the course is a sellout. We should have a reporter there."

"What's the matter with Roger? He's on nights this week." Roger MacGillivray was a general assignment reporter married to Sharon Hanstable, Mildred's daughter.

"Sharon is assistant demonstrator for the course, so Roger has to stay home and baby-sit Wednesday night," Riker explained. Then his usually bland expression changed to a roguish one. "However, Roger could cover the story, and you could baby-sit. Or Sharon could stay home with the kids, and you could help Mildred with the demonstration."

Gruffly Qwilleran said, "Tell Roger to stay home. What time does the class start? Where's it being held?"

"Seven-thirty at the high school, in the home ec department. Take a camera."

"What's the deadline?"

"Thursday noon, firm. Earlier if possible."

"What is Mildred going to teach these guys? How to make grilled cheese sandwiches?"

Riker ignored the remark. "Most men who signed up want to master one or two specialties, like barbecued spare ribs or Italian spaghetti. If I do say so myself, I make a memorable stuffed cabbage, but nothing else."

"How come I've known you since kindergarten and never tasted your memorable stuffed cabbage?"

Shrugging off the question, Riker went on. "Some of the requests made by the class are meatloaf, Oriental stir-fry, pan-fried trout, Swiss steak, and so on."

"Okay, Arch. If I do this for you," Qwilleran said, "you owe me one."

"Any time you say, friend."

On the way out of the building, Qwilleran picked up a paper from a bundle that had just come from the printing plant. The headline read: SEARCH TWO COUNTIES FOR BOMB MURDERER. He planned to read it with his lunch at Lois's.

Lois herself was waiting on tables. "Is that today's paper?" she asked. "Is Lenny's picture in it?"

Qwilleran scanned the front page, the carry-over on three, and the photo spread on the back page. "Doesn't look like it," he said, "but Lenny had his picture in the paper when he won the silver, and I imagine he looks better in a helmet than a bandage. How's he doing?"

"Not good. He's down in the dumps. Him and Anna Marie were gonna get married, you know . . . What'll it be for you today, besides three cups of coffee?"

He ordered a Reuben sandwich and reserved a piece of apple pie, one of Lois's specialties that sold out fast. While waiting for the sandwich, he perused the paper. There were photos of the shattered interior of room 203; the fallen chandelier lying on the reservation desk; the hotel exterior, windowless and draped with debris. There was also a photo of Anna Marie copied from her driver's license, found in her handbag in the employees' locker room.

Of unusual interest was the computer-composite of the suspect's probable likeness, this being the first time such a technical advance had appeared in the local paper. It would also be running in the *Lockmaster Ledger,* and the good folk of two counties would carry it around and peer suspiciously into every passing face.

The lead story was set in large type, giving it importance and concealing the embarrassing truth that there was little to report that was not already generally known:

Law enforcement agencies are combing two counties in their search for the suspect who allegedly planted a bomb in the New Pickax Hotel, killing one employee, injuring two others, and causing extensive property damage. The explosion occurred Friday at 4:20 P.M. No guests were on the premises at that time.

Pronounced dead at the scene was Anna Marie Toms, 20, of Chipmunk, a part-time housekeeping aide at the hotel and nursing student at Moose County Community College.

Desk clerk Leonard Inchpot, 23, of Kennebeck sustained a head injury when a chandelier dropped from a ceiling above the registration desk. Manager Isabelle Croy of Lockmaster was thrown to the floor in her second-floor office. Both were treated at the Pickax Hospital and released.

"Several members of the staff were shaken up," said Croy. "Because it was late Friday afternoon, all the commercial travelers had checked out, and the dinner hour hadn't started yet. We feel terribly upset about Anna Marie. She was new and trying so hard to do a good job."

Major damage occurred at the front of the building on the second floor, with the bomb allegedy planted in room 203. A police spokesperson said that a white, middle aged, clean-shaven man entered the hotel at approximately four o'clock to deliver what he said was a birthday gift and also a bouquet of flowers for the occupant of 203. Shortly after, Toms was seen entering the room with a vacuum cleaner "because the flowers had made a mess on the rug," Croy said. The explosion occurred within minutes.

PPD chief Andrew Brodie said, "A couple of thousand bombings are reported in the U.S. every year. Dynamite and blasting caps and other components of homemade bombs are easy to buy, and too many nuts out there have the know-how. You can even make a bomb with fertilizer."

Room 203 had been occupied for the last two weeks by a woman registered as Ona Dolman of Columbus, OH. She has not been seen since the bombing. A spokesperson at the airport reported that a woman using that name returned a rental car at 5:20 P.M. Friday and boarded the shuttle flight to Minneapolis. The *Moose County Something* has not been able to locate anyone of that name in Columbus, OH.

Local police are being assisted in the investigation by detectives, bomb experts, and forensic technicians of the SBI, as well as the sheriff departments of Moose and Lockmaster counties.

The photo of room 203 was a scene of incredible destruction: walls gouged, doors ripped off, ceiling panels hanging down, and furnishings shredded and flung about the room like confetti. Qwilleran read the lead story twice; there was no mention that the desk clerk allowed the stranger to take the gift upstairs himself. Then Qwilleran wondered, If the "clean-shaven" stranger had worn a shaggy beard and long hair, and if he had been carrying a six-pack of beer instead of flowers, would he have been allowed to go up to 203? He also wondered about the manager's remark that commercial travelers checked out Friday afternoon. Did that fact have anything to do with the timing of the explosion? If the Lockmaster management firm had indeed plotted the incident, as some believed, did the in-house manager (from Lockmaster) suggest the best time to pull it off?

There was more on the front page. A bulletin stated: "Do not open gifts or other unexpected packages delivered to your home or place of business—if the sender is unknown. Play it safe! Contact the police!"

A human interest anecdote with an ironic twist was included as a sidebar:

> After the "birthday gift" had been delivered to room 203, the desk clerk notified the kitchen that it was Dolman's birthday, and the chef, Karl Oskar, prepared to bake her a birthday cake. He was mixing the batter when the bomb exploded, and both he and the batter ended up on the floor.

Qwilleran finished his lunch and went to Amanda's Design Studio to speak with Fran Brodie. The designer was cloistered in a consultation booth with an indecisive client and a hundred samples of blue fabric. Fran saw him and made a grimace of desperation, but he signaled no-hurry and ambled about the shop. He liked to buy small decorative objects once in a while, partly to please the daughter of the police chief.

When Fran finally appeared at his elbow, he was examining a pair of carved wooden masks painted in garish colors. "That woman!" she muttered. "She's a sweet little lady, but she can never make up her mind. She'll come back tomorrow with her mother-in-law and again on Saturday with her husband, who couldn't care less. He'll point to a sample at random and say it's the best, and she'll place the order. . . . What do you think of my Sri Lanka masks?"

"Is that what they are? I'd hate to meet one of them in a dark alley." They were mythical demons with wicked fangs, bulging eyes, rapacious beaks, and bristling head-dresses.

"By the way," Fran said, "you made a big hit with the new banker's wife. She came in this morning, and all she could talk about was you and your barn. She thinks you're charming. She loves your voice. She loves your moustache. Don't let Polly hear about Danielle; she'll have a relapse. But thanks for giving me credit for the barn, Qwill. She'll be a good customer. She hates blue."

"Did you sign her up for the theatre club? I hear she's had stage experience."

"Well . . . yes. She was a night-club entertainer in Baltimore. Her stage name was Danielle Devoe . . . Is that today's paper you're carrying?"

"Take it. I've read it. There's nothing new," he said. "You probably know more than the newspaper."

"I know they've run a check on Ona Dolman. Her driver's license is valid, but there's no such address as the one she gave the hotel. The suspect was described as wearing a blue nylon jacket and a black baseball cap with a 'fancy' letter D on the front. He got into a blue pickup behind the hotel."

Qwilleran thought, Nine out of ten males in Moose County drive blue pickups and wear blue jackets; they also wear high-crowned farm caps advertising fertilizer

or tractors. Baseball caps are worn chiefly by sport fishermen from Down Below. The suspect's black one
sounds like a Detroit Tigers cap; the letter D is in Old
English script.

To Fran he said, "I think I'll take these hideous
masks. Would you gift-wrap them and deliver them to
Polly on Gingerbread Alley? I'll write a gift card."

Dubiously the designer said, "Will she like them?
They don't represent her taste in decorative objects."

"Don't worry. It's a joke." On the card he wrote: "A
pair of diet deities to bless your kitchen: Lo Phat and Lo
Psalt."

TEN

As Qwilleran fed the cats on Tuesday morning, a hundred questions unreeled in front of his brain's eye:

Who had bombed the hotel—and why? Would he strike again?

What would happen to the hotel now? Would it ever be restored? Was this the beginning of the end for downtown Pickax?

Were mall developers from Down Below implicated in the bombing? Did they want to see the demise of downtown shopping?

What was J. Willard Carmichael's true reason for moving to Moose County? Did Pickax People's Bank have an interest in promoting mall development?

And what about Iris Cobb's cookbook? Would it ever be found?

And what about the Food Forum? Was it just another of Hixie's harebrained ideas? Why should he waste his time dummying a column for her when he had problems of his own?

Feeding words and thoughts into the bottomless maw of the "Qwill Pen" was one problem. Feeding two fussy felines was another, more immediate, more exasperating problem. They had been on a seafood binge, and he had stocked up on canned clams, tuna, crabmeat, and cocktail shrimp. Today they were turning up their wet black noses at a delicious serving of top-quality red sockeye salmon with the black skin removed.

"Cats!" he muttered. Koko was the chief problem, having spent his formative years in the household of a gourmet cook. That cat wanted to order from a menu every day! Yum Yum merely tagged along with her male companion. She was the type of cat who could live on love: stroking, hugging, sweet words, a ready lap.

Qwilleran found himself yearning for other times, other places—when Iris Cobb was his housekeeper, when he lived in Robert Maus's high-class boarding house, when Hixie was managing the Old Stone Mill and sending the busboy over with cat-sized servings of the daily specials. He was aware of the conventional wisdom: If they get hungry enough, they'll eat it. But he, unfortunately, was the humble servant of two sovereign rulers, and he knew it. He admitted it. What was worse, they knew it.

Qwilleran left the two plates of untouched salmon on the kitchen floor in the feeding station and went to breakfast at Lois's, knowing she often had interesting leftovers in the refrigerator, waiting to go into the soup pot. It was raining, so he drove his car.

He sat in his favorite booth and ordered pancakes. Lois's son was serving. The rather large adhesive bandage on his forehead indicated that he had looked up when the bomb exploded and the chandelier dropped.

"Will you be able to ride in the bike-a-thon Sunday?" Qwilleran asked him.

"I don't much feel like it, but everybody tells me I should." Lenny Inchpot had the lean and hungry look of a bike racer, the neatly groomed look of a hotel clerk, and the stunned look of a young man facing tragedy for the first time.

"If you bike, I'll sponsor you at a dollar a mile."

"Take it!" Lois shouted from the cash register. "Give him a green card!" It was not really a shout; it was Lois's usual commanding voice.

Qwilleran asked Lenny, "What's the best place to get some good pictures?"

"About a mile south of Kennebeck, where the road runs between two patches of woods. Know where I mean? We're just starting out—no drop-outs—no stragglers. It's some sight! You see a hundred bikers come over the hill! The paper's gonna print a map of the route on Friday, and everybody knows that's the best place to shoot, so get there early. Take a lotta film. There's a prize, you know, for the best shot."

As they talked, Qwilleran felt someone staring at them from a nearby table. It proved to be a husky man with a pudgy face and long white hair. He was eating pancakes.

"Good morning," Qwilleran said. "How are the flap-jacks today?"

"They're good! Almost as good as my mom's. Lois

always gives me a double stack and extra butter. I bring my own honey. D'you like honey on flapjacks? Try it. It's good." The beekeeper leaned across the aisle, offering Qwilleran a plastic squeeze bottle shaped like a bear-cub.

"Thank you. Thank you very much . . . How is Mr. Limburger? Do you know?"

"Yeah. I took him a jar of honey yesterday, and he threw it at the window, so I guess he's feeling pretty good. Coulda broke the glass. He wants to come home. The doctor says: No way!"

Qwilleran dribbled honey on his pancakes and staged a lip-smacking demonstration of enjoyment. "Delicious! Best I've ever tasted!" Then he noticed the front page of Monday's newspaper on Aubrey's table. "What did you think of the hotel bombing?"

"Somebody got killed!" the beekeeper said with a look of horror on his face. He stared at his plate briefly, then jumped up and went to the cash register.

"Aubrey, don't forget your honey!" Qwilleran waved the squeeze bottle.

The man rushed back to the table, snatched it, and left the lunchroom in a hurry.

Lenny ran after him in the rain. "Hey, you forgot your change!"

Lois said, "What's the matter with him? He didn't even finish his double stack."

"He's wacko from too many bee stings," her son said.

"Well, you wash his table—good! It's all sticky . . . How'd you like the flapjacks, Mr. Q?"

"Great! Especially with honey. You should make it available to your customers."

"Costs too much."

"Charge extra."

"They wouldn't pay."

"By the way, Lois, could I scrounge a little something for the cats? Tack it on to my check."

"Don't be silly, Mr. Q. I always have a handout for those two spoiled brats. No charge. Is ham okay?"

With a foil-wrapped package in the trunk of his car, Qwilleran drove to the public library for a conference with Homer Tibbitt, but the aged historian was not to be found in his usual chair. Nor was he in the restroom, taking a nip from his thermos bottle. One of the clerks explained that rainy weather made his bones ache, and he stayed home.

A phone call to the retirement village where the nonagenarian lived with his octogenarian wife produced an invitation. "Come on over and bring some books on lake shipwrecks. Also the file on the Plensdorf family." At ninety-five-plus, Homer Tibbitt had no intention of wasting a morning.

The historian was sitting in a cocoon of cushions for his back, knees, and elbows when Qwilleran arrived. "I need all this padding because I'm skin and bones," he complained. "Rhoda's trying to starve me to death with her low-fat-this and no-fat-that. I'd give my last tooth for a piece of whale blubber."

"Homer, dear," his wife said sweetly, "you've always been as thin as a string bean, but you're healthy and productive, and all your contemporaries are in their graves." She served Qwilleran herb tea and some cookies that reminded him of Polly's dietetic delight.

He said to Homer, "Under these circumstances, my mission today may prove painful. I want to know what food was like in the old days, before tenderizers and flavor-enhancers."

"I'll tell you what it was like! It tasted like *food!* We lived on a farm outside Little Hope when I was a boy. We had our own chicken and eggs, homemade bread made with real flour, milk from our own cow, home-grown fruit and vegetables, and maple syrup from our own trees. I never even saw an orange or banana until I went away to normal school. That's what they called teacher training colleges in those days. I never found out why. Rhoda thinks it's a derivation from the French . . . What was I talking about?"

"The food you ate on the farm."

"Our fish came from Black Creek or the lake, and sometimes we butchered a hog. Anything we didn't eat we took to Little Hope and exchanged for flour, sugar, and coffee at the general store."

"And calico to make dresses for your womenfolk," Rhoda added.

Qwilleran asked, "What happened when the mines closed and the economy collapsed?"

"With no jobs, there was no money for food, and no market for our farm produce. We all tightened our belts."

Rhoda said, "Tell him about the rationing in World War One."

"Oh, that! Well, you see, sugar was in short supply, and in order to buy a pound of it, we had to buy five pounds of oatmeal. We ate oatmeal every day for break-fast and sometimes dinner and supper. I haven't eaten the stuff since! After the war I went away to school and discovered fancy eating, like creamed chicken and peas, and prune whip. I thought that was real living! Then I came home to teach, and it was back to boiled dinners, squirrel pie, fried smelt, and bread pudding. What a let-down! Then came the Great Depression, and we majored in beans and peanut butter sandwiches."

Qwilleran said, "You haven't mentioned the foremost regional specialty."

The Tibbitts said in unison, "Pasties!"

"If you write about them," Homer said, "tell the green horns from Down Below that they rhyme with *nasty,* not *hasty.* You probably know that Cornish miners came here from Britain in the mid-nineteenth century. Their wives made big meat-and-potato turnovers for their lunch, and they carried them down the mine shaft in their pockets. They're very filling. Takes two hands to eat one."

Rhoda said, "There's disagreement about the recipe, but the real pasty dough is made with lard and suet. I don't approve of animal fat, but that's the secret! The authentic filling is diced or cubed beef or pork. *Ground meat is a no-no!* It's mixed with diced potatoes and rutabagas, chopped onion, salt and pepper, and a big lump of butter. You put the filling on a circle of dough and fold it over. Some cooks omit the rutabagas."

Qwilleran said, "There's a Pasty Parlor opening in downtown Pickax on Stables Row."

"Unfortunately," she said, "pasties are no longer in our diet. Homer and I haven't had one for years . . . Have we, dear?"

They turned to look at the historian. His chin had sunk on his chest, and he was sound asleep.

Having been briefed in Pasty Correctness by the knowledgeable Tibbitts, Qwilleran went to Stables Row to check out the Pasty Parlor, not yet open for business. Behind locked doors there were signs of frantic preparation, but he knocked, identified himself, and was admitted. A bright young couple in paint-spattered grubbies introduced themselves as the proprietors.

"Are you natives of Moose County?" he asked, although he noted something brittle about their appearance and attitude that indicated otherwise.

"No, but we've traveled up here on vacations and eaten a lot of pasties, and we decided you people need to expand your horizons," the young man said. "We made a proposal to the K Fund in Chicago and were accepted."

"What was your proposal?"

"A designer pasty! Great-tasting! Very unique! Choice of four crusts: plain, cheese, herb, or cornmeal. Choice of four fillings: ground beef, ham, turkey, or sausage meat. Choice of four veggies: green pepper, broccoli, mushroom, or carrot—besides the traditional potato and onion, of course. Plus your choice of tomato, olive, or hot chili garnish—or all three—at no extra charge."

"It boggles the mind," Qwilleran said with a straight face. "I'll be back when you're open for business. Good luck!"

From there he hurried through the rain to Lori Bamba's brainchild: The Spoonery. It was not yet open for business, but the energetic entrepreneur was lettering signs and hanging posters. He asked her, "Are you serious about serving only spoon-food?"

"Absolutely! I have dozens of recipes for wonderful soups: Mulligatawny, Scotch broth, Portuguese black bean, eggplant and garlic, and lots more. Soup doesn't have to be boring, although I'll have one boring soup each day for the fuddy-duddies."

"What does your family think about it?"

"Nick's very supportive, although he's working hard at the turkey farm. My kids are taste-testing the soups. My in-laws are helping set up the kitchen . . . How are

Koko and Yum Yum? I haven't seen them since Breakfast Island.

"They're busy as usual, inventing new ways to complicate my life."

Lori said with her usual exuberance, "Do you know what I read in a magazine? Cats have twenty-four whiskers, which may account for their ESP."

"Does that include the eyebrows?"

"I don't know. They didn't specify."

"Are there twenty-four whiskers on each side, or is that the total?" he asked.

"I don't know. You journalists are such fuss pots!"

"Well, I'll go home and count," Qwilleran said. "And good luck, Lori! I'll drop in for lunch someday."

It was still raining. He went home to give the Siamese the ham he had begged from Lois, and he found Koko doing his grasshopper act. The cat jumped in exaggerated arcs from floor to desktop to chair to bookshelf. It meant that there was a message on the answering machine. The faster he jumped, it appeared, the more urgent the call. How did the cat know the content of the message? Perhaps Lori was right, Qwilleran thought; cats have ESP whiskers.

The message was from Sarah, the office manager, who had never phoned him at the barn before. "Sorry to bother you at home," said the deferential voice, "but an express letter came for you. I thought I should let you know."

He got her on the phone immediately. "Sarah, this is Qwill. About the express letter, what's the return address?"

"It's just hotel stationery. No one's name. It's from Salt Lake City."

"I'll pick it up right away. Thanks." Qwilleran felt a tingling on his upper lip; he had a hunch who was writing to him. He drove to the newspaper via the back road, to make better time.

Sarah handed him the letter. "Shall I slit the envelope for you?" she offered.

"Not this time, thanks."

He carried it to an empty desk in the cityroom and tore it open, looking first at the signature: Onoosh Dolmathakia. The handwriting was hard to decipher, and she spoke English better than she wrote it. She had trouble with verbs, and she was nervous, frightened. The brief note dripped with emotion:

> Dear Mr. Qwill—
>   I sorry I leave and not say thank you—I hear it on radio about hotel bomb—I panick—he is threttan me many time—he want to kill me—I think it good I go away—long way away—so he not find me—how he find me in Pickacks is not to know—now I afraid again—I not feel safe if he alive—always I run away where he not find me—I leave this hotel now—I sign my right name—
>   Onoosh Dolmathakia

When Qwilleran finished reading the letter for the second time, he felt his neck flush and beads of perspiration drench his forehead—not at the thought of Onoosh being terrorized by a stalker, but at the realization that Koko had been feeding him this information ever since the bombing, and even before. Koko had been stalking Yum Yum boldly and repeatedly, in a way that looked like a purposeful campaign.

Qwilleran telephoned the police station. "Stay there!" he barked at Brodie. "I have some curious information." A few minutes later, he walked into the chief's office.

"What've you got?" Brodie demanded gruffly.

"A letter from Onoosh Dolmathakia, a.k.a. Ona Dolman. Don't ask any questions till you read it. She addressed it to me at the paper."

Brodie grunted several times as he read it, then threw it down on the desk. "Why the hell didn't she tell us his name—and how to find him? Stupid!"

"Not stupid," Qwilleran protested. "She's in panic. She's not thinking straight."

"We can assume he lives Down Below. That means he transported explosives across a state line—a federal offense. The FBI will get into the act now. My God! Did the guy fly up here on the shuttle with a homemade bomb on his lap—in fancy wrappings? Crazy woman! Why didn't she give us more information? She's left Salt Lake City by now."

Qwilleran said, "Dolman is obviously an Americanization of Dolmathakia and not the name of her ex-husband. All we know about him is that he might be a fan of the Detroit Tigers, judging by the description of his cap."

"There's gotta be a local connection. How would he know she was here? Who drove the getaway vehicle? Did the same blue truck pick him up at the airport?"

"Well, the ball's in your court, Andy. I have unfinished business at home. Give me Onoosh's letter."

"I'll keep the original," the chief said. "You can have a copy."

Qwilleran went home and counted whiskers. He counted Koko's first and then Yum Yum's. It was just as he had surmised. He telephoned Polly immediately.

At the sound of his voice, Polly was convulsed with merriment. She said, "Lo Phat and Lo Psalt have just arrived, and I laughed so hard I almost ruptured my thoracic incision! When I saw the gift box, I thought it was a bomb, but it came from Amanda's, so I felt safe in opening it. I'm going to hang them in my kitchen. Qwill, you're so clever!"

"Yes, I know," he said tartly. "I should get a job in advertising."

"You sound rushed. Is something on your mind?"

"I want you to count Bootsie's whiskers and call me back," he said. "Include the eyebrows."

"Is this another joke?"

"Not at all. It's a scientific study. I plan to introduce it in the 'Qwill Pen' after the Food Explo. Cats all over the county will be having their whiskers counted."

"I still think you're being facetious," she said, "but I'll do it and call you back."

In a few minutes she phoned. "Bootsie has twenty-four on each side. Is that good or bad? Some are long and bold; others are shorter and quite fine."

"That means he's normal," Qwilleran said. "Yum Yum has twenty-four also. Koko has thirty!"

ELEVEN

The Great Food Explo was about to blast off, with Mildred Riker's cooking class lighting the fuse:

Wednesday evening: First in a series of cooking classes for men only, sponsored by the *Moose County Something*.

Thursday: Introduction of the *Something*'s weekly food page, featuring a Food Forum for readers.

Friday noon: Official opening of Stables Row with ribbon-cutting, band music, and balloons.

Friday evening: Open-house hospitality on Main Street, with all stores remaining open until 9:00 P.M. and offering refreshments and entertainment . . . to be followed by fireworks and a street dance in front of Stables Row.

Saturday: Food Fair and Pasty Bake-off at the county fairgrounds, sponsored by the Pickax Chamber of Commerce.

Saturday evening: Celebrity Auction sponsored by the Boosters Club to benefit the community Christmas fund.

Sunday: Wheels for Meals bike-a-thon staged by the Pedal Club to benefit the home-bound.

Qwilleran was involved in many of the week's activities, not entirely by choice. Reluctantly he had consented to cover the opening session of the cooking class. Without much enthusiasm he would join Mildred Riker and the chef of the Old Stone Mill in judging the Pasty Bake-off. With serious misgivings he would go on the auction block as a potential dinner date for who-knows-whom. In addition, he was committed to writing the "Qwill Pen" with a food slant for the duration of Explo.

Qwilleran's life seldom proceeded according to plan, however. On Wednesday he went to Lois's for lunch. Her Wednesday luncheon special was always turkey, and he always took home a doggie bag. Lois's Luncheonette was on Pine Street not far from Stables Row, and as he approached he saw a crowd gathered on the sidewalk—not a friendly crowd. He quickened his step.

Milling about, waving arms and expounding vehemently, were men in work clothes and business suits. A few women office workers and shoppers wore anxious expressions and raised shrill voices.

Qwilleran asked loudly, "What goes on here? What's happened?" No one answered, but there was a general hubbub of indignation and complaint. Then he saw the hastily crayoned sign in the window: CLOSED FOR GOOD. The protesters were yelling:

"Where'll we get ham and eggs? There's no place for breakfast!"

"Where'll we get lunch?"

"There's the new soup kitchen, but who wants soup every day?"

"There's the new pasty place, but I get pasties at home."

"Who'll have apple pie that's any good?"

Qwilleran asked some of the quieter protesters, "Why did she close? Does anyone know?"

"Could be she's afraid of the new competition," a City Hall clerk suggested.

"If you ask me," said a salesman from the men's store, "she's tee'd off because Stables Row got all slicked up by the K Fund. If she wanted to fix up her place, her customers had to pitch in and do it."

An elderly man said, "Some people in town want her to quit so they can get the building and tear it down."

It was indeed a sad old structure. Qwilleran had often dropped a twenty into a pickle jar near the cash register to help defray the cost of shingles or paint. The labor was willingly donated on weekends by a confraternity of loyal customers. They enjoyed doing it. To work on Lois's beloved lunchroom was the Pickax equivalent of knighthood in the court of King Arthur. There was, in fact, a large round table where the in-group met for coffee and conversation. And now she was leaving the food business after thirty years of feeding Pickaxians. It was a calamity! First the hotel bombing—and now this!

Qwilleran went to the Old Stone Mill for lunch. He said to the excessively tall young man who was his waiter, "I hear you've enrolled in the Restaurant Management course, Derek."

"Yeah, Liz talked me into going to MCCC," said the scion of the Cuttlebrinks. "In two years I can get an associate degree. I'm carrying a full load. The boss here gives me flexible hours."

"I'm glad you've decided to stay in the food business."

"Yeah, Liz thinks I have a talent for it. Acting is something I can do as a hobby, she says."

"What's today's special, Derek?"

"Curried lamb stew."

"Is it good?" Qwilleran was aware that this was a senseless question; what waiter would denigrate the chef's daily special? Yet, restaurant-goers everywhere had been heard to ask it, and now Qwilleran repeated it. "Do you recommend it?"

"Well, I tried it in the kitchen before I came on duty," Derek said, "and I thought it bombed. You'd be better off to take the beef Stroganoff."

The cooking class at the high school was scheduled for 7:30 P.M., but Qwilleran arrived early, hoping to glean some quotable comments from the participants. Eleven men were present, some of whom he knew; all of them knew Qwilleran, or recognized his moustache. They included the new banker, a commercial fisherman, and even the tall waiter from the Old Stone Mill. They had an assortment of reasons for attending:

Mechanic from Gippel's Garage: "My wife went back to work, teaching school, and she says I've gotta do some of the housework. I like to eat, so maybe I'll learn how to cook."

J. Willard Carmichael: "Cooking has replaced jogging as the thing to do! Besides, Danielle is no bombshell in the kitchen, and it behooves me to set a good example."

Hardware salesman: "I'm a single parent with two kids, and I want to impress them."

Derek Cuttlebrink: "Liz gave me the course for a birthday present."

Commercial fisherman: "My wife sent me to find out how to cook fish without so much grease. She just got out of the hospital, and she's on a diet."

Qwilleran was tempted to say, I've got a good cookie recipe for you. Instead he said, "You must be Aubrey's brother. His honey farm was the subject of my column yesterday."

"Yeah! Yeah! We all read it. The family was glad to see him get some attention. He's kinda shy, you know. Stays by himself, mostly. But he's got a lot on the ball, in some ways."

There was an unmistakable aroma of Thanksgiving dinner in the classroom. Qwilleran decided it was Mildred's crafty psychology to put the class in a good food mood. Promptly at 7:30 she appeared, her ample figure filling out an oversized white bib-apron. A floppy white hat topped her graying hair, and the insouciance of its floppiness made her audience warm up to her immediately.

After a few words of welcome, she began: "Thanksgiving is not far off, and some of you checked turkey on your list of requests, so tonight we'll take the mystery out of roasting the big bird and make you all instant turkey experts. This will be a two-bird demonstration, because roasting takes several hours. Bird Number One has been in the oven since four o'clock and will be ready for carving and sampling at the end of the session."

Qwilleran's interest in the class increased as he visualized a take-home for the Siamese. He clicked his camera as Sharon Hanstable entered the arena with Bird Number Two on a tray—plucked, headless, raw, and sickly pale. In bib-apron and floppy hat, she was a younger, thinner

version of her mother, with the same wholesome pretti-
ness and outgoing personality. Smiling happily and bantering with the audience, she handed out notepads,
pencils, and brochures containing roasting charts and
stuffing recipes.

Mildred said, "This handsome gobbler, which weighs a
modest twelve pounds, arrived in a frozen state from the
new Cold Turkey Farm and has been defrosting for two
days in the refrigerator. Please repeat after me: *I will
never . . . thaw a frozen turkey . . . at room temperature.*"

A chorus of assorted male voices obediently took the
oath.

"Now for Step One: Preset the oven at three hundred
twenty-five degrees. Step Two: Release the legs that are
tucked under a strip of skin, but do not cut the skin."

Eleven pencils and Qwilleran's ballpoint were busily
taking notes.

"Step Three: Explore the breast and body cavities and
remove the plastic bags containing neck and giblets.
These are to be used in making gravy. Step Four: Rinse
the bird and drain it thoroughly."

Qwilleran thought, This is easy; I could do it; what's
the big deal?

"Meanwhile, Sharon has been mixing the stuffing. It's
called 'Rice-and-Nice' in your brochure. It consists of
cooked brown rice, mushrooms, water chestnuts, and
other flavorful veggies. So . . . Ready for Step Five: Stuff
the cavities lightly with the rice mixture."

Mildred tucked in the legs, placed the bird breast-up on
a rack in the roasting pan, brushed it with oil, inserted a
thermometer, and explained the basting process. By the
time Bird Two was ready to go into the oven, Bird One
was ready to come out—plump-breasted, glossy, and
golden brown. She demonstrated the carving and the

making of giblet gravy. Then the men were invited to help
themselves.

"Good show!" Qwilleran said to Mildred as he filled
his paper plate for the second time.

"Stick around," she said in a whisper. "You can have
the leftovers for Koko and Yum Yum."

The day after the cooking class, Qwilleran's rave re-
view appeared on the newspaper's new food page, along
with a feature on fall barbecues, an interview with the
chef of the new Boulder House Inn, and the Food Forum.
The comments and questions submitted to the Forum
were signed with initials only, and they were interesting
enough to have readers guessing: Who was B.L.T. in
Pickax? Who was E.S.P. in Mooseville?

> Does anyone know a good way to cook musk-
> rat? My grandmother used to bake hers with
> molasses. It sure was good!
>
>   —*E.S.P., in Mooseville.*

> If they reopen the dining room at the Pickax
> Hotel, I hope they do something about those
> ghastly streetlights on Main Street. They
> shine in the windows and turn the food green
> or purple.   —*B.L.T., in Pickax.*

> I once ate a delicious coconut cream cake with
> apricot filling that a dear lady made for a
> church bazaar. She has since passed away. Her
> name was Iris Cobb. Does anyone know the
> recipe?   —*A.K.A., in Brrr.*

I don't have time to cook anything with more than three ingredients, and here's a casserole that my kids are crazy about. A can of spaghetti in tomato sauce, a can of lima beans, and six boiled hot dogs cut in chunks.

—*A.T.T., in Sawdust City.*

My pet peeve—those restaurants so dark you can't read the menu without a flashlight. I won't mention any names, but you know who I mean.   —*I.R.S., in Pickax.*

Help! Does anyone know the secret of the wonderful meatloaf that Iris Cobb used to bring to potluck suppers at the museum? My husband still raves about it. Help save our marriage!

—*B.S.A., in Kennebeck.*

I think that I shall never see
A better cheese than one called Brie.
My brother goes for Danish blue;
My boss is nuts for Port du Salut.
Some folks in Pickax all declare
The tops in cheese is Camembert.
To each his own, but as for me,
I cast my vote for creamy Brie.

—*J.M.Q., in Pickax.*

The *Something* celebrated the debut of the food page with an in-house party in the cityroom. Staffers drank champagne and ate turkey sandwiches, thriftily made from the meat of Bird Number Two. They praised Mildred for her barbecue story, Jill for her interview with the chef, and Hixie for her brilliant idea of reader participation. Everyone was surprised that the Food Forum was such a success in the first issue. The identity of J.M.Q was guessed, of course, and Qwilleran explained Jack Nibble's theory: If people can't pronounce it, they won't eat it, and Pickaxians have a problem with the French cheeses. What Qwilleran did not explain was his complicity in ghostwriting the entire Food Forum. No one noticed the frequent dead-pan glances that passed between him and Hixie.

Friday was the big day in Pickax. A yellow ribbon, a block long, was tied across the front of Stables Row. At 11:00 A.M. the public started to gather for the noon ribbon-cutting. There were loafers, retirees, young people who looked as if they should be in school, mothers with small children, and a middle-aged newsman with a large moustache, who was there to see what he could see and hear what he could hear.

What he saw was a row of seven new business enterprises, encouraged and subsidized by the K Fund, intended to enrich life in the community and dedicated to clean windows and tasteful displays. Reading from south to north, they were:

The Pasty Parlor, with its exclusive, all-new, great-tasting designer pasties.

The Scottish Bakery, featuring scones, shortbread, meat-filled bridies, and a death-defying triple-chocolate confection called Queen Mum's cake.

Olde Tyme Soda Fountain, offering college ices (sundaes), phosphates (sodas), and banana splits at an antique marble soda bar with twisted wire stools and a peppy soda jerk pulling the taps.

Handle on Health, selling vitamins, safe snacks, organ-

ically grown fruits and vegetables, and diet-deli sandwiches.

The Kitchen Boutique, with displays of salad-spinners,
wine racks, espresso-makers, cookbooks, woks, exotic
mustards, and chef's aprons.

Sip 'n' Nibble, with assortments of wine and cheese
hitherto unknown to many in Moose County.

The Spoonery, dedicated to fast-feeding with a spoon,
either at a sit-down counter or a stand-up bar. Opening-
day specials: sausage gumbo, butternut squash soup with
garlic and cashews, borscht, and tomato-rice.

For the festivities, the entire block was closed to traffic,
and as noon approached, it began to be crowded with
downtown workers, shoppers, mothers with preschoolers
in tow, and members of the Chamber of Commerce.
Voices bounced between the stone facade of the old stables and the rear of the stone buildings facing Main
Street. Not all was excitement and anticipation; there
were cynical observations and dire predictions:

"They'll never make a go of it—not in this tank town!
It's too fancy."

"I hear the prices are jacked up outasight."

"The mayor'll get his ugly mug in the paper again. Did
you vote for him? I didn't."

"He's gonna be in that auction. I wouldn't let my wife
bid a nickel to have dinner with that four-flusher!"

"Who needs a Pasty Parlor? What we need is a hot dog
stand."

"Who's runnin' the soup kitchen? They must be nuts!
Whadda they think this is—a hobo camp?"

"Why'd they string up all that ribbon? A coupla yards
would be enough. They better not charge it to the taxpay-
ers!"

If the sour comments were heard by Dwight Somers,

they failed to dent his professional exuberance. He dashed around and talked on his cellular phone. "The school bus just arrived with the band. Alert the mayor to leave City Hall in five minutes." Then, seeing Qwilleran, he said, "How about this, Qwill? We're halfway through the Explo—and no more bombs, no homicides, no civil disturbance!"

"The game ain't over till it's over," Qwilleran quoted wryly. "The judges at the Pasty Bake-off could get food poisoning."

Larry Lanspeak pushed through the crowd to speak to the newsman. "The Celebrity Auction's a sellout! Carol is gonna bid on all the guys—just to inflate the bidding."

"Tell her to exercise caution," Qwilleran advised. "She might win Wetherby Goode. Are you staying open till nine tonight?"

"Sure! All the merchants are cooperating. Susan Exbridge didn't like the idea of idle browsers in her uppity-scale shop, but we talked her into it."

"Do you have any trouble with shoplifting, Larry?"

"Only in tourist season. One nice thing about a small town: Everybody is watching everybody."

The high school band was tuning up. A police siren could be heard, and the mayor's car approached. No one cheered; rather, the crowd became grimly silent. Then the band crashed into the *Washington Post March* with the confidence of young musicians who know most of the notes, and a police officer cleared the way for the mayor. Gregory Blythe was a middle-aged, well-dressed stockbroker, handsome in a dissipated way and insufferably conceited. Yet, he was always reelected; after all, his mother was a Goodwinter.

Dwight Somers led the applause as Blythe mounted a small podium and spoke into the microphone. "On this festive occasion I want to say a few words about the future of Pickax."

"Make it short!" someone yelled from the crowd.

"Excellent advice!" Blythe replied with a smile in the heckler's direction. Then he proceeded to speak too long, despite murmurs in the audience and the lack of attention.

Finally a child's shrill voice cried out, "Where's the balloons?"

"Let there be balloons!" the mayor decreed.

Two photographers rushed forward. Scissors were produced. The ribbon was snipped. Then, as the band struck up *Stars and Stripes Forever,* multicolor balloons rose from behind Stables Row, and the crowd converged on the new shops, which had promised souvenirs and food-tasting.

Qwilleran caught sight of a husky, heavily bearded young man lumbering about like a bear. "Gary!" he shouted. "What brings you to town? Souvenirs, refreshments or balloons?"

"Just checking on my competition," said the proprietor of the Black Bear Café. "I think I'll add pasties to my menu, but only the traditional kind. I know a woman who makes the crust with suet."

"What do you think of the Stables?"

"The building's neat. The Spoonery's a good idea. But the Pasty Parlor is off the wall. It's run by a couple from Down Below—nice kids—but they don't know a pasty from a pizza . . . Well, so long! Don't forget the bike-a-thon Sunday."

Qwilleran observed the crowds for a while and then went into the shop that was attracting the fewest visitors. The Kitchen Boutique was being managed by Sharon Hanstable.

"I loved your report on the turkey roast!" she greeted him. "Does it mean you're going to start cooking?"

"Only if hell freezes over. I attended the class under duress." He glanced around at the gadgets so foreign to his lifestyle: garlic presses, nutmeg grinders, pastry brushes. "What are those knives with odd blades?"

"Cheese knives," Sharon said. "The wide blade is for crumbly cheese; the pointed one for hard varieties; the narrow squarish one is for soft and semisoft."

"I'll take a set. Since Sip 'n' Nibble opened, I'm becoming a cheese connoisseur. So are the cats! . . . What are those round things?" He pointed to some circles of floppy rubber imprinted with the name of the shop.

"Take one to Polly," she said. "They're for unscrewing hard-to-open jars and bottles. They really work!"

Both of them looked suddenly toward the entrance. The band had stopped playing, and there was a roar of voices, including some angry shouting.

"Sounds like a riot!" Qwilleran said, dashing for the door just in time to hear glass shattering. A siren sounded. People were flocking to the south end of the block; others were running away. Witnesses were yelling to the police and pointing fingers. And the young couple who had opened the Pasty Parlor were looking in dismay at their smashed window.

As Qwilleran looked on, Lori Bamba came up behind him. "What happened, Qwill?"

"An anti-pasty demonstration," he said. "Militant right-wingers protesting against subversive ingredients in the filling."

He left Pine Street with an uneasy feeling that things were changing in Pickax—too fast. The locals were not ready for "designer pasties." The economic development division of the K Fund was partly to blame. Their theories sounded good, but they failed to understand a community 400 miles north of everywhere. Their ideas needed to be screened by a local commission. There was no one with whom he could discuss his apprehension. His friends in the business community were afire with optimism, and he hesitated to be a wet blanket. His closest confidante was recuperating from major surgery, and it would be unwise to trouble her. He did, however, take Polly the jar opener, and he praised the soup at the Spoonery.

She said, "We're going to watch the fireworks from our upstairs porch tonight. Would you like to join us, Qwill? Lynette has invited her bridge club, and there'll be refreshments."

"Thank you," he said, "but when one has seen fireworks over New York harbor, it's hard to get excited about a shower of sparks over the Pickax municipal parking lot."

When he returned to the barn, he found a mess in the lounge area. Someone had destroyed the Lanspeaks' potted mums that had been standing on the hearth. Someone had uprooted the vintage burgundy blooms and scattered them all over the white Moroccan rug.

Koko was sitting on the fireplace cube, waiting for Qwilleran's reaction.

"You, sir, are a *bad cat!*" was the stern rebuke.

Koko flicked a long pink tongue over his black nose.

Then Qwilleran relented. "I didn't think much of them myself. They look like dried blood . . . Sorry, old boy."

He stayed home for the rest of the day. When his antique sea chest arrived from Exbridge & Cobb, he had it placed outside the back door to receive packages. Finding a weathered wood shingle in the toolshed, he made a crude sign for it: DELIVERIES HERE. For dinner he hacked enough meat for two cats and one man from the carcass of Bird Number One. Later he read to the Siamese. Koko chose *Poor Richard's Almanac,* which provided such pithy tidbits as *A cat in gloves catches no mice.*

As the evening wore on, however, Qwilleran frequently tamped his moustache and consulted his watch. Koko was nervous, too. He prowled incessantly after the reading. Did he sense the forthcoming fireworks as he did the approach of a storm? The merchants on Main Street would serve their cookies and punch until nine o'clock; then the crowd would move to the Stables block for the sky show.

Promptly at nine the fireworks began, and Yum Yum hid under the sofa, but Koko was agitated. He growled; he raced around erratically. Qwilleran could hear, faintly, the crackling, thudding, and whining of the rockets; no doubt the cats could feel more than they could hear. A tone juncture Koko howled as if in protest.

The radio was tuned in to WPKX, broadcasting live from their van parked on the Stables block. Later, they would jockey the discs for the street dance. When the dance music started, Qwilleran stayed tuned, waiting for the ten o'clock newscast. He was in the kitchen scooping up a dish of ice cream when an announcer broke in with a bulletin:

"The Food Explo festivities in Pickax tonight were marred by the killing of a downtown merchant in the course of an armed robbery. Police have not released the victim's name, pending notification of family. The shooting took place while Explo crowds were watching the fireworks. Further information will be broadcast when available."

TWELVE

The WPKX bulletin reporting a homicide in downtown Pickax struck Qwilleran like the bomb that wrecked the hotel. In horror his mind raced through a roster of his friends who were merchants on Main Street: the Lanspeaks, Fran Brodie, Susan Exbridge, Bruce Scott, and more. He knew virtually everyone in the central business district.

First he called the newspaper, and the night editor said, "Roger is camping out at police headquarters, waiting for them to release the victim's name. An entire block of Main Street is taped off, between Elm and Maple, if that's a clue."

"It isn't," Qwilleran said. "That block has the highest

concentration of retail stores." As a wild shot he then phoned the police chief's home.

"Andy isn't here," Mrs. Brodie said. "He got a phone call and took right off. There's been a murder. Isn't that terrible?"

"Did he say who was killed?"

"Only that it wasn't our daughter, thank the Lord. I don't know when he'll be back. He told me not to wait up. If he calls, I'll tell him you phoned."

Qwilleran tried to read, but the radio was blaring soccer scores, weather reports, and country music; the murder had put an abrupt end to the street dance. Hoping for another news bulletin, he was afraid to turn it off. Even the eleven o'clock newscast had no further information on the crime. That meant the police were having trouble locating next of kin. The Siamese sensed that he was upset and knew not to bother him; they merely comforted him with their calm presence. Around midnight the telephone rang, and he sprang to lift the receiver.

"Brodie here," the chief barked. "Did you hear the news? They took out one of our witnesses."

"No! Which one?"

"I'll stop by the barn on my way home, if you're gonna be up. I could use a drink, and that's no lie!"

Within a few minutes, Koko's ears swiveled, and he ran to the kitchen to look out the window. Seconds later, headlights could be seen bobbing through the woods. Qwilleran turned on the exterior lights and went out to meet his friend.

"They got Franklin Pickett," were Brodie's first words. "Poor guy died with flowers clutched in his hand."

Qwilleran poured a Scotch and a glass of Squunk water, and they sat at the bar within reach of a cheese platter.

"The cash drawer was rifled," Brodie went on, "but the

robbery was a red herring. The real motive was obviously to silence a witness. Notice the timing! Nobody was looking or listening. The fireworks were shooting off, and everybody was gawking at the sky. You could shoot a cannon down Main Street. They were all at Stables Row or the big parking lot. The SBI detectives flew up again, second time in a week."

"Who discovered the crime?"

"Danny was on patrol, cruising Main Street. The stores were supposed to be locked up and lights out, except for security night-lights. Pickett's lights were on full blast. Danny checked and found the door unlocked—nobody in sight—no answer to his shout. Then he saw the cash register open and found Pickett in the backroom, face down in front of the flower cooler. The cooler door was open."

Qwilleran said, "If the killer had bought flowers on the day of the bombing, shouldn't Pickett have recognized him?"

"He could've worn a disguise, or it could have been his local accomplice on a mopping-up mission. We already decided there was a local connection. That would account for the timing. Somebody around here would know the schedule of events and when to hit. Might even be somebody Pickett knew. He could mingle with the crowd until nine o'clock, then go into the flower shop and take a long time making up his mind. Might even have bought a fifty-cent birthday card. That would take time, too, and Pickett wasn't one to pass up a fifty-cent sale, even if he had to stay open all night."

"What kind of flowers was the victim clutching?" Qwilleran asked with grim curiosity.

"Something dark red."

"Have some cheese, Andy."

"Is it the good stuff you gave me last time? I forget what you called it."

"It's a kind of Swiss cheese called Gruyère."

"YOW!" came a startlingly loud comment from under the bar. Koko knew by experience where to wait for crumbs.

Qwilleran said to Brodie, "If it's witnesses they're after, what about Lenny Inchpot? He's riding in the bike-a-thon Sunday. The three medalists are riding. The paper printed their names and shirt numbers in today's paper—also the route."

"We're trying to find him. He was seen at the street dance tonight but didn't go home, apparently. His mother's visiting her sister in Duluth, and you can bet Lenny's crashing with his bike buddies. We may have to nab him at the starting gate Sunday and ship him off to Duluth. He won't like being grounded. I hear he's got a lot of sponsors."

"Has the SBI come up with any leads on the bombing suspect?"

"Well, with no name and no car license and no fingerprints, they're working against odds, you might say, but . . . if you hang in there long enough, something usually happens to bust the case wide open. The homicide tonight may be the thin edge of the wedge." Brodie downed one more quick Scotch and said it was time to go home, adding, "Why doesn't your smart cat come up with some clues?" It was half in jest and half in wonder at Koko's past performances.

"He's working on it, Andy." Qwilleran was thinking about the cat's frenzy during the fireworks . . . his trashing of the dark red mums . . . his ominous howl at one particular moment. Were his psychic senses registering a gunshot on Main Street?

Now Lenny Inchpot was in danger. He was Lois's youngest. She'd crack up if anything happened to him.

Qwilleran checked his green pledge cards for the bike-a-thon and found only two. There had been three of them—for Gary, Wilfred and Lenny—on the telephone desk under the brass paperweight. The missing card was Lenny's. A search turned it up in the foyer—on the floor—well chewed. Neither cat was in sight.

Saturday was the day of the Pasty Bake-off. As Qwilleran fed the cats that morning, he said, "You guys have it made. You don't have to judge contests, go on the auction block, or write a thousand words twice a week when there's nothing to write about!"

At one-thirty he reported to the exhibit hall at the fairgrounds, the site of the Food Fair and Pasty Bake-off. At the door, he identified himself as a judge and was directed to a room at the rear; the directions could hardly be heard above the din of amplified music and reverberating voices in the great hall. Local cooks were exhibiting and selling homemade baked goods, preserves, and canned garden produce. Some of the items had already been honored with blue ribbons. Fairgoers wandered through the maze of edibles, stunned into silence by the ear-piercing music.

The judges' chamber was a bleak, ill-furnished cubicle, but Mildred Riker's greetings and light-hearted banter warmed the environment. She welcomed Qwilleran with a hug and a judge's badge. "Qwill, it's good of you to donate so much of your valuable time to Explo!" she shouted above the recorded noise.

"Think nothing of it," he said loudly. "I'm a food freak. But couldn't we turn down the volume, or disconnect the speaker, or shoot the disc jockey?"

Without another word, Mildred hurried from the room;

the music faded to a whimper; and she returned with a triumphant smile.

"Now," Qwilleran began, "tell me how many hundred pasties I have to sample today."

"I hate to disappoint you," she said cheerfully, "but the preliminaries have narrowed the field down to fifteen. First the crust judges eliminated about a third of the entries. I feel sorry for the cooks who got up at four o'clock this morning to bake, and were scratched in the first heat. The next group of judges checked ingredients and correct prep of the filling. No ground meat! No disallowed vegetables! We'll do the final testing for flavor and texture."

"How many judges have been nibbling at the fifteen pasties before we get them?" he asked.

Before she could reply, a tall, gangling youth shuffled into the room. He threw his arms wide and announced, "Guess what! You got me instead of chef-baby."

"Derek! What happened to Sigmund?" Mildred cried in disappointment and some annoyance. Derek, after all, was only a waiter.

"He slipped on a sun-dried tomato and sprained his ankle. The sous-chef had to take over lunch, and the prep cooks are working on dinner already, so you're stuck with everybody's favorite wait-person."

"Well, I'm sure you're a connoisseur of anything edible," she said dryly. "Let's all sit down at the table and discuss the procedure. First I'll read some guidelines. The purpose of the competition is to preserve and encourage a cultural tradition, thus forging a spiritual link with the past and celebrating an eating experience that is unique to this region of the United States."

"Who wrote that?" Derek asked. "I don't even know what it means."

"Never mind. Just taste the pasties," she said sharply.

She went on: "Entries are limited to twelve inches in length, with traditional crust and ingredients."

"What about turnips?" Qwilleran asked. "I hear the anti-turnip activists are quite vocal."

"We're awarding two blue ribbons—for pasties with and without."

"I must confess: I hate turnips" he said. "And parsnips. Always have."

"Taste objectively," Mildred advised. "A great pasty transcends its ingredients. It's an art, requiring not only culinary skill but an act of will!"

"Okay, let's get this show on the road," Derek said impatiently. "I'm starved, and I've got a four-o'clock shift."

Mildred opened the door and gave the signal, whereupon the no-turnip pasties were brought into the room. Reduced by the preliminaries to half their size, they were cut into bite-sized chunks and served to the judges, whose comments were brief and emphatic: "Too much onion . . . Rather dry . . . Good balance . . . Flat; needs seasoning . . . Too much potato . . . Excellent flavor." After some retasting, Number 87 was named winner in the no-turnip category.

Next came a tray of pasties identified with a T for turnip. One in particular was praised by the two male judges, but Mildred tasted it and said indignantly, "This is turkey! Dark meat of turkey! It's disqualified. How did it slip past the other judges?"

Qwilleran said, "But it deserves some kind of recognition. I detect a superior act of will in its fabrication. I wonder who baked it."

"I bet it was a guy," Derek said.

"Well, we can't accept it," Mildred said firmly. "Rules are rules when you're judging a contest. Emphasis is on tradition, and tradition calls for beef or pork."

"You can't convince me," Qwilleran said, "that the
early settlers didn't make pasties with wild turkey—or
venison or rabbit or muskrat or anything else they could
shoot or trap."

"That may be true, but if we break the rules, all future
competitions will lose significance. And do you realize
what a controversy we'll have on our hands?"

Derek said, "Take a chance. Start a war."

Qwilleran had a suggestion. "Throw the superpasty out
of the running, but find out who baked it and do a special
feature on him or her on some future food page."

Mildred agreed. The crisis was past, but another crisis
was yet to develop. When they emerged from the judges'
chamber and handed the two winning numbers to the
chairperson of the bake-off, he stepped to the microphone.

"Attention, please," he announced on the public address
system. "Two blue ribbon winners in the Pasty Bake-off
have been selected by our esteemed judges, and each will
receive a prize of one hundred dollars, but we have a slight
foul-up here. In order to preserve the anonymity of contes-
tants during the judging, their names were deposited in the
safe at our accountant's office, MacWhannell & Shaw, and
since their office is closed until Monday, we regret we can-
not identify the winners at this time. They will be notified,
however, on Monday morning, and the winning names
will be announced on WPKX and in the *Moose County
Something.*"

As the judges left the exhibit building, Mildred said to
Qwilleran, "Weren't you shocked by last night's murder?
It was a case of armed robbery, they said. We've never had
anything like that in Moose County!"

Qwilleran knew more than he wanted to disclose to the
publisher's wife. He said, "The SBI is on the case, and we
can assume it's a criminal element from Down Below

that's responsible—not some bad boy from Chipmunk . . .
By the way, the cats want to express their gratitude for
Bird One. The carcass is getting thinner, and Koko and
Yum Yum are getting fatter." That was not quite true, but
it sounded good. Actually, Qwilleran monitored their in-
take, believing that Siamese were intended to be sleek.
Even when he gave them a crumb of cheese for a treat, it
was no larger than a grape seed. Yet, they chomped and
bobbed their heads and washed their whiskers and ears for
ten minutes, as if it had been a Delmonico steak.

For Qwilleran, one more Explo commitment remained:
the Celebrity Auction. He dressed for the event with care.
In his days as a hard-working journalist Down Below,
there had been neither time nor money to waste on sartor-
ial splendor. His new lifestyle supplied both, and the
owner of Scottie's Men's Store was his mentor. For the
auction, Scottie recommended a bronze, silk-blend sports
coat, olive green trousers, and a silk shirt in olive, to be
worn open-neck.

On the way to the high school auditorium, Qwilleran
drove to Gingerbread Alley to obtain Polly's okay on his
outfit. She said he looked distinguished and romantic.
"Call me when it's over, no matter how late," she re-
quested. "I won't sleep until I know who gets you."

The crowd that gathered for the auction had paid plenty
for their tickets and were convinced they were going to
have a good time. The auctioneer, Foxy Fred, circulated in
his western hat and red jacket, whipping up their enthusiasm. His spotters, also in red jackets, handed out numbered
flash cards to those intending to bid. Poster-sized pho-
tographs of the celebrities were displayed onstage, either
hanging on the back wall or displayed on easels.

The celebrities themselves were assembled in the Green

Room backstage, where they would be able to hear the proceedings on the PA system. Besides Qwilleran, there were the mayor, the WPKX weatherman, the town's leading photographer, and the ubiquitous Derek Cuttlebrink, plus five attractive women: the heiress from Chicago, the personable young doctor, the glamorous interior designer, the theatre club's popular ingenue, and the chic vice president of the *Moose County Something*.

Qwilleran said to them, "I expect Foxy Fred to hawk me as 'a gen-u-wine old news-hound in fair condition, with the patina of age and interesting distress marks.' Then the bidding will start at five dollars."

The balding John Bushland said, "You're bananas! They'll hock their teeth to bid on you, Qwill. You have more hair than all the rest of us put together."

Hixie Rice assured them all, "Dwight has some shills in the audience to liven up the action if it's too slow, or if the bids are too low."

Fran Brodie muttered to Qwilleran, "Wouldn't you know the mayor would have the chutzpa to wear a dinner jacket and paisley cummerbund? You're dressed just right, Qwill! If I were in the audience, I'd bid a month's commissions on you. Danielle Carmichael was in the studio yesterday, looking at wallpaper. They're both here tonight. Willard is going to bid on me, and she's going to bid on you, although he won't let her go over a thousand."

"Have you heard any more about the shooting?"

"Only that they know what kind of handgun was used, but it happened less than twenty-four hours ago. Give them a break!"

At that point, Pender Wilmot of the Boosters Club arrived in the Green Room to brief the somewhat nervous celebrities. "Packages will be auctioned in the order that appears in the printed program. Foxy Fred will open the bidding with a suggested starting price. If the bids start low, don't worry; he's a master at milking the audience. When your package is knocked down, the winner will come to the platform, and you'll walk out to meet your dinner date. Relax and have fun. It's all for a good cause."

Foxy Fred banged the gavel, and the bidding commenced. The mayor's package—dinner at the Purple Point Boat Club—was knocked down for $750, and the woman he went onstage to meet was Elaine Fetter—widow, champion volunteer, gourmet cook, and grower of mushrooms.

Fran whispered to Qwilleran, "She's been running after the mayor ever since she lost her husband. She lives in West Middle Hummock. I did her house. She has a fabulous kitchen."

Her own package—dinner at the Palomino Paddock—brought $1,000 from Dr. Prelligate. After meeting him onstage, she said breathlessly to Qwilleran, "He's not at all like a college president; he's quite sexy! I wonder what I should wear for the dinner."

"Maybe you can get a decorating job out of it," he suggested. "Find out if he likes blue."

After Derek Cuttlebrink's motorcycle cook-out brought $325 amid screams from his young adherents in the audience, Jennifer Olsen was heard to complain in the Green Room, "That's unfair! Those girls pooled their money and drew straws. A hairdresser won, and she had hundreds of dollars to bid. Nobody will have nearly that much to bid on me."

The pretty young actress stopped pouting, however, when her all-you-can-eat package brought $400. She went onstage in a state of shock to meet her dinner date, and the others in the Green Room heard her shriek "Dad!"

"That's parental love!" declared Dr. Diane backstage. "Poor Mr. Olsen will have to eat the Hot Spot's ghastly food and sit through two hours of ear-blasting rock. He'll be at the clinic Monday morning, complaining of deafness and heartburn."

Qwilleran's package—a complete makeup and hair styling, followed by dinner at the Old Stone Mill—was the last to go on the block. While other packages had been greeted with murmurs of interest and a few youthful shrieks, this one brought a storm of clapping, cheering, and stamping of feet.

Foxy Fred shouted, "Who wants to have dinner with a famous journalist?" He had been instructed not to mention money or moustache. "Shall we start with five hundred? Who'll give me five hundred? . . . Five hundred do I see? . . . I hear four hundred. No money! Go back to the hills . . . Who'll make it four-fifty?"

"Hep!" shouted a spotter, pointing at a flashcard.

"Four-fifty I've got. Make it five-fifty. Do I see five-fifty?"

"Hep!"

"That's the ticket! Now we're rollin'. Who'll bid six-fifty? Waddala waddala bidda waddala . . . Six-fifty I've got. Make it seven! Seven hundred for a thousand-dollar dinner date! . . . Who'll make it seven?"

"Hep!"

"Make it eight! Chance of a lifetime, folks! . . . I see eight in the back row. Do I see nine? Waddala waddala bidda waddala bidda bidda . . . Nine I've got over there at the left. Make it a thou! Let's hear from the heavy artillery! Dinner date you'll never forget! . . . A thousand I've got! Who'll bid twelve hundred? . . . Twelve I've got from the lady in the back row! Make it fifteen! Fifteen? Fourteen is bid. Make it fifteen! Where's that card in the back row?"

Qwilleran and Fran exchanged anxious glances. Had

Danielle exceeded her thousand-dollar cap? He passed a hand ruefully over his warm face.

"Do I hear fifteen? Shoot the works! Don't lose him now! Make it fifteen!"

"Hep!"

"Fifteen is bid! Who'll go sixteen? Sixteen? Sixteen?. . . Fifteen once, fifteen twice!" The gavel banged down. "Sold for fifteen hundred to the lady back there with number 134. Don't faint, ma'am! The red jackets will escort you to the stage."

Qwilleran said, "Oh, God! Who can it be?" A list flashed into his mind: women who had been pestering him for the last five years . . . women who could afford fifteen hundred dollars . . . women he liked . . . women he didn't like. If only Polly could have been in the audience! They could have rigged it: She'd bid; he'd pay.

His colleagues in the Green Room were applauding; the crowd in the auditorium was going wild! Derek and Bushy pulled him to his feet and pushed him toward the stage.

Foxy Fred shouted, "Come on out, Mr. Q. Don't be bashful!"

Theatrically, Qwilleran's timing was perfect; suspense was building. The auctioneer was bawling, "Here's the lucky lady! Come right up, sister. Feeling a little weak in the knees?"

Qwilleran tidied his moustache, took a deep breath, and squared his shoulder. Walking onstage, he bowed modestly toward the bright lights and the hundreds of upturned faces, and the sight of the famous moustache increased the uproar. He looked across the stage to see a red-jacketed spotter assisting a little gray-haired woman up the steps.

"Sarah!" he shouted in astonishment.

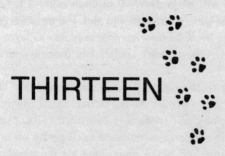

THIRTEEN

At the newspaper everyone called her Sarah. Now she was giving her name as Sarah Plensdorf. Qwilleran walked across the stage toward the nervous little woman, extending two reassuring hands. Tears of excitement or triumph were streaming down her face. His own reaction was: How could she—or why would she—spend that kind of money on a dinner date with *anyone?* It must be a practical joke, he decided, financed by the unholy three: Riker, Hixie, and Junior. It was the kind of trick they would play—an expensive joke, but tax-deductible . . . Well! He would spoil their fun; he would put on a good show! He grasped Ms. Plensdorf's two trembling hands, bowing over them courteously, and mumbling his pleasure that she had won. Then he brought down the house by giving her a bear hug.

The red-jacketed attendant ushered the two of them to a table in the wings, where Pender Wilmot invited them to set a date for their dinner.

"Would Monday evening be too soon?" Ms. Plensdorf asked shyly. "I'm so thrilled, I can hardly wait."

"Monday will be perfect," Qwilleran said. "I'll reserve the best table at the Mill and pick you up at seven o'clock." She lived, he now learned, in Indian Village, a good address, where many singles had upscale apartments.

Returning to the Green Room he reasoned that he could have done worse. At the office Sarah always dressed tastefully and spoke in a cultivated voice. Furthermore, she regularly commented intelligently on his current column and never mentioned his moustache. With the complete makeup and hair styling included in the package, she would be a presentable dinner date. Besides, it was all for a charitable cause. He was, in fact, glad that Sarah Plensdorf had edged Danielle Carmichael out of the running.

Back at the barn he wasted no time in phoning Polly to report the news.

"Sarah Plensdorf! What a surprise!" she exclaimed. "Well, I'm glad she won you, Qwill. She's a very sweet person."

"I know her only as office manager at the paper, and she seems to bring efficiency and a pleasant manner to the job. What I wonder is: Can she afford fifteen hundred dollars?

"I'm sure she can. She donates generously to the library. The Plensdorfs made their fortune in lumbering in the early days, and I imagine she inherited a handsome amount."

"I see," Qwilleran said. "Do you know anything about her personal interests?"

"Only that she collects buttons."

"Buttons!" he repeated in disbelief. "Did I hear right?"

"Well, yes. Didn't you see her collection in the library display case last year? It was featured in your paper, too."

"I didn't see the display, and I didn't read the feature!" he declared defiantly.

"When are you taking her to dinner?"

"Monday night."

"If you want to bone up on buttons before then, you'll find one or two books on the subject at the library."

"Thank you for the suggestion, but . . . no thanks. I'll wing it."

Early rising was not a Qwilleran habit, but on Sunday morning he left the barn at seven-thirty and drove toward Kennebeck. The wooded hill south of the town was lined with cars, vans, and pickups on both shoulders. Those who had arrived early for a good vantage point were having tailgate breakfasts. By eight-thirty their cameras were at the ready.

First, a sheriff's car came slowly over the crest of the hill and started down the long gentle slope, followed by more than a hundred elegantly lightweight cycles with helmeted riders crouched over the handlebars. Qwilleran hoped he would not see Lenny's green jersey with number 19 on the back. There was a burst of applause for the gold and bronze medalists when they passed, but the silver medalist was nowhere in sight. The PPD had successfully grounded him; he might even be on his way to Duluth.

The ride was a joyful sight—until a rifle shot rang out. The crowd became suddenly silent. A second shot was heard, and parents pushed their children into their vehicles. "Just a rabbit hunter," someone yelled. Still, the motorcycle escort talked into a cellular phone, and the sheriff's car returned.

Qwilleran thought, Everyone's edgy. All their lives they've been used to hearing hunters' rifle shots. What a difference a homicide makes!

When he returned to the barn, he took a quick look into the sea chest before unlocking the back door. To his surprise, there was a carton labeled: "Product of Cold Turkey Farm. Weight, 12 pounds. Keep frozen until ready to use, then defrost in refrigerator."

Payola, Qwilleran thought, but then he remembered that payola was a big-city breach of ethics. In the country, 400 miles north of everywhere, neighbors helped neighbors and received neighborly expressions of gratitude, which they accepted with good grace. The question was: What to do with the bird? Actually, as he remembered Mildred's demonstration, prepping a turkey was not a staggering problem, and the oven did the rest. If one followed the instructions, it could be no harder than changing a tire—easier, perhaps. He would need a large pan with a rack. There were two turkey roasters in the apple barn, but they were being used for other purposes. Meanwhile, the cats were yowling in five octaves, and he banished them to the broom closet until he could open the carton and put the plastic-wrapped turkey into the refrigerator.

On the hour he tuned in WPKX, expecting to hear a report on the bike-a-thon: how many riders had started, how many had dropped out, and what milepost the leaders had reached. Instead, he heard a startling news bulletin:

"A fisherman was found dead this morning, as a result of multiple bee stings. According to the medical examiner, the insects had attacked in such numbers that the victim was virtually smothered. The body was found in a rental cabin belonging to Scotten Fisheries on the bank of Black Creek. No further details are available at this time, but police say . . . he was not . . . a resident of Moose County."

That last statement, spoken with significant emphasis, was typical of WPKX. It meant: Relax; he was not one of us.

Qwilleran had a sudden urge to visit Aubrey Scotten.

As usual, he liked to take the public pulse whenever an unusual happening occurred, so he stopped at the Dimsdale Diner. On a Sunday morning there were no pickups in the rutted parking lot and no farmers smoking and laughing around the big table. He sat at the counter on the only stool that still had a seat on its pedestal; the others stood like a row of grim stakes in a tank trap. To the half-awake counterman he said, "I'll have a cup of your famous bitter coffee and one of your special three-day-old doughnuts." The man shambled away to fill the order. A cheap radio spluttered in the background.

Qwilleran asked, "Where did you buy that radio? It has excellent tone."

"Found it," said the counterman.

"Did you hear about the guy who was stung to death by bees?"

"Yep."

"Who was he? Do you know?"

"Fisherman."

"Has that ever happened around here, to your knowledge?"

"Nope."

"Apparently he was allergic to bee venom."

"Guess so."

Someday Qwilleran would write a column about the laconic subculture in Moose County. Engaging them in conversation was a hobby of his. "Best coffee I ever drank! Great taste!" he declared. "What's your name?"

"Al."

"Thanks, Al. Have a nice day."

It was indeed a nice day, Moose County style: sunny —just cool enough for a sweater. On such a day Gustav Limburger's red brick mansion rose out of its green weeds with a forlorn grandeur. He drove into the side yard and tooted the horn. The door of the honey shed was open, and after a second blast of the horn, a dejected figure appeared in the doorway. He was not the big, fleshy man who had enthused about his bees, Lois's flapjacks, and the German Bible he would inherit. His whole frame drooped, and his pudgy face sagged.

Qwilleran jumped out of his car and went toward him, saying, "Remember me? Jim Qwilleran. I came to buy a couple of jars of honey."

Without a word Aubrey disappeared into the shade of the shed and returned with two of the flattened jars. The transaction was made in silence.

"Beautiful day, isn't it?" Qwilleran asked.

Aubrey looked around to see what kind of day it was, and then nodded absently.

"How's Mr. Limburger?"

"Same, I guess," he said in his squeaky voice.

"Did you hear that Lois has closed her restaurant?"

The beekeeper nodded in a daze.

"How do you like your new job at the turkey farm?"

The man shrugged. "It's . . . okay."

"Look here, Aubrey! Are you all right? Is something worrying you?" Qwilleran asked out of curiosity and concern.

Two tears ran down the soft face and were wiped away with a sleeve.

Qwilleran slipped into his big-brother role. "Come on, Big Boy, let's sit down and talk about this. It'll do you good." He took the young man by the elbow and steered him to a weather-beaten bench outside the honey shed. They sat in silence for a few moments. "I was sorry to hear about the accident at your cabin. Did you know the man?"

Aubrey's breathing was a series of heavy sighs. "He was my friend."

"Is that so? How long had you known him?"

"Long time."

"Had he ever been up here before?"

There was more weary nodding.

"And the bees had never bothered him?"

There was no response.

"Where were you when it happened?"

"In the house." He jerked his head toward the brick mansion.

"He evidently did something that frightened or upset the bees."

Aubrey shrugged shoulders that seemed weighted by a heavy burden.

"I wish I could think of something to say or do that would help you, Aubrey. You must keep up your spirit. Go to see the old man in the hospital; do your job at the turkey farm; take care of your bees. It takes time to recover from the shock of a tragedy like this. Keep busy.

Face one day at a time." While he was babbling plati-
tudes, he was thinking about a recent morning at Lois's
when the bombing was mentioned, and the sensitive
young man said, "Somebody was killed." Then he
rushed from the restaurant without finishing his pancakes. Now a longtime friend had been killed—and by
his own bees, compounding the anguish. If bees died
after stinging, did it mean that Aubrey had lost much of
his swarm? He was a lonely person who seemed to yearn
for a friend. He liked Lois because she was friendly;
Gary at the Black Bear was friendly; his bees were his
friends. Taking that thought as a cue, Qwilleran said,
"At a time like this, it helps to talk to a friend, Aubrey. I
want you to think of me as a friend and call me if I can
help . . . Here's my phone number." The sincerity of
Qwilleran's attitude said as much as his words.

Aubrey took the card and nodded, while drawing his
sleeve across his face again. Then he surprised Qwilleran by following him to his car. "The police were
here," he said anxiously.

"That's standard procedure in the case of accidental
death. The police and the ambulance crew and the medical examiner are required to respond. What did the police say?"

"They kept asking about the bees. Could they arrest
me for what my bees did?"

"Of course not! Cops always ask a lot of questions.
They may come back and ask some more. Just answer
them truthfully without going into a long-winded expla-
nation. If they give you a hard time, let me know."

On the way home, Qwilleran frequently tamped his
moustache with his fist. Instinct, and a sensation on his
upper lip, told him there was more to this story than appeared on the surface. Furthermore, Koko had been agi-

tated all weekend, a sure sign that he was trying to communicate. For one thing, he kept knocking *A Taste of Honey* off the bookshelf.

From the desolation of blighted Black Creek, Qwilleran drove to West Middle Hummock, where fine estates nestled among rolling hills and winding roads. The Lanspeaks lived there. So did the Wilmots. Elaine Fetter had suggested Sunday afternoon for the mushroom interview because her weekdays were consumed by volunteer work.

In preparation he had consulted the encyclopedia and had learned that the edible fungus is a sporophore consisting largely of water and having a curious reproductive system—what they called the sexuality of the mushroom. Although he was no gardener, he knew that one could plant a radish and get a radish, but there was something murkily mysterious about the propagation of mushrooms.

Mrs. Fetter specialized in shiitake, which she pronounced *shee-tock-ee*. The Japanese word with a double-i would confuse the proofreaders at the *Something*. After several years they were still uncomfortable with the QW in his name.

The Fetter residence was an old farmhouse on which money had been lavished, with open decks and ramps, giving it a contemporary look. The woman who greeted him was the same statuesque, self-assured, well-groomed shopper who had suggested short-grain rice at Toodle's Market.

"Do come in and let us start with a cup of tea in the keeping room," she said. She led the way through spacious rooms furnished with antique pine and cherry—to a large kitchen with a six-burner range, a bank of ovens, and shelves filled with cookbooks. Separated from the cooking center by an iron railing was an area with a fireplace and Windsor chairs around a trestle table. The railing looked like the missing section of the Limburger fence.

Qwilleran said, "This would make a spectacular feature for our new food page. John Bushland could take photos, if you'd permit it. Did you have a professional designer?"

"No, this is all my own idea, although Amanda's studio ordered a few things for me. I call this the nerve center of the house. I spend my mornings here, testing recipes and experimenting with new dishes. I'm writing a cookbook, you see, in addition to supervising the one for the Friends of the Library."

He set up his tape recorder, with her consent, and then asked, "Could you describe briefly the procedure in growing shiitake?"

"Of course! First you find a young healthy oak tree and cut it down after the leaves begin to fall and before it leafs out in spring. It should be four to six inches in diameter, with just the right thickness of bark."

"How thick is the right thickness? Already this sounds somewhat esoteric."

"Ah! This is a matter of study and experience. After cutting your logs in four-foot lengths, you buy commercial spawn; drill holes in these bed-logs, as they're called; then inoculate them with the spawn and seal the holes, after which they incubate for three months."

"Do you ignore them during the incubation?"

"Not at all! You must maintain the humidity by occasional deep-soaking or frequent watering with a gentle spray. An electric gauge measures the interior moisture of the logs." She explained the process glibly and concisely, like a lesson memorized from a textbook. "After inoculation you can expect fruiting in six to nine months."

"And what do you do with your crop?"

"Sell them to restaurants and the better markets in Lockmaster. Local grocers consider them too expensive, although shiitake are considered more delicious and nutritious than ordinary mushrooms. After we've visited the growing arbor, I'll sauté some for you—with parsley, garlic, and freshly ground black pepper."

From the kitchen they stepped through sliding glass doors to a patio, then down a ramp and along an asphalt-paved path to a wooded area on the bank of a stream. In the partial shade the bed-logs were stacked in a crisscross pattern; others stood on end around a central pole. Some were sprouting little buttons. "Just beginning to fruit," she said. "And over there is a flush ready to crop." She pointed to logs ringed with ruffles of large mushrooms, the caps as big as saucers and furrowed in a pattern of brown and white.

Qwilleran thought, By comparison, ordinary mushrooms look naked. "Are mushrooms still considered aphrodisiacs?" he asked, remembering a reference in the encyclopedia.

"There have been all sorts of superstitions in the past, and always will be," she replied. "There was a time when women weren't allowed in mushroom-growing establishments; it was thought the presence of a female would ruin the crop."

"When was that? In the Dark Ages?"

"Surprisingly, the superstition continued into the beginning of the twentieth century. And did you know that scientists used to battle over the question of whether the mushroom was a plant or an animal?"

On the way back to the kitchen, he said, "This shiitake project sounds like a lot of work, considering all your other activities."

"Oh, I have a little help," she said nonchalantly.

While she sautéed shiitake, Qwilleran perused her large collection of food-related books: Larousse, Escoffier, and Brillat-Savarin, as well as ethnic cookbooks of all kinds and the recipe collections of famous chefs. He wondered how original her own cookbook would be, and how much plagiarism occurred among food writers. Before he had a chance to examine the books, she called him to the table, and he tasted the best mushrooms he'd ever eaten.

Later, he reported the entire incident to Polly as they took their walk. "After five minutes with the encyclopedia and an hour with Elaine Fetter, I am now a mycological expert. I know that a mushroom cap is called the *pileus;* the gills underneath are *lamellae;* and the stem is the *stipe.* Also, there are three strains of shiitake, one of which is called *Koko.*"

"You overwhelm me with your erudition," Polly said. "What did you think of Elaine?"

"Well, I'm impressed by her vitality and expertise and collection of cookbooks, but . . . ." He patted his moustache. "I have a sneaky feeling she wasn't telling the whole story. During my career I've interviewed about forty thousand individuals, and I get certain vibrations when they're holding something back—or lying."

"Did she mention her son?"

"No, the conversation was all about mushrooms and her personal activities. She didn't even mention the auction, and she's the one who snagged the mayor. What about her son?"

"Donald lives with her. He was driving the car when it crashed and killed her husband, and he's quite incapacitated. He's confined to a wheelchair, but growing shiitake is his therapy, and it gives him a reason for living."

"Hmmm . . . that puts a different slant on the story," Qwilleran said. "And actually it's a better story—one that could be rather inspirational. Also, it explains the ramps and asphalt pathways and the spaciousness of the house . . . Now what to do?"

"Perhaps I shouldn't have mentioned it."

"I'm glad you did—very glad! The question is: Why did she withhold that aspect of the mushroom enterprise? Does Donald avoid publicity because of his physical condition? Or does his mother keep him under wraps? Does she want the publicity for herself?"

"An astute observation," Polly said. "She's a very proud woman, and she has a powerful ego. It makes it hard for her to get along with other volunteers. She's always taking credit for what the others do . . . What *will* you do about it?"

"Put the column on hold until I can get to the bottom of the problem."

"I hope you'll handle it tactfully."

"Don't worry, and I won't involve you in any way. But it puts me in a bind. I'd scheduled it for this week, and now I'll have to find another topic in a hurry."

He declined an invitation to have tea with Polly and Lynette. He said he had to make some phone calls. He didn't mention it, but there was more than the shiitake situation that bothered him.

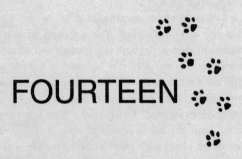

FOURTEEN

Following his interview with Elaine and his enlightening conversation with Polly, Qwilleran hurried home to the barn. He waved at Celia Robinson, getting out of her red car in front of the carriage house. He looked into the sea chest at the back door—empty! He let himself in and went directly to the telephone without even speaking to the welcoming cats. He called Celia.

"Hi, Chief!" she hailed him in her usual cheerful manner. "Were you trying to reach me earlier? I've been out all day. I sang in the choir and then served at the coffee hour. Then Virginia Alstock took me to dinner with her folks, and we took them for a ride. It was a beautiful day! Did you do something special?"

"No, I'm just a working stiff," he said. "I did an inter-

view out in West Middle Hummock. That's why I'm
calling. Do you happen to know a Donald Fetter?"

"Sure! I know Donald very well. He's a subscriber to
Pals for Patients. He's confined to a wheelchair, you
know. It was an auto accident. His father was killed, and
he'll never walk again. His mother says he was driving
too fast on those winding roads and hit a tree. He's quite
young . . . Why did you ask?"

"It's a long story—too long for the phone. Why don't
you hop into your car and drive down here before dark?
I have some new cheese for you to try—"

"Isn't that funny?" she interrupted. "I was just thinking about you when you called. Virginia gave me a new
recipe for macaroni and cheese, and—"

"If you need a guinea pig, I'm willing to volunteer.
Meanwhile, I may have a new assignment for you."

"Whoops!" she cried in her youthful way. "Give me
ten minutes to feed Wrigley, and I'll be right there."

Qwilleran hung up and turned to the Siamese, who
had heard the word cheese and were waiting in anticipation. "Our neighbor is coming for a conference, and I
want you two heathens to behave like civilized human
beings. Or, at least, civilized beings," he corrected himself. He arranged a cheese board for his guest and gave
the cats a crumble or two: Havarti for Yum Yum, feta
for Koko.

While waiting for Celia, he played the tape of his interview with the Mushroom Queen, as he now thought
of her, uncharitably. She gave evasive answers to some
questions and textbook answers to others, never striking
a personal note. She never said, "I maintain the humidity" or "We inoculate the logs."

Postponing the mushroom column in light of the new

information would be an inconvenience, but, for the moment, there was another matter on his mind.

Celia arrived in a flush of smiles. "What's that box outside the door? Where are those good kitties?"

Qwilleran replied, "The kitties, as you call them, are guarding the cheese. The box is a historic sea chest to be used for deliveries of macaroni and cheese if I'm not home."

As she went to the lounge area and dropped her large handbag on the floor at her feet, the Siamese followed her. They knew that handbag! Sometimes it contained a treat. "The autumn color is terrific this year," she said. "Especially on Ittibittiwassee Road. Virginia said it's because of the sharp frost we had . . . What's the new cheese?"

"Goat cheese from the Split Rail Farm. I wrote about it in my column Friday. This one has garlic . . . this one is flavored with dill . . . and that one is feta, quite salty."

"Yow!" said Koko.

"When my husband was alive," she said, "we kept a few goats and sold milk to folks in town who had trouble with cow's milk. I loved our she-goats. They're so sweet, the way they look at you with sleepy eyes! I called them April, May, June, and Holiday. The buck was March. My! He was a smelly critter." Celia gazed into space with a bemused expression. "Seems a long time ago." Then she snapped back to the present. "How was the autumn color in West Middle Hummock?"

"Spectacular! I went out there to interview Elaine Fetter about her mushrooms."

"*Her* mushrooms? Is that what she told you? The whole thing was Donald's idea! He was very depressed until he heard about growing—what do you call them?"

"Shee-tock-ee. They're a Japanese mushroom."

"Well, it gave him something to live for. We send Junior Pals out there, and they help with the heavy work—those big logs, you know. Did you taste the mushrooms? Did you see the kitchen? I wouldn't know how to act in such a big one. What's his mother like? I only met her once. Donald doesn't get along with her too good."

"She's a prominent club woman and volunteer—accustomed to running the show—somewhat conceited, they say—a gourmet cook—and she's writing a cookbook."

"Did you see the cookbooks she has in her kitchen? I never saw so many!"

"That, madame, is precisely why you are here," Qwilleran said in the declamatory style that always made her laugh.

"Okay. Shoot!" she said merrily.

"First, a little background information: Have you heard of Iris Cobb? She died before you moved up here."

"Virginia talks about her. She made wonderful cookies."

"She contributed greatly to the community, but she's chiefly remembered for her cooking. Her collection of personal cooking secrets was left to me in her will, but it disappeared before I could put my hands on it."

"You don't cook, Chief! What good would it do?"

"She also left me that pine wardrobe over there, a Pennsylvania German *schrank*. The cookbook, I think, was supposed to be a joke, but I planned to publish it and donate the proceeds to charity, in her name."

"That's pretty nice. Yes, I like that!" Celia said. "Any notion what happened to it?"

"There are three possibilities: It was in a piece of furniture that was sold to an out-of-state dealer when her apartment was liquidated. Or it was thrown out as junk, being a greasy, spotted, scuffed notebook with a broken spine and loose pages. Or it was simply stolen. A request for its return, with no questions asked, produced no results."

"Sounds like something I wouldn't mind reading myself," Celia said.

"You may get a chance. When I was in Mrs. Fetter's kitchen this afternoon, I noticed a battered black book among all the colorful jackets of slick new cookbooks. I didn't think too much of it at the time; I was concentrating on how to handle all the technical stuff on spawn and inoculation and incubation without boring my readers. Later, though, I remembered that the spine of the black book had been repaired with transparent tape. That's when my suspicions arose." He touched his moustache tentatively. "The next time you go to see Donald—if you do go, that is—you might sneak a peek. Could you manage that?"

"Could I! You know me, Chief! I'll go there with one of the junior trainees. Is there anything special I should look for, besides grease spots?"

"I don't imagine Iris ever put her name on it. If she did, no doubt it's been obliterated. But first you should look for almost illegible handwriting. Next you might look for certain recipes that made her a legend in her time, like butter pecan ginger snaps and lemon coconut squares. She also had a secret way with meatloaf and macaroni and cheese."

"Oh, this will be fun!" She rummaged in her large handbag for a notepad and made a few jottings. "If it turns out to be Mrs. Cobb's book, how will you go about getting it?"

"That's the difficulty. In a small town you don't send a

cop with a search warrant and a court order to seize stolen property—especially when the suspect is a prominent woman who has a dinner date with the mayor . . . Although—off the record, Celia—the mayor himself has a few shadows falling across his illustrious past."

"Oh, this town is a hoot!" Celia squealed with laughter. "Somebody should write a book! . . . But look! It's getting dusk. I should get home before it's dark in the woods." She gathered up her large handbag and struggled to rise from the deep cushions of the sofa.

"Better check your handbag for stowaways," Qwilleran suggested, noticing that one cat was missing from the top of the fireplace cube. He escorted her to her car and then returned to check out the Siamese. Yum Yum had jumped down from the cube and was doing extravagant stretching exercises. Koko was sitting in front of the refrigerator, staring at the door handle. Inside, the frozen turkey was still hard as a rock.

The next morning a delegation arrived at the barn on official business. They were there to discuss arrangements for the cheese-tasting party: the two men from Sip 'n' Nibble, who were catering the event; Hixie Rice as volunteer publicist; Carol Lanspeak and Susan Exbridge, representing the Country Club. The male-dominated service organization had recently voted to allow women members to serve on committees.

"Not because they were suddenly conscious of women's rights," Susan explained dryly, "but because they need help with their projects."

"So true!" Carol said.

Jerry Sip and Jack Nibble, who had never seen the barn before, were overwhelmed by its size and rustic contemporary magnificence. The main floor was a hun-

dred feet across, minus the space occupied by the fireplace cube, and living areas on all sides of the cube were
roomy, to say the least.

"This is some place!" Jack said, "We can handle a
hundred people here without a hitch. We'll have the
punch bowls on the dining table and set up two eight-
foot folding tables on either side—for the cheese service. With white tablecloths, of course."

"And flowers," Susan added. "For the dining table
I'm bringing two very tall silver candelabra and a silver
bowl for a low arrangement of fall flowers. They're
coming from a florist in Lockmaster. I ordered several
arrangements from Franklin a week ago, but now . . . his
shop is full of police, and all his plants and flowers are
dying, and no one knows exactly what's going on."

Carol said, "I hear the body is being shipped to his
home town in Ohio. It's all too dreadful!"

There was a moment of respectful silence. Then
Qwilleran asked about parking. "With a hundred guests
there could be as many as fifty cars."

"Guests will park in the theatre lot," Carol explained,
"and jitneys from County Transport will deliver them to
the party. We purposely scheduled it for after-dark, because the exterior of the barn looks so spectacular under
the floodlights, and the interior looks magical. The whole
evening is going to be gala! I've special-ordered several
evening dresses for my customers, and if the merchandise
doesn't come in today's delivery, I'm in deep trouble!"

"Do you think I should lock up the cats?" Qwilleran
asked.

"No, let them mingle with the guests. They're a
delightful addition to a party—so elegant, so well-
behaved."

He uttered a grunt of doubt. "Who'll be guarding the

sixteen running feet of cheese table? We're talking about cheese bandits here."

"No problem," said Jack Nibble, the cheese maven. "A bunch of students will be coming from the college to help serve, pick up empties, and all that."

"And what kind of punch are you serving?"

"None of your sissy-pink punches," said Jerry Sip. "The non-alky bowl will have three kinds of fruit juices plus a slug of strong cold tea and a dash of bitters. With the tea and the cranberry juice, it'll have a good color. The wine punch is amber-colored, like Fish House punch but nowhere near as potent."

"Smoking prohibited, I assume?"

"Definitely!" said Hixie, who had become militantly anti-tobacco since giving up cigarettes herself.

Carol said, "The hosts who greet people and hand out programs will also circulate and be sure no one lights up. The programs list the cheeses being served."

"Yow!" came a loud comment from the kitchen. Jack and Jerry, startled, turned their heads quickly in that direction.

"That's only Koko," said Qwilleran. "He always has to put in his nickel's worth, no matter what the conversation . . . Well, it looks as if you've covered all the bases."

"Everything will run smoothly," said Jack. "Trust me."

And Carol added, "Everyone will have a perfectly fabulous time." Then, as the delegation was leaving, she said to Qwilleran, "Your dinner date was at the store as soon as we opened the doors this morning. Sarah wanted something special to wear. She bought a rust-colored silk with a Chanel jacket piped in black, and we're doing rush alterations for her."

Hixie also had a private comment to make to him as

she handed him an advance copy of the program. "This should remind you of a cheese-tasting you and I went to Down Below. You were covering it for the *Daily Fluxion*, and you invited me."

He nodded. "It was held at the Hotel Stilton, and you wore a hat with vegetables on it."

"My God!" she said, rolling her eyes. "The things I wore when I was young and foolish! We've both come a long way since then, baby!"

Having said goodbye to the group, Qwilleran found Koko sitting in front of the refrigerator in rapt concentration, as if willing the door to fly open and the turkey to fly out. "Sorry, old boy," he said. "You'll have to wait a couple of days. How about a read instead?" He waved the program for the cheese-tasting.

With mumbles of appreciation, the Siamese ran to their positions: Koko jumping on the arm of Qwilleran's favorite chair and Yum Yum waiting patiently for his lap to become available. First he read the preface aloud. It said that cheese is mentioned in the Bible and in Shakespeare's plays, and that there are hundreds of different cheeses in the world today. It said that tonight's event would feature imports from nine countries. It said that those selected could be considered the Bach, Beethoven, and Brahms of the cheese world.

At each mention of cheese, Koko responded with an emphatic yowl.

"What is this? The Anvil Chorus?" Qwilleran complained. "I appreciate your interest, but your comments get boring after a while." It occurred to him that Koko might confuse "cheese" with "treat," or even "read." He wondered if a cat's ear is tuned to vowels and not consonants. As a test he tried using the French word for cheese:

"If Roquefort is considered the king of *fromages*, Cheddar must surely be the Houses of Parliament. The centerpiece on each *fromage* table tonight is a large wheel of Cheddar, one from Great Britain and one from Canada. Even so, be sure to sample all twenty *fromages* in this unique adventure in tasting."

Koko yowled at every mention of *fromage*, leading Qwilleran to conclude that the cat was not comprehending words; he was reading minds, and the extra whiskers were probably responsible.

The program then listed the twenty cheeses with country of origin and kernels of information:

FROM FRANCE:

Roquefort, the king of cheeses—blue-veined, patented five centuries ago.

Brie, the queen of cheeses—soft, buttery, salty, and capricious—once an influence in French politics.

Camembert, invented by a woman—a soft, elegant dessert cheese associated with affluence.

Port du Salut, first made by Trappist monks—nothing monastic about its rich, ripe flavor.

Neufchâtel—small, white, creamy, mild-flavored— becomes pungent with age.

FROM GERMANY:

Tilsiter—full-bodied ripe flavor, pleasant to the nose and palate. More respectable than Limburger.

FROM ITALY:

Bel Paese—pearly white, sweetly mild, and agreeably rubbery in texture.

Fontina—yellowish and sometimes slightly smoky. A table cheese that also melts well for cooking.

Gorgonzola—blue-veined like Roquefort but less salty and more creamy than crumbly.

FROM SWITZERLAND:

Emmenthaler—the big cheese with big holes. Wheels weigh up to 160 pounds. Flavor: Swiss.

Gruyère—a smaller, saltier, creamier, more delicious Swiss with smaller holes (called "eyes").

Raclette—a rich cheese made for fondue and the melt-and-scrape ritual called "raclette."

FROM DENMARK:

Havarti—mild, clean, slightly acid flavor that becomes sharper with age.

Samsoe—similar to Cheddar in flavor with a slightly sweet, nutty flavor.

FROM THE NETHERLANDS:

Edam—popular low-fat cheese with cushiony shape and red rind. Texture: like soap but pleasant.

Gouda—yellow, fairly hard, and blessed with a strong flavor minus bite. Smoked version is great!

FROM CANADA:

Cheddar—with the famous flavor and famous black rind. Need we say more.

FROM GREECE:

Feta—soft, white, heavily salted. Crumble it on salads, pizza, and other dishes.

FROM GREAT BRITAIN:

Cheddar—from the country where it all began. Complicated to make, easy to love.

Stilton—a magnificent blue-veined cheese that slices well. A classic with port wine.

As Qwilleran read this list aloud, Yum Yum fell asleep on his lap with a foreleg over her ears, but Koko listened attentively. Three times he yowled—at Brie, Gruyère, and feta. Because they're salty, Qwilleran reasoned, but so is Roquefort . . . Yet, Koko was unimpressed by the king of cheeses.

At midday he walked to the newspaper office and handed in his copy on eating in the good old days. It began, "Where are the foods of yesteryear?"

He also picked up his fan mail, but Sarah was not there to slit the envelopes for him. The office boy said with a grin, "She took the day off to get her hair and face done. Whoo-ee!" Officially the speaker was a "systems aide," but to Qwilleran he was still an office boy.

For lunch he went to the Spoonery, where the day's soup specials were New Orleans gumbo, Viennese goulash, oxtail, and turkey-barley. He had a bowl of the oxtail and pronounced it sensational. He also asked Lori if the turkey-barley soup really had any turkey in it.

"It's loaded! Big chunks! Want a bowl? The second bowl is twenty percent off," she said.

"No thanks, but I'd like a quart to take out." He planned to fish out a few chunks of turkey for the

Siamese, avoiding the barley. That should satisfy them until the bird in the refrigerator was ready to fly.

Before he left the Spoonery, several copies of the Monday paper were delivered for customers to read with their soup, and Qwilleran grabbed one. The weekend had been an editor's delight, with the Celebrity Auction, the Pasty Bake-off and the bike-a-thon. Qwilleran chuckled as he read about the pasty winners' names being locked in a safe overnight—accidentally. More likely, he thought, Hixie had engineered the trick to delay the newsbreak until the *Something*'s deadline. The news story read:

PASTY WINNERS HERALDED

Two local cooks were elected to the new Pasty Hall of Fame Saturday after their contest entries survived three batteries of judges.

Lenore Bassett of Trawnto Beach placed first among the turnipless entries. George Stendhup of Sawdust City won in the turnip category. Each will receive a blue ribbon and a $100 prize.

After the process of blind judging—with entrants identified only by number—the suspense was prolonged by an accidental misunderstanding. Entrants' names were locked in a safe in the office of MacWhannell & Shaw. The bakers of the winning pasties were not known until this morning.

Stendhup, a toolmaker, was one of an unexpected number of male entrants. "I always knew the guys made better pasties than the gals," he said when contacted with the good news. Pork was his meat of choice. "I always add turnip for more guts."

Bassett could not be reached for comment, but her husband, Robert, said, "She's out of town on family business, but I'm gonna phone her the good news after five o'clock. Me and the kids always said Mom makes the best gol-danged pasties anywhere."

Mildred Riker, food editor of the *Something* and one of the final judges, said, "The response to this celebration of a cultural legend exceeded our wildest expectations, with more than a hundred entries. The overall quality was excellent, and the final judges were hard-put to name winners."

The sponsors of the Food Fair and Pasty Bake-off was the Chamber of Commerce.

Another headline caught Qwilleran's attention, although it was buried on page four. Notable for its brevity, it covered the who, what, when, and where of the newspaper rule book, but not the why.

BIZARRE INCIDENT IN BLACK CREEK

The body of a tourist from Glassville, OH, was found in a riverbank cabin Sunday morning. Victor Greer, 39, renting the cabin for a weekend of fishing, had been stung to death by bees, according to the medical examiner. The incident was reported by the beekeeper, Aubrey Scotten. The cabin is owned by Scotten Fisheries.

The item, Qwilleran knew, was played down for two reasons: The victim was not a local man, and the county disliked adverse publicity. It was commonly believed that the metropolitan media, bored with ordinary shootings and beatings, watched the small-town newspapers like vultures, hoping to spot a bizarre country crime. Most country crimes reported Down Below were "bizarre," and the use of the word in the *Something* headline was a mistake, in Qwilleran's opinion. He wondered who had written it. The wire services would pick it up, and the TV networks would fly crews to the "grim ghost town" with nothing but a "haunted house" and a "death cottage" where "killer bees" attacked an innocent fisherman from Down Below. They would fluster the poor beekeeper and trick him into saying something stupid that would sound suspicious to a coast-to-coast audience, and the cameras would zoom in on the buzzing bees and make them look like monsters. Qwilleran hoped the intruders would be stung; it would serve them right!

Further, he sensed the need to steer the nervous, distraught Aubrey out of harm's way. His motive was not entirely altruistic; as a journalist he was drawn to a newsworthy character with an exclusive story to tell.

He walked home briskly to pick up his car keys. The quart of turkey soup he put in the refrigerator, closing the door as quietly as possible. Then he left the barn without disturbing the sleeping cats.

Arriving at the Limburger house, he parked in the side yard. For the first time the door of the honey shed was closed. First he went to the front door and clanged the old-fashioned doorbell; there was no response. He banged on the door without results. Yet, Aubrey's blue pickup was parked in the yard. He might be down at the creek with his bees.

Qwilleran rang the bell again and peered through the etched glass. A shadowy figure was shambling toward the front door. "Aubrey! It's your friend from Pickax!" Qwilleran yelled. "I need some more honey!" Purposely he used two buzz words: "friend" and "honey." The door opened slowly and Aubrey said in his squeaky voice, "Threw it all out. I'm gonna let my bees go wild."

"Have the police been talking to you again?"

Aubrey shook his mop of long white hair. "They come back, but I hid in the cellar."

"Well, let me give you some friendly advice. You should get away from here. Strangers will be coming up from Down Below, and they're worse than the police. Go and stay with your family for a while. Where do your brothers live?"

"Up the road."

"Okay, I'll drive you there. Do you want to pack a bag—or anything?"

"I don't need nothin'." Then, as Qwilleran steered him toward his car, Aubrey added, "I wanna go to my mom's."

"That's fine. That's even better. Tell me where to go."

On the way Aubrey mumbled brief, half-hearted answers to questions intended to fill the awkward silence: Does your mother live alone? Do you see her often? How long has your father been gone? Have you talked to her since the accident?

A large old farmhouse between Black Creek and Mooseville was the Scotten homestead. It had a well-kept lawn and what seemed like acres of mums in bloom, some of them the color of dried blood. It looked like a commercial flower business. A woman was digging up clumps of mums and transferring them to pots. When the car pulled into the long driveway, she stuck the pointed spade in the ground and came forward—a tall woman like her sons, but her weathered face was gaunt under a large straw hat. She wore denims, with kneepads buckled on her legs.

"You poor boy!" she said, throwing her arms around her big son. "You look terrible! You need something to eat!" She looked at Qwilleran's moustache. "Do I know you? You must be the man from the paper. You wrote about the bees."

"I'm also a customer of Aubrey's. I stopped at the house to buy honey and thought he looked in need of some home cooking."

"Poor boy! Come in the house and I'll make you a big stack of flapjacks," she said. "I'd better give you a haircut, too. How long since you went to the barber, son?"

Qwilleran caught her eye and mumbled, "I want to speak to you."

"Aubrey, go in and wash up. I'll get rid of these muddy boots and be right there."

Qwilleran said, "Don't let anyone know he's here, not even your sons. All sorts of people will be pestering him—for various reasons. Wait till it blows over. Can you keep him for a few days?"

FIFTEEN

Convinced that he was doing the right thing, Qwilleran left Aubrey with his mother and went home to dress for his dinner date with Sarah Plensdorf. First he fed the cats, scooping turkey chunks from the Spoonery carton and warming them in some of the broth, minus barley and carrots. "This will have to do," he told them, "till the real bird comes along."

Then he showered, shaved, trimmed his moustache, and dressed in his navy blue suit with white shirt and red paisley tie. He thought it was an appropriate getup for an evening with a button collector; whimsically, he chose a button-down collar.

On the way to Indian Village to pick her up, he reflected that she had donated $1,500 to charity for the privilege of a few hours in his company, and it was his responsibility to make the evening enjoyable, if not memorable. Making conversation with strangers or virtual strangers was no problem; it was one of his professional skills. In fact, asking questions and listening to the answers had made him a popular companion in Moose County. He hoped only that the cosmetician would not make the modest Sarah look like a china doll, or worse.

When he arrived at her apartment, she was ready and waiting—somewhat breathlessly, he thought. In her new rust-colored dress with Chanel jacket, she looked quite smart, and Brenda's Salon had given her a flattering hairdo and natural makeup that gave her a certain glow.

Gallantly he said, "I've been looking forward to this evening, Sarah."

"So have I, Mr. Q," she said excitedly. "Would you care for an apéritif before we leave?"

"I'd like that, but we have a reservation for seven-thirty, and I think we should be on our way." Then he added sternly, "And if you don't start calling me Qwill, I'll cancel the reservation!"

Amused and pleased, she concurred. She wondered if she would need a wrap. He said it might turn chilly later in the evening, and it would be wise to take one.

While she went to pick up her handbag and, presumably, have a last look in the mirror, Qwilleran appraised the interior: large rooms, evidently two apartments made into one . . . heavy on blue . . . antique furniture, old oil paintings, good Orientals. He was surprised, however, to see a dog. Dogs were not permitted in apartments in the Village. This one was a Bassett hound. Strangely, it was standing on hind legs with forepaws on a library table. He stared at the dog, and the dog stared at him.

Sarah returned. "That's Sir Cedric," she said. "A Victorian piece, carved wood. Realistic, isn't it?"

"I must say it's unique," Qwilleran said. The table was dark pine with ordinary carved legs at one end, while the other end was supported by the dog. "Clever! Very clever!"

As they drove away he asked his passenger, "Do you like living in Indian Village?" It was not the most intelligent question he had ever asked, but it was a start.

"I do indeed," she replied. "Every season of the year has its delights. Right now it's the autumn color, especially beautiful this year."

"Polly Duncan, whom you must know, would take an apartment out here, if it weren't for the long drive into town."

"You tell her," Sarah said emphatically, "that it's no trouble at all, after one does it for a week or so."

"How do you like working at the newspaper?"

"It's most enjoyable! Everyone seems to be having so much fun, and yet they manage to put the paper out on time. It was Junior Goodwinter who suggested me for the job. It's the first one I've ever had."

"Is that so?" he asked in surprise. "You handle it with great aplomb."

"Thank you. I attended an Eastern college and could have had a fine position in Boston, but my parents wanted me at home. I was an only child, you see, and we had a lovely family relationship. I went to Europe with my mother and on business trips with my father. Then there was community service, which is both social and rewarding. So I've had a busy life. My one regret is . . . that I never had a career. I think I would have been quite successful."

"I'm sure of that!" he said. Then, to introduce a light

note to the conversation, he added, "My only regret is . . . that I was born too late to see Babe Ruth at bat or Ty Cobb in centerfield."

"That's right! You're a baseball fan! I clip and save all your columns on baseball—for old time's sake. My father never missed a World Series, and he started taking me along when I was seven. My mother didn't care for spectator sports, so he and I flew all over the country, and I learned to keep a detailed scorecard and figure batting averages. I believe it gave me a knack for math and a taste for minutiae."

Qwilleran glanced at her with admiration. "Minutiae" was a word he had never heard on a blind date. He said, "Do you remember the historic game in 1969 when the Mets took the series from the Orioles?"

"I do! I do! In 1968 the Mets had ended in ninth place, and since Father and I always rooted for the underdog, we were strong Met supporters. When they won—after that last exciting game—I remember the Met fans running out on the field and digging up the grass. . . . Do you have any particular ball club allegiances, Mr. Q? . . . I mean, Qwill?"

"Well, I was a Chicago Cubs fan before I could walk, but I seldom see a big league game these days. Do you still follow the sport?"

"No," she said sadly. "Not since Father died. It was baseball that killed him. The 1975 Series between Cincinnati and Boston was unbearably suspenseful. It ran seven games. There were delays because of rain. Scores teetered back and forth. Incredible performances! Surprises and twists of fate! It was too exciting for Father. He had a heart attack." She sighed, and Qwilleran mumbled consolations.

When the two baseball fans arrived at the Old Stone Mill, they were shown to the best table—one with a bouquet of fresh flowers—and there was applause from other diners; everyone in Pickax knew about the $1,500 dinner date. Sarah blushed, and Qwilleran bowed to the smiling faces at other tables.

The waiter served them one dry vermouth and one Squunk water, and Sarah said, "When you write about Koko and Yum Yum in your column, Qwill, you show a wonderful understanding of cats. Have you always been a cat fancier?"

"No, I was quite ignorant of feline culture when I adopted them, but they soon taught me everything I needed to know. Now I'd find it difficult to live without them. What attracts me is their secret energy. It makes a cat a forceful presence at all times."

He was interrupted by the forceful presence of Derek Cuttlebrink, presenting the menus and reciting the specials: "Chicken breast in curried sauce with stir-fried veggies . . . roast rack of lamb with green peppercorn sauce . . . and shrimp in a saffron cream with sun-dried tomatoes and basil, served on spinach fettucine."

Sarah said, "I developed a taste for curry when we traveled in India, so that would be my immediate choice."

Derek asked Qwilleran, "You want a sixteen-ounce steak and a doggie bag?"

"You don't happen to have any turkey, do you?"

"Come back on Thanksgiving day. The soup du jour is oxtail."

"I had oxtail for lunch at the Spoonery. Who stole the recipe from whom?"

"You wanna know the truth," Derek confided, "our chef got the recipe from *Joy of Cooking.*"

When the waiter had left the table, Sarah said, "He's rather outspoken, isn't he? But he's refreshing."

Qwilleran agreed. "He gets away with it because he's six-feet-eight. If he were five-feet-six, he'd be fired . . .

Now, where were we? Speaking of cats, I assume you like animals."

"Very much. I volunteer my services at the animal shelter every Saturday."

"What do you do?"

"I wash dogs."

"Small ones, I hope," Qwilleran said.

"All sizes. Every dog gets a bath when he arrives at the shelter, and not one has ever given me any trouble. They seem to know we're doing something nice for them. Last Saturday I bathed a Great Dane. He jumped right into the tub. I put cotton in his ears and salve in his eyes, then wetted him down with the hose, applied shampoo, talked to him, hosed him off, and dried him. He loved it!"

"Apparently you're accustomed to dogs."

"Yes, we always had them at home. Now all I have is Sir Cedric. When I go home at the end of the day, he greets me, and we have some conversation, rather one-sided, I'm afraid . . . I wouldn't tell this to anyone else, Qwill."

"I understand exactly how you feel," he said with sincerity.

When the entrées were served, he took a deep breath and asked, "Didn't you have a display of buttons at the library a while ago?"

"You remembered! How nice!" she exclaimed.

"How, why, and when did you start collecting?"

"My father had a valuable collection of historic military buttons, and when we went to large cities for ballgames, he would search for Civil War buttons in the antique shops, and I would look for pretty glass ones. Now I have over a thousand—all kinds. My miniature paintings on porcelain are small works of art that I can hold in my hand. I also specialize in animal designs on ivory, silver, brass, copper, and even Wedgwood. I have a shell cameo of a dog's head carved from the Cassis Tuberca from the West Indies. You may remember it in my exhibit."

"Yes," he murmured vaguely.

Then she said, "If it isn't too presumptious, Qwill, I'd like to give you a memento of this occasion." She reached into her handbag and gave him a carved wood button depicting a cat's head.

"Well, thank you. That's a charming thought," he murmured.

"You might like to attend a meeting of the tri-county button club, too. Quite a few men belong."

"That's something to keep in mind . . . Shall we have dessert?"

The meal ended with crème brûlée for her and apple pie with cheese for him, and she declared it the most delightful dining experience of her entire life. As he drove her home, the conversation turned to shoptalk: the newspaper's fast-growing circulation, Wilfred's glory as a biker, and Mildred's new Thursday food page.

Sarah asked, "Did you notice the references to Iris Cobb in the Food Forum? She's greatly missed."

"Did you know her?"

"Very well! When I was a volunteer at the museum, she'd invite me to have lunch with her, knowing how I loved her pasties. I have an educated palate, you know—another of Father's legacies." She sighed and went on. "Did you know I was one of the preliminary judges for the pasty contest Saturday?"

"No. Filling or crust?"

"Filling. And now I must confide in you: There was one pasty that was extraordinary! To me it tasted as good as Iris Cobb's! It was made with turkey, which was disallowed, but the other judges and I were mischievous enough to pass it through to the finals." They were turning into the gates of Indian Village. Shyly, Sarah said, "Would you care to come in for a while and see my collection of buttons?"

"Thank you, but I have some scheduled phone calls to make. Another time, perhaps," he said, "but I'll see you safely indoors and say goodnight to Sir Cedric."

The animal holding up the library table, who had been standing on his hind legs for a hundred years, looked eerily alive. There was the shading of the brown coat, with the delineation of every hair, and there was the sad hound-dog expression in the eyes. Qwilleran patted his head. "Good dog! Good dog!"

On the way home he reflected that the evening would have been quite different if his auction package had been knocked down to Danielle Carmichael for her mandated cap of a thousand dollars. The conversation would have been about malls, football, and kinkajous instead of buttons, baseball, and carved wooden dogs, and she would never have referred to minutiae. Instead of a simple dress with Chanel jacket, she would have worn a sequinned cocktail sheath, thigh-high, and the other diners would not have applauded. Rather, they would have gasped, and some would have snickered. (This was Pickax, not Baltimore.) And the Christmas fund would have been five hundred dollars poorer. And he would not have heard the comment on the extraordinary pasty in the bake-off. By raising the ghost of Iris Cobb, Sarah might well be supporting his growing suspicions.

As soon as he arrived home, he made some phone calls. It was late but not too late for certain night owls of his acquaintance.

At the Riker residence, Mildred answered. "How was your fifteen-hundred-dollar dinner date?"

"Never mind that. Read about it in the 'Qwill Pen,'" he replied briskly. "Right now I'm interested in what the accountants' safe divulged. I read the winners' names in the paper today. Who baked the superpasty?"

"If I tell you, will you promise not to leak it? We're planning a feature, you know—the way you suggested."

He promised.

"Promise you won't even tell Polly?"

He promised again.

"Why are you so interested?"

"I'm writing a book on the origin and evolution of the pasty, from miner's lunch to gourmet treat."

"At this time of night? Come on, Qwill! You're keeping secrets."

"You're the one who's keeping secrets. I'm telling you flat-out that I'm writing a book." He was always on the verge of writing a book, but not about pasties.

"Okay. It was Elaine Fetter of West Middle Hummock."

"I suspected as much."

"Do you know her?"

"Everybody knows her. And if I were you, I'd put that superpasty feature on hold."

"What's the matter? What's this all about?"

"Tell you tomorrow. I'm in a hurry. Thanks for the information. Wake up your husband and tell him I said goodnight."

He hung up the phone without further civilities and called Celia Robinson. There had been lights in the carriage house when he drove in, and he knew she would be sitting up, reading the latest espionage thriller. In an undercover voice he asked, "Any luck?"

"You were right. I found what you wanted." She spoke in a hushed voice with abstract references. "There wasn't any name on it, but I checked what you mentioned. It's the real McCoy, all right."

"Good going!" he said. "Talk to you later."

And now, he wondered, how do we get our hands on it without embarrassing anyone? He sprawled in a lounge chair with his feet on an ottoman and cudgeled his brain. The Siamese sat quietly nearby, sensing that he was doing some concentrated thinking.

Suddenly, in one impulsive move, he swung his feet off the ottoman and went to the telephone desk. He called Hixie Rice at her apartment. There was no answer. He left a message on the machine.

Two minutes later she called back. "Sorry, Qwill. I've been avoiding someone. What's on your mind? How was your dinner date? What did you two talk about?"

"We talked about cats, dogs, baseball, buttons, pasties, and Iris Cobb, and that's why I'm calling you. I need to enlist your cooperation in a small, private, legal, innocuous intrigue."

"That's my specialty," she said.

"I want to run an ad in tomorrow's paper, if it isn't too late, but I must not be identified with it in any way. Can you handle that?"

"How big an ad?"

"Whatever it takes to be seen across the room: bold headline, sparse copy, plenty of white space."

"What's the message? Can you give it to me on the phone? I don't think I'm bugged."

He dictated about twenty words.

"Hmmm . . . interesting!" she said. "Do you expect results?"

"I don't need results," he told her. "This is a bluff. Stay tuned."

SIXTEEN

The cheese-tasting was scheduled for Tuesday evening, and Qwilleran spent much of the day hanging out downtown. The reason was simple. The redoubtable Mrs. Fulgrove was coming to clean the main floor. The amiable Mr. O'Dell would do the floors and vacuum the furniture, but she would dust, scrub, polish, and complain—about public morals, politicians, the younger generation, popular music, and the cat hair, which she considered a Siamese conspiracy to make her work harder. The white-haired Pat O'Dell, on the other hand, usually had something constructive to say in his pleasing Irish brogue.

"Faith, an' it's a foine woman livin' upstairs o'er the garage," he said on this occasion.

"Yes, Mrs. Robinson is a cheerful and energetic soul," Qwilleran agreed.

"Her windows are in need of washin', I'm thinkin', what with so many cars in the parkin' lot and the exhaust leavin' a scum on the glass."

"Make arrangements with her to clean them, Mr. O'Dell, and send the bill to me." Celia had already remarked about the considerate and good-natured maintenance man; she thought she might invite him to dinner some evening and give him a good Irish stew.

So Qwilleran locked the Siamese in their loft apartment and made his getaway before Mrs. Fulgrove loomed on the scene. First, he stopped at the library to see if they had any books on button collecting, in case he should want to write a column on the hobby at some future date. They did. He leafed through one of them and was pleased to find his cat-button pictured and described as a valuable collectible.

Then he went to breakfast at the Scottish Bakery: scones, clotted cream, and currant jam served by a bonnie lassie wearing a plaid apron. The coffee was not bad, either.

Next he visited the health food store, whose bearded proprietor was the husband of the *Something*'s new feature editor. "Welcome to Pickax!" Qwilleran said. "We're always glad to give asylum to defectors from Lockmaster."

"Thank you. We like it here, although the bombing and the murder shook us up, I don't mind telling you."

"It's not a local crime wave, I assure you. It's a spillover from Down Below." Qwilleran patted his moustache with confidence. "Okay if I just browse around?"

He wandered among the vitamin bottles with strange names, trays of muffins with unusual ingredients, meatless sandwiches, and fruit and vegetables without the waxed finish that made them look so good at Toodle's Market. Then there were the snacks. What looked like a chocolate chip cookie had no butter, no sugar, and no chocolate. What looked like a potato chip was made without fat, salt, or potato.

Qwilleran said, "I have a friend who'll be a good customer of yours. Tell me honestly, do your kids eat this stuff?"

"Oh, sure! Our family goes in for alternatives. Our kids were brought up that way, and they think junk food is weird."

From there Qwilleran walked to the police station to inquire about Lenny Inchpot. The witness to the bombing had been found and put on a plane to Duluth, where he would stay with his aunt for a while.

At the Chamber of Commerce across the street, he found them making plans for a Lois Inchpot Day in Pickax, in an effort to lure her back to town and reopen her lunchroom. The mayor would issue a proclamation to that effect, and loyal customers were painting the walls and ceiling, water-stained from the last roof leak.

Then it was time for a bowl of soup at the Spoonery. The day's specials were bouillabaisse, roasted peanut with garlic, sausage and white bean, and chicken with rice and dill. Qwilleran played safe with the bean soup.

After that he visited the Kitchen Boutique to buy a thermometer, basting syringe, and roaster with rack. He was going to roast that blasted bird if it was the last thing he ever did in his life.

Triumphantly, Sharon said, "Mother and I knew you'd break down and start cooking—someday."

"Don't bet on it," he said. "I'm just picking these up

for a friend." It was one of the impromptu prevarications that he had developed into an art.

By that time the Tuesday edition of the paper was on the street, and he read his ad. Within a few hours the entire county would be talking about it:

$10,000 REWARD

for information leading to the recovery of the late Iris Cobb's personal recipe book, missing since her death. Confidentiality guaranteed. Write to P.O. Box 1362, Pickax City.

When Qwilleran returned to the barn, the cleaning crew had gone and there was not a cat hair or mite of dust to be seen. He climbed the ramp to the top level and opened the door to the loft apartment. "Okay, you can come out and start shedding," he said.

In the kitchen he tested the progress of the thawing turkey, and before he could close the door, Koko executed a *grand jeté* over the bar and landed in the refrigerato with the bird.

"Out!" Qwilleran yelled, dragging him from the refrigerator and slamming it shut. The cat howled as if his tail had been caught in the door. "Don't overreact, you slyboots! Cats are supposed to be known for their patience."

Koko went slinking away, licking his wounded feline ego.

Qwilleran dressed for the cheese-tasting in dinner jacket and black tie, with a rare set of black studs in his shirt-front. They were from India, inlaid with silver and gold—a gift from Polly. Appraising himself in the full-length mirror, he had to admit that he looked good in evening clothes.

It was dark when the jitneys started delivering the well-dressed guests, and the exterior lights transformed the barn into an enchanted castle. Indoors, mysterious illumination from hidden sources dramatized the balconies and overhead beams, the white fireplace cube and its soaring white stacks, the contemporary tapestries, and the clean-cut modern furniture. Add to that the glamor of beaded dinner dresses, the courtliness of men in evening wear, and the bonhomie of such an occasion; it had all the ingredients of a magical evening, one never to be forgotten in Pickax, for more reasons than one.

John Bushland was on hand with a camcorder, the idea being to sell videos of the festivities and raise an extra thousand or two for a good cause. Although distinguished guests received ample coverage, the Siamese received more than their share of footage. They sat on the fireplace cube, watching in an attitude of wonder. Later they would sail to the floor like flying squirrels, Koko on the trail of cheese crumbs and Yum Yum on the lookout for shoelaces. As the proliferating number of feet endangered her tail, she fled to the first balcony and watched from the railing.

Among those present were the Rikers, Lanspeaks, and Wilmots; the mayor in his red paisley cummerbund; Don Exbridge with his new wife and his former wife; and the new banker with the flashy Danielle. If one wanted to count, there were three attorneys, four doctors, two accountants, one judge, and five public officials coming up for re-election. One of them was the cranky but popular Amanda Goodwinter, running again for city council and wearing a dinner dress she had worn for thirty years.

The focus of attention was the dinner table, with its silver punch bowls and lighted candles. Flanking it were the two white-skirted buffets, each with eight cheese platters and a large wheel of Cheddar. Jerry Sip and Jack Nibble presided at the buffets, assisted by college students looking professional in white duck coats.

Jack Nibble was heard to say, "We have three blues on the cheese table. Try all three and compare; it's the only way to learn. The one from France is crumbly; the Italian is spreadable; the one from England slices well."

And Dr. Prelligate replied, "Do I detect nuances in your observation?"

"Anyway you eat it," said Amanda Goodwinter, "it's still moldy cheese."

Then Jerry Sip said, "If you like a rich, creamy cheese with superb flavor, try the double-cream Brie."

"Yow!" came an endorsement from the floor.

Amanda said, "That cat and yours truly are the only ones here who tell it like it is!"

Pender Wilmot, who had cats of his own, said, "They all know the word 'cream' when they hear it."

"I have it on good authority," said Big Mac, "that Qwill feeds his on caviar and escargots. Too bad he can't take them as dependents."

"They're so elegant!" Dr. Diane enthused. "We have to dress up for special occasions, but Siamese always look formally attired." She gazed up at Yum Yum on the balcony railing, and the little female turned her head this way and that to show off her left and right profiles. "They're also vain!"

Not all the conversation was about cats and cheese. There were speculations about the bombing, the murder, and the $10,000 reward. Riker pulled Qwilleran aside and demanded, "Did you run that ad? You're crazy! Who's going to pay off?"

"Don't worry, Arch. No one will claim it, but it's large enough to put a lot of sleuths on the trail. I'm betting that the guilty person will mail the cookbook anonymously to the P.O. box, rather than be exposed."

Qwilleran circulated, listening and looking for ideas. He was always the columnist, always on duty, always hoping for material to fill the space on page two above the fold. What he heard was mostly small talk:

Don Exbridge: "It's never safe to recommend a restaurant. If you do, the chef quits the next day, the management replaces him with a hash-slinger, and your friends think you have a tin palate."

Larry Lanspeak: "Has anyone been to the Boulder House Inn? The chef grows his own herbs and knows how to cook vegetables—with a bone in them."

Carol Lanspeak: "Qwill, there's a fuchsia silk blouse at the store that Polly would love—scarf neck, drop shoulder. In fact, I've laid one aside in her size. If you want me to, I'll gift-wrap it and drop it off here."

Pender Wilmot: "Who's interested in starting a gourmet club? I'm taking applications."

Arch Riker: "Deal us in—but not if it's just another dinner club where you talk about the national deficit while you're eating. I want to learn something about food and wine."

Mildred Riker: "Someone has said that food worth eating is worth talking about."

Qwilleran: "Would this be a club for gourmands, gourmets, or gastronomes?"

Don Exbridge: "Get the dictionary, somebody!"

Dr. Diane: "How would it work? Would we flock around to restaurants? Or would we have to cook?"

Willard Carmichael: "In Detroit we belonged to a hands-on group. The host planned the menu and prepared the entrée. Other members were assigned to bring the other courses. Recipes were provided—all unusual, but not freaky. No fried grasshoppers."

Danielle Carmichael: "You had to follow the recipe exactly or pay a forfeit—like running the dishwasher or paying for the wine."

Qwilleran: "I'll join if I can be permanent dishwasher."

Amanda Goodwinter: "Don't put my name on the list. The last time I attended a gourmet dinner, I had indigestion for a month!"

The evening wore on, with much consumption of cheese and the amber-colored punch. Voices grew louder. A few couples started to leave. Suddenly there was a commotion in the kitchen—a thumping and growling, followed by a shattering crash! Conversations stopped abruptly, and Qwilleran rushed to the scene. Koko was having a cat fit. He raced around the kitchen in a frenzy, flinging himself at the refrigerator.

When Qwilleran tried to intervene, the cat leaped over the bar and crashed into a lamp, sending the shade and the base flying in opposite directions. Women screamed and men yelled as he zipped around the fireplace cube and headed for the cheese tables.

"Stop him!" Qwilleran shouted as the cat skidded through the cheese platters and scattered crumbs of Roquefort, cubes of Cheddar, slices of Gouda, and gobs of runny Brie, before leaping to the punch table and knocking over the lighted candles.

"Fire!" someone shouted.

Qwilleran dashed to a closet for a fire extinguisher, at the same time bellowing, "Grab him! Grab him!"

Three men tore after the mad cat as he streaked around the fireplace cube with fur flying. Pender, Larry, and Big Mac tore after him, bumping into the furniture and each other. Around and around they went.

"Somebody go the other way!"

Somebody did, but the trapped animal only sailed to the top of the cube and looked down on his pursuers.

"We've got him!"

A moment later Koko swooped over their heads and pelted up the ramp, not stopping until he reached the roof, where he perched on a beam and licked his fur.

Qwilleran was embarrassed. "My apologies! The cat went berserk! I don't know why."

"He drank some of Jerry's amber punch," Big Mac suggested.

Truthfully, Koko wanted everyone to go home, Qwilleran suspected, leaving him unlimited access to the cheese tables.

The guests were understanding but decided it was time to think about leaving. The dinner jackets on Larry, Pender, and Big Mac looked more like gray fur than black wool. A few cat hairs might have been an annoyance, but a million cat hairs—thanks to the amber punch—made it a joke. It was a merry crowd that boarded the jitneys, twelve at a time, for the ride back to the parking lot, and the students cleaning up the mess grinned to each other; it was the best thing that would happen all semester.

The Sip 'n' Nibble partners were philosophical. Jerry said, "Don't feel bad about it, Qwill. There's nothing like a minor catastrophe to make a party a success. They'll talk about this for the rest of the century."

"That's what I'm afraid of."

"I just hope they mention the name of our store," Jack added, "including the address and telephone number."

Carol said, "It was really funny to see three adult males chasing a little cat in a cloud of flying fur! I wonder if Koko has any left. It was better than a car chase! Aren't we lucky that Bushy got it on tape? We'll sell loads of videos."

Jack Nibble summed it up. "I'd say we achieved our goals: to show everyone a good time and educate a few palates. And it doesn't have to be double-cream to be good; the feta we brought is low-fat."

"Yow!" came a loud affirmative from somewhere overhead.

When everyone had gone, with promises to send a clean-up crew the next day, Qwilleran changed into a jumpsuit and went into the kitchen. Koko was ahead of him, trying to claw his way into the refrigerator.

"You rascal!" Qwilleran said. "So that's why you wanted everyone to go home! If you'll just cool it, we'll prep the turkey tonight and throw it in the oven first thing in the morning. Stand back!" He opened the refrigerator door cautiously, expecting a flank attack, but Koko knew when the battle was won. He watched calmly as the prepping began.

Qwilleran remembered Mildred's instructions: Remove the plastic wrap; release the legs without cutting the skin; explore the two cavities. He put his hand gingerly into the breast cavity and withdrew a plastic bag containing the neck. Then he turned the bird around and, with more confidence, explored the body cavity. It was cold but not frosty. Koko was watching with ears back and whiskers bristled. Qwilleran groped for the plastic bag. Instead, he found something hard and very,

very cold. His first thought was: a block of ice. His second was: a practical joke! He threw everything back into the tray and shoved the naked bird into the refrigerator. Then he called Nick Bamba at home.

"Hope I'm not calling too late, Nick. Just wanted to thank you for the *cold* turkey. I'm getting it ready to roast tomorrow . . . Yes, thanks to Mildred, I know how. But I have one question: Was there supposed to be anything *special* about the bird you delivered to me? . . . No, there's nothing wrong with it. I just had a . . . *special feeling* about it." He tamped his moustache. "Thanks again, Nick. I'll let you know how it turns out."

Hanging up the phone, Qwilleran kept his hand on the receiver. Should he, or should he not, call the police chief at home again? He punched the number that he knew by heart, and when the gruff voice answered, he said, "We had the cheese-tasting here tonight, you know, and Jerry and Jack left a variety of cheeses. Why don't you run over for a nibble—and a sip? Also . . . I have something peculiar to report—very peculiar!"

"I'll be there in two shakes," Brodie said. He arrived in a matter of minutes, and his first comment was: "You've got a big box at your back door."

"That's an antique sea chest. It's for package deliveries."

"And you've moved the furniture around."

"That was to accommodate the crowd. We had a hundred guests. The committee is coming tomorrow to put everything back the way it was."

They sat at the bar, where Qwilleran had ready a Scotch and a plate of leftover party cheeses. He pointed out Cheddar, Gouda, Bel Paese, Emmenthaler, Stilton, and Port du Salut.

"Where's the one I like so much?"

"Try the Emmenthaler, Andy. There wasn't any Gruyère left. Everyone liked the Gruyère."

"Yow!"

"Including our smart cat."

When Brodie had finished his first Scotch, Qwilleran said, "Before I top your glass, Andy, I'd like you to look at a gift I received Sunday." Keeping one eye on Koko, he brought the turkey from the refrigerator and pushed the tray toward the chief. "What would you say this is?"

"Are you pullin' my leg? It's a turkey!"

"Do you know how to stuff a bird?"

Brodie scowled. "That's my wife's job."

"Well, let me explain. This is the head-end, and that's the tail-end. There are two cavities. Put your hand in the breast cavity and see what you find."

Reluctantly and suspiciously, the chief did as instructed and drew out a plastic bag. "That's the neck! Are you playin' games?"

"Now put your hand in the body cavity. That's where they always store the sack of giblets."

With a glowering glance at his friend, Brodie thrust his hand into the bird. Immediately, a strange expression spread across his craggy face. It was a mixture of shock and disbelief. "What the hell!" he blurted as he drew forth a small handgun. "Who gave you this bird?"

"Nick Bamba. It was frozen solid when it arrived—probably part of a shipment going Down Below. It's been thawing in the fridge for two days, and Koko's been going crazy. Do you want a plastic bag for the evidence?"

"Gimme a trash bag," Andy said. "I'm taking the whole bird."

*　　*　　*

"There goes your turkey," Qwilleran said to Koko. To his surprise, the cat seemed unconcerned, sitting on his haunches in his kangaroo pose and grooming a small patch of fur on his chest. Could it be that Koko sensed there was something not quite right about that turkey? Qwilleran himself sensed there was something not quite right at the Cold Turkey Farm. Nick Bamba, he knew, needed a large work force, since young turkeys required much attention. Supervisory and technical posts were held by full-time workers with special skills, but there were jobs for college students and others needing part time employment or a second source of income. Nick's contingency payroll included off-duty police officers, clerks from the public library, the beefy installer from the design studio, an alterations apprentice from the men's store, and two of Mrs. Toodle's grandchildren. Lenny Inchpot wanted to sign on, after his job at the hotel blew up, but his mother vetoed it for reasons of her own.

Did one of these employees shoot the florist and hide the gun in a turkey to be shipped Down Below? Was it assumed that the bird would be lost in a labyrinth of human chaos in some distant metropolis? That was hardly smart thinking; the plastic wrapper clearly identified its source. On the other hand, the lucky recipient might consider it a wonderful Crackerjack prize—something to keep handy for the next prowler, attacker, mugger, burglar, carjacker, or other urban menace.

So . . . who was guilty of the homicide, and was he the accomplice of the original bomber? Certainly it was not the fresh-faced Toodle grandchildren . . . nor the fun-loving bumpkin who installed wall-to-wall

SEVENTEEN

The morning after the cheese-tasting and Koko's calamitous catfit, the Country Club sent a crew to remove the folding tables and silver punch bowls and return the furniture to its normal arrangement. Meanwhile, Qwilleran spent the morning in his balcony studio, writing a thousand words about cheese. In two weeks he had learned a great deal from Jack Nibble and quoted him at length: "Never grate cheese in advance . . . To get your money's worth from cheese, serve it at room temperature . . . Cheese belongs with a good meal and makes a bad one better."

In the afternoon, Qwilleran went for a long bike ride, hoping to clarify his thinking on various matters; too much had been happening too fast. He walked through the woods to the carriage house, where his bike was parked in one of the stalls, and waved to Celia Robinson. She was having a jolly conversation with Mr. O'Dell, who was there to blow fallen leaves into huge piles for the city's vacuum truck.

"Nice man," she commented to Qwilleran as he tested the air in his tires. "Isn't this a wonderful day for a bike ride? Where are you going?"

"Out Ittibittiwassee Road to the stone bridge and back the same way."

"Oh, my! That's quite a ways! How long will it take?"

"Couple of hours."

"Well, be careful. Get back before dark!"

Ittibittiwassee Road, part of the route for the Labor Day Race, still had the orange-and-white markers planted on the shoulder by the Pedal Club. They would remain in place until November, at which time the county snowplows would send them flying through the air like toothpicks. When Qwilleran turned onto the highway at the Dimsdale Diner, the first milepost he encountered was number 15. From there he ticked off his thoughts by the mile:

Milepost 16: What to write for Tuesday's paper? Should be about food. The dictionary says turnips are edible. How about a thousand derogatory words about turnips? People live on them in times of famine or war; that's why they're such a depressing vegetable. We call a bad play or movie a turkey; in France they call it a turnip. The *Larousse Encyclopedia* says that turnips can be boiled, scalloped, glazed, stuffed, creamed, molded, puréed, or souffléd. I say: Any way you mash it, it's still a turnip. Has it ever been used as fertilizer? Brodie says you can make a bomb out of fertilizer. Is there such a thing as a turnip bomb?

Milepost 18: Too bad about the shiitake. It would make a good column, but not until the family situation is straightened out. Are the mushrooms his or hers? Where was Donald during the interview? She never even mentioned him. Is she hiding something? If so, what? Celia says mother and son don't get along well.

Milepost 19: How to handle it tactfully? Down Below they'd try to probe family secrets and make a scandal out of it.

Milepost 20: The shiitake had a great taste. Butter, garlic, parsley, and freshly ground pepper, she said. Polly will be interested, except for the butter.

Milepost 22: First, shiitake; and now Iris's cookbook. What's going on in Madame Fetter's kitchen? Did she pilfer the book from the museum? Or is she a receiver of stolen goods? She must have known it was hot. The museum had appealed for its return, no questions asked.

Milepost 25: Everyone's talking about the reward and P.O. Box 1362. How will Madame Fetter react? Will she have any qualms about an exposé? Will she take some sort of action? If she takes the book to the post office to be weighed for postage, those savvy postal clerks will notice that it's local—going to Box 1362—with no return address. They'll recognize her. They know everyone who's ever bought a stamp.

Milepost 26: Even if she mails it from Lockmaster, it's risky. The *Ledger* picked up the story of the reward. So maybe she won't try to mail it at all. She could burn it—after copying a few of the recipes. She could plant it in someone else's kitchen and claim the reward herself. Just a thought; she can't be that low. Or someone who's seen the book in her kitchen could squeal, and I'd have to fork over money for information I already have.

Milepost 29: Too bad I didn't take the book myself

when I was there. I was lawfully on the premises, and the book is lawfully mine. No crime! And she couldn't accuse me without incriminating herself. I could have Celia sneak it out of the kitchen, but that's burglary; it's not her own property. I can't involve Celia in anything that might blow her cover. She's too valuable to me.

At that point, Qwilleran reached the stone bridge, took a breather, and biked home, arriving just before dusk. After stabling his bike in the carriage house, he walked to the barn on bicycle legs—with bent knees and bouncing gait. In the sea chest he found two deliveries: a Lanspeak Department Store bag and a foil-wrapped brick, slightly warm. The Siamese knew what it was and gave him a clamoring welcome.

"Okay! Okay! Later!" he said, tossing the brick into the refrigerator for security reasons. Then he turned his attention to the Lanspeak bag. Before opening it, he said to himself, Hey, wait a minute; it's too heavy for a silk blouse! It was indeed heavy. It was a thick, black, scuffed, greasy notebook with loose pages.

"Ye gods!" he said aloud. "It's Iris's cookbook!" He rushed to the phone, followed by two demanding cats. "Later! Later!" he shouted at them.

After two rings he heard Celia's voice saying playfully, "Carriage House Inn-on-the-Park. May I help you?"

"I'd like to reserve a table for six for dinner," he said.

"Oh, I'm sorry, Chief. I thought it was—someone else. Did you find my meatloaf?"

"Yes, and we all thank you profusely, but that's not all I found!"

"Were you surprised?"

"That's putting it mildly. I didn't expect you to . . . help yourself to the evidence."

"I didn't!" she cried defensively. "It was given to me!"

"Well! That's a surprise. Did Mrs. Fetter explain its illegal presence on her bookshelf?"

"No! No! Donald gave it to me! He saw me reading it and said, 'Why don't you take that *something-something* piece of *something* home and keep it? Mom's not supposed to have it anyway. But don't tell her I gave it to you.' Those aren't his exact words, but that's the idea."

"Well! What can I say? Was that on Monday?"

"Yes, when I went out there with the junior trainee. Sorry I didn't deliver it to you right away. I wanted to copy a few of the recipes. I hope you don't mind."

"Celia, not only do I not object; I'm promoting you to Senior Executive Assistant in charge of Sensitive Investigations."

Her laughter rang out as he said good night. For a while he stared at the phone. He was thinking, If Donald had waited another twenty-four hours, he could have turned in his own mother and collected the reward . . . although he might have had to split it with her.

He examined the cookbook, oblivious of the caterwauling around him. The black cover was gray with decades of spilled flour; Iris had always boasted of being a sloppy cook. It bulged with loose pages and yellowed newspaper clippings, liberally spotted and smeared. Qwilleran thought he could identify bacon grease, tomato juice, olive oil, chocolate, coffee, and blood. Splashes of liquid had blotted some of the handwriting, which was virtually indecipherable even at its best. He went to his studio and typed a release for the *Moose County Something* and *Lockmaster Ledger*:

A missing cookbook, originally owned by Iris Cobb, has been anonymously returned to its rightful owners, the Klingenschoen Foundation, which intends to publish it. The announcement of a $10,000 reward for information leading to its recovery produced no tips or clues, according to a spokesperson for the K Fund. The return of the book was voluntary, and no inquiries will be made.

It was while he was giving the Siamese a couple of slices of meatloaf that the phone rang. His hello brought only labored breathing. "Hello?" he repeated with a questioning inflection.

Then he heard a high-pitched voice say, "I'm gonna kill myself." The words were spoken in a monotone, but desperation made them almost falsetto.

"What? What did you say? Is this Aubrey?"

"I'm gonna kill myself."

"Where are you? Are you at your mother's house?"

"I come home. I come home to get a gun. I'm gonna shoot myself."

Qwilleran had heard suicide threats before. Aubrey needed to talk to someone.

"What did your mother think about your leaving?"

"Di'n't tell her."

"How did you get home?"

"Walked."

"Where was she when you left?"

"Diggin' in the yard."

"Don't you think you should have told her?"

"She don't need me. She's got her grandkids. I'm gonna shoot myself."

"But who would take care of your bees? They need you! You told me yourself, they're your friends."

"They're gone. I smoked 'em out."

"Did you blame them for what happened? They didn't know what they were doing."

There was a breathy pause. "I'm goin' crazy. Can't eat. Can't sleep. I'm gonna shoot myself."

"Now, wait a minute, Big Boy. We have to talk about this. I'm your friend. I want to know what's troubling you."

"I got the old man's gun. I'm gonna put it under my chin and pull the trigger."

"Okay, but don't do anything until I get there! I'm leaving right away—do you hear? I'll be there in ten minutes. Turn the outside lights on."

Qwilleran grabbed his jacket and car keys and had the presence of mind to throw the remainder of the meatloaf in the refrigerator. Without saying goodbye, he rushed out the door to his car. Gunning the motor, he bumped through the darkening woods and made a tire-screeching turn onto Park Circle, heading for Sandpit Road. Traffic was light at that hour, and he could speed. Reaching Black Creek, he looked across the forlorn landscape and saw the yardlights of the Limburger house in the distance. It meant that Aubrey had been listening; he was obeying orders.

Qwilleran parked at the curb and hurried to the lighted veranda. As he climbed the crumbling brick steps, the front door opened, and a ghost of a man stood there, his shoulders drooping, his face almost as white as his hair, and his eyes unfocused.

"Thanks for turning on the lights," Qwilleran said, following the shuffling feet into the front hall. A single dim lightbulb burned in the branched chandelier. The door to the gun cabinet was open. "Look here, Big Boy," he said. "Let's go somewhere and have a good talk, friend-to-friend. Let's get away from this gloomy place. Everything will turn out all right. Don't worry. You need to talk to someone who understands, when you're feeling down. Come on. Let's go. Turn out the lights. Lock the door."

Aubrey needed someone to take charge. He did as he was told, moving slowly as if in a trance. Then Qwilleran took him by the elbow and piloted him down the steps and into the car.

He could write a thousand words for his column with the greatest of ease, but he had to work hard to fill the silence that amplified the rumble of the motor as they drove to Pickax. "It's a nice night. Crisp but not chilly. Just what you expect in early October. Soon it will be Halloween—then Thanksgiving, before we know it. We haven't had Indian summer as yet, though. After that, anything can happen. Dark, isn't it? No moon tonight. You can see the glow on the horizon from the Pickax streetlights. Not much traffic tonight. No one goes out on Wednesday night . . . There's the Dimsdale Diner. They stay open all night. You never see any trucks in the parking lot, though. I think the cook sleeps behind the counter. His pancakes are the worst I've ever eaten. I wonder what he does to them. They say Lois is going to open her lunchroom again."

While he talked about everything and nothing, his passenger slumped in a stupor. Qwilleran hoped that his planned shock treatment would work. They turned off Park Circle, crossed the theatre parking lot, and plunged into the woods. As they emerged from the dark stand of evergreens, Qwilleran reached for the remote control, and instantaneous floodlights turned the towering barn into something unreal. Aubrey sat up and stared.

"An old apple barn," Qwilleran told him. "Built more than a hundred years ago. Wait till you see the inside."

As they walked through the kitchen door, he pressed a single switch that illuminated balconies, ramps, beams, and the giant fireplace cube. Two cats who had been sleeping on the sofa rose, arched their backs, stretched, and jumped down to inspect the visitor. They circled him inquisitively, sniffing his field boots and finding them quite fascinating.

"What are they?" Aubrey asked.

"Siamese cats. Very friendly. You can see they're attracted to you. They know you like animals. The little female is Yum Yum; the male is Koko. Talk to them. Tell them your name."

"Aubrey," the man said hesitantly.

"Yow!" Koko replied in his piercing Siamese baritone.

Qwilleran said, "See? He's pleased to meet you. Take off your jacket and sit down in that comfortable chair. Would you like some cheese and crackers? What do you drink? Coffee? Beer? Wine? Ginger ale?"

"Beer," Aubrey said in a daze as he sank into the deep-cushioned chair. He could not take his eyes from the cats, who were milling about gracefully, striking poses, gazing at him, doing all the right things, as if they had been assigned to patient therapy.

Yum Yum made a half-hearted pass at the laces of the field boots before jumping into Aubrey's lap and kneading in the crook of his elbow, purring loudly. Then she looked up at him with soulful eyes.

Qwilleran thought, She's a witch!

"Big eyes," Aubrey said. "Why's she lookin' at me like that?"

"She wants to play Blink. She stares at you, you stare at her, and the first one who blinks loses the game." He put a can of beer and a plate of cheese at Aubrey's elbow.

Then it was Koko's turn to do his mesmerizing act. He jumped to the arm of the big chair and sniffed Aubrey's sleeve. Then the cold wet nose traveled up his sleeve and sniffed his ear.

"It tickles," he said, almost smiling.

"Do you know that cats have twenty-four whiskers on each side? They're all guaranteed to tickle. Count them and see if I'm right."

Aubrey turned his head and met the hypnotic gaze, eyeball to eyeball.

Qwilleran thought, They know he's troubled. Cats have a natural aptitude for care-giving. He said, "Give Koko a taste of cheese, and he'll be your friend for life."

The man followed orders and was pleased when both cats took crumbs of cheese from his fingers. "Just like a dog I used to have," he said. "His name was Spot— black and white—mixed breed. On'y way he'd eat was from my hand. I never saw cats like these . . . You let 'em in the house!" he added in surprise.

"This is where they live. They never go outdoors."

Aubrey stroked their silky fur constantly while he talked.

Qwilleran thought, It's a miracle; he's talking!

Aubrey went on, as though some healing flow of energy was passing from the cats to the man. "When Spot was killed, I di'n't want another dog. I joined the Navy. I was gonna learn electronics. I like that stuff. But I had an accident. I hadda come home."

Cautiously and with all the kindliness he could muster, Qwilleran asked, "What kind of accident?"

"I come near drownin'. When I come to, I thought I was dead. I felt different. But I wasn't dead. I was in sick bay. The medics said I owed my life to my buddy. Vic, his name was. He jumped in after me. They said there was sharks all around."

"Frightening experience."

"When somebody saves your life, you owe 'im one. That's what they say."

"Do you still keep in touch with . . . Vic?"

Aubrey turned a horrified face to Qwilleran. "That was him in the cabin!" He broke down in a fit of sobbing, covering his large face with his hands.

"That's all right," Qwilleran said soothingly. "It's good to let go. Get it off your chest."

The Siamese were alarmed but stayed nearby—each a silent but sympathetic presence. When the sobbing finally subsided and Aubrey started wiping his face on his sleeve, Qwilleran offered handfuls of tissues. The man clutched at them.

"Now you'll feel better," Qwilleran said.

He was right. Aubrey relaxed into dazed tranquility.

"Perhaps you're ready for something to eat now—a meatloaf sandwich?"

"Yeah. I'm hungry."

"Let's go and sit at the bar. We'll take the cheese with us, so the cats don't get it."

Aubrey hunched over the bar and devoured cheese and crackers and drank beer while Qwilleran threw together sandwiches with Celia's meatloaf, mustard, and dill pickle. Then, after two sandwiches and three cans of beer, Aubrey wanted to talk. Words poured forth in a torrent of disconnected thoughts and naive remarks.

Qwilleran listened attentively. Suddenly he said, "Excuse me a moment. I'll be right back." He spiraled up the circular staircase that led from the kitchen to his studio and made a phone call. At the first gruff hello, he thundered, "Where's Koko's turkey? He wants his turkey!"

"It's at the lab," Brodie said, sounding grumpy. "Buy him another one. You can afford it. Is that all you called about?"

"Not by a long shot. Seriously, Andy, I hate to bother you again, but I think you should haul your bagpipe over here on the double. It's important. I want you to meet someone."

"What the hell kind of invitation is that?" the chief demanded. He sounded as if his favorite TV program had been interrupted.

"Trust me. You won't be sorry."

"Business or pleasure?"

"Tonight it's just a friendly get-together. You're off-duty. You just happen to drop in for a drink . . . But tomorrow it may be police business. Tonight it's off-the-record, off-the-cuff, and off-the-wall."

"Get out the Scotch," Brodie said. "I'll be right there."

EIGHTEEN

Qwilleran and his guest had finished eating their sandwiches at the bar and were back in the lounge area with mugs of coffee. The Siamese were still hanging around, having been fed crumbs of cheese and crumbles of meatloaf by their new friend. Without warning, Koko's body stiffened and his head jerked toward the back door. Then he scampered to the kitchen to look through the window.

"Koko can see headlights and hear motors when they're half a mile away," Qwilleran explained.

Minutes later, a weird noise came from the parking lot, and he jumped up to investigate. Andrew Brodie was approaching the kitchen door, his bagpipe skirling a Scottish tune.

"Is this the place where they give free drinks to pipers?" he called out as Qwilleran went to meet him.

"Depends how good you are. As a matter of fact, I've always wanted to hear bagpipe music in the barn. The acoustics are phenomenal."

Brodie dropped his bagpipe in the kitchen and swaggered into the lounge area, where a hefty young man with white hair was sitting with one cat on his lap and another on his shoulder. "Aubrey! What are you doing here, for Pete's sake?" he barked. "Playing St. Francis?"

"Hi, Andy. I had a big sandwich and a coupla beers, and now I'm talkin' to the cats. They're friendly. We play Blink. D'you know how to play Blink?"

Qwilleran said, "You guys seem to know each other."

"Cripes, I've known Aubrey ever since he was in high school and I was with the sheriff. I know all his brothers, too. And his mother grows the best flowers in the county! How's she doin', Aubrey?"

"Mom's got some arthritis, but she's doin' all right. She still makes flapjacks better'n Lois's. D'you know Lois's lunchroom is closed?"

"Don't worry. She'll be back in business again. She's always threatening to close . . . Who are your two friends?"

"This one's Yum Yum, and this one's Koko. He wants to tickle my ears with his whiskers."

Qwilleran said to Brodie, "Make yourself comfortable. Have some cheese. Aubrey was telling me an interesting story. As an old friend of the family, you ought to hear it."

Turning to the young man, the off-duty chief said, "Aren't you the one that reported the body down by the river?"

"Yeah. I found him in my cabin. That's where I live.

The family used to have five cabins for rent. Now there's only one left, and I live there with my bees. The hives are on the side that gets the sun and not the north wind. They gave me a lot of honey this summer. Did you ever taste my honey? It's darker than most. It has a lot of flavor." He turned to Qwilleran. "You've tasted my honey. Do you think it's got a lot of flavor?"

"It's the best!" said Qwilleran, wondering if Aubrey had forgotten that his bees were gone.

Brodie took a gulp of his drink. "How come this fisherman was renting your cabin last weekend?"

"I knew him a long time. He liked to come up and fish for bass sometimes. I always let him use my cabin, and the old man would let me sleep in the big house. He's in the hospital now. Did you know he's in the hospital, Andy?"

"Yes, I heard he was in a bad way."

"It's the kidneys and pros—pros—"

"Prostate," Qwilleran said.

"When he kicks the bucket, I'm gonna get his Bible. That's what he told me. It's German. I can't read it, but it's got gold edges and gold letters on the cover." He turned to Qwilleran again. "You saw it. Is it real leather?"

"Yes, it's real leather and a very handsome book." Then, to get the story back on track, he asked, "Aubrey, didn't you say your friend spent his honeymoon in your cabin, some years back?"

"Yeah. He married a nice lady, but she di'n't like fly-fishin', so she never come up again. He always come alone. He tied his own flies. He was real good at it. D'you like fly-fishin', Andy?"

"Can't say that I do. Had your friend ever had trouble with the bees before?"

Aubrey shook his head solemnly, and Qwilleran re-

minded him, "Didn't you mention that he'd been drinking heavily Saturday night? From what I've learned of
honeybees, that might have antagonized them . . . Tell
Andy how you met this guy, Aubrey."

"Yeah." Without a flicker of emotion he related the
story of his near-drowning and the heroic act that saved
his life. "Vic always said I owed him one for saving my
life. That's why I always let him use my cabin for free
anytime he wanted. His name was Victor, but I called him
Vic. He'd call up from Down Below and say, 'How's
about usin' your shanty for a coupla days, Big Boy?' He
always called me Big Boy. He'd fly up here, and I'd pick
him up at the airport. He'd do some fishin' and I'd do my
chores, and we'd eat his catch for supper, and I'd boil
some turnips. I make 'em like my mom does—mashed
with butter and salt and pepper." He turned to Qwilleran.
"D'you like turnips?"

"No!" was the vehement reply.

"You'd like 'em mashed with butter and salt and—"

Brodie interrupted. "What did Vic do for a living?"

"Electronics. That's what I wanted to do, but I di'n't
get a chance. I hadda come home."

"Another Scotch, Andy?" Qwilleran asked. "How
about you, Big Boy? Some more coffee? Then tell us
about seeing Vic's wife at the Black Bear Café a couple
of weeks ago."

"Yeah. They weren't married anymore. She got a di-
vorce. I don't know why. She was a nice lady. I saw her
at the Black Bear. She was with some man. Her hair was
different, but I could tell it was her. She di'n't see me.
When Vic called me long distance next time, I told him.
He was surprised. I knew he'd be surprised. Coupla days
after, he called me up again. I like gettin' long-distance

calls, don't you?" He looked at his two listeners, who
nodded. "He told me to meet him at the airport."

"But at Lockmaster, not Mooseville," Qwilleran said
with a significant glance at Brodie.

"Yeah. Lockmaster. Nice airport. Bigger'n ours.
Takes longer to get there, but I di'n't care. He was my
best friend. I owed him one. That's what Vic always
said. He was kinda quiet when I picked him up. He said
he still loved his wife—I forget her name—and he
wanted to make up. He had a birthday present for her.
He said he paid a lotta money for it. It was all wrapped
in silver paper and fancy ribbons. He said it would be a
big surprise."

"Damn right it was a big surprise," Brodie muttered.

"Go on, Aubrey," Qwilleran encouraged.

"Next day, he borrowed my truck and drove around.
Don't know where he went, but he put a lotta miles on
it. I hadda buy gas. Come afternoon, I drove him to the
hotel so he could leave the present and a bunch of flowers he bought somewheres. Then I drove him back to
Lockmaster."

Brodie asked, "When did you find out the birthday
present was a bomb?"

"Goin' to the airport. I di'n't know what to think. I
di'n't know what to say. I asked him why. He said he
loved her and di'n't want nobody else to get her. He told
me to keep my mouth shut or I'd be arrested. He said I
hadda buy a paper and see what they printed about it. I
hadda cut it out and send it to him. I wanted to call him
long distance, but he said no. I di'n't feel good about it,
but . . . I owed him one."

"How did you feel when you learned the bomb killed
the housekeeper?"

"I felt sick. She was Lenny's girl friend—Lenny Inchpot. They were gonna get married." Aubrey jumped up. "I hafta go outside a minute."

"There's a bathroom right off the kitchen," Qwilleran said, but Aubrey had rushed out.

Brodie said, "I hope he's not gonna steal my car and go fugitive."

"He'll be back. He's accustomed to outdoor plumbing."

"Can we believe this story?"

"Wait till you hear the rest of it, Andy. It fits together like a jigsaw puzzle: mystery woman in room 203—battered wife with scarred face—divorced and trying to escape a stalking ex-husband—coming to this remote town for refuge—never thinking she'd be recognized. That's where she made her mistake."

"And he made his mistake by buying flowers; he killed the wrong woman," Brodie said grimly. "Aubrey seems to enjoy telling the story."

"It's doing him good. A few hours ago he was in a suicidal depression. Now he's blabbing like a guest on a TV talk show with an audience of millions. I think he likes the attention. He's lived a lonely life since getting out of the Navy."

"Strange guy. Strange situation."

When Aubrey returned, he said he had walked around the barn; he'd never seen a round barn before. Qwilleran offered him more coffee and said, "Tell us how Vic came up again the next weekend."

"Yeah. I picked him up in Lockmaster again. He said two people described him to the police—that's what it said in the paper. He wanted to know if I could get at the old man's guns."

"How did he know about them?"

"He seen 'em the week before—and the Bible—and

the cuckoo clock. He liked the clock. Did you ever see a cuckoo clock, Andy?"

"My mother-in-law has one," the chief said gruffly.

"Okay," Qwilleran said. "Tell us about the handgun."

"Yeah. Vic took one and loaded it, and I drove him to the flower shop on Main Street. He wanted to go there. Wasn't nobody around. They was all at the fireworks. When he come out, I wanted to stay and watch the fireworks, but he wanted to get outa there. That's when he told me I hadda get rid of the gun or I'd be arrested. I di'n't know what to do."

"Whose idea was it to hide it in a turkey?"

"We talked about it. I hadda go to work at midnight. They hadda get a shipment ready for Down Below. Vic said it'd be funny if somebody bought a turkey and found a gun in it."

"Very funny," Brodie growled.

"When I come home from work, I hadda get some sleep. I dunno what Vic did, but he had it all figgered out. He said we hadda get the hotel clerk. That meant Lenny. We hadda hide in the woods and pick him off with a rifle when the bikers went by. The paper printed Lenny's number, and there was a map. Then he said it was my turn to do it because I'm a good shot with a rifle. He was drinkin' whiskey, and I thought he di'n't mean it, but he did. I said I couldn't kill anybody, and he said I hadda do it."

"Because you owed him one," Brodie put in.

"Yeah. I didn't know what to do. I got all hot and sticky, so I went down and talked to my bees. When I come back, the whiskey bottle was empty and he was workin' on the old man's schnapps. Pretty soon he was dead drunk. I hadda lug him to the cabin in my truck and dump him in the bed. There was a quilt that my mom made—red stars and green circles—but he had the cold shakes, so I got him the old man's heavy German blanket. He won't need it no more. He's gonna kick the bucket."

"Did the blanket help?" Qwilleran asked, urging him on.

"I dunno. He'd been sick, and the cabin stunk. I opened a window and got outa there."

"And the next morning?"

"He di'n't come up for cornflakes, so I went to the cabin, and he was dead. His hands and face was all swelled up. I ran outa the cabin and cried. I cried because I wouldn't hafta shoot Lenny."

His two listeners looked at each other. Brodie said, "If you had shot Lenny, you'd be the next victim. Vic would steal your truck and disappear. Nobody but you knew he was here, and nobody but you knew *why* he was here. You can thank your bees for what they did."

"They're gone," Aubrey said. "I smoked 'em out."

"You can hive another wild swarm," said Qwilleran, displaying his recently acquired knowledge.

"Yeah. I know where there's some in an old tree."

"And now I'll play you a tune before I go home," Brodie said. He carried his bagpipe to the top balcony and then spiraled down the ramp at a slow rolling gait as he piped "Amazing Grace." The bagpipe wailed like a banshee, the sound bouncing off the vast interior. Koko howled, and Yum Yum buried her ears in Aubrey's armpit.

When Qwilleran accompanied Brodie to the parking lot, the chief said, "I remember that kid when he was in high school and played football and worked the fishing fleet on weekends. He was a helluva rifle shot. He sure changed, and now he's got himself in a pickle, but when he makes his statement to the prosecutor, it'll wrap up the whole damn case."

"He'll never be charged—under the circumstances," Qwilleran predicted. "It's a clear-cut case of exploitation and coercion. I'm calling George Barter in the morning. He's handled other sensitive legal matters for me, and we're on the same wavelength . . . Thanks for coming over, Andy."

"Glad to see this nasty business come to a head." Brodie stepped into his car and then rolled down the window. "Say, how much was your smart cat involved in this case?"

"Well . . . " Qwilleran said. "More than I thought."

Indoors, Aubrey was on his hands and knees, frolicking with both cats on the Moroccan rug. Yum Yum squirmed deliriously as he pummeled her and spun her around. Koko attacked Aubrey's other hand, wrestled with it, bit it gently, and kicked it with his hind legs. Then the big man rolled on his back, and they climbed all over him. They had never paid so much attention to a stranger.

Qwilleran thought, Do they sense that he needs friends? Or have I been doing it all wrong—too many intellectual pursuits and not enough roughhouse?

He let Aubrey give them their bedtime snack, then sent him up to the guestroom on the second balcony. With the Siamese locked up in their apartment above, Qwilleran settled down for some quiet reading. He was just beginning to feel drowsy when the phone rang, and he heard the brisk, wide-awake night editor of the *Something* saying, "Qwill, this is Dave on the night desk. Sorry to call so late, but there's a long-distance call for you on the other line—from California. It's a woman. She doesn't realize the difference in time zones."

"What's her name?"

"It's a tricky one. I'll spell it. O-n-o-o-s-h."

"Get her number and tell her to hang up. I'll call her immediately."

Within minutes he was talking with Onoosh Dolmathakia.

"Oh, Mr. Qwill! I hear about it!" she said breathlessly. "I see little thing in *USA Today*—man stung to death. He was marry to me. Is too bad I not feel sad. Now I go back to Pickax and start new restaurant with partner. I cook Mediterranean."

"How soon can you get here?" Qwilleran asked.

"We fly. We stay at Hotel Booze."

"Get in touch with me as soon as you arrive." He gave her his phone number and hung up with a sense of satisfaction. Now he would get his stuffed grape leaves.

In the morning he phoned Celia first thing, saying, "I have a houseguest, and I need to rustle up some kind of breakfast. Could you come down here and make pancakes for a couple of starving castaways? Lois has left her customers beached and desperate."

"Sure," she said. "Do you have a griddle?"

"There's a large, oblong stainless-steel thing in the top of the range—is that what you mean? It has pawprints on it, but I'll clean them off. There's plenty of butter and honey here. What do you need to make the pancakes?"

"Don't worry about that. I'll mix the batter here and bring it down there. How soon?"

"Soonest."

Qwilleran went to the second balcony to wake Aubrey. The guest room door was wide open, and the guest had gone. But there were sounds of hilarity on the third balcony; he and the Siamese were having a ball.

Celia arrived with her infectious laugh and bowl of batter, and while she flipped pancakes, Qwilleran phoned the attorney.

The first thing Aubrey said to George Barter when he arrived was: "I'm gonna get me a cat."

NINETEEN

In all, Aubrey Scotten told his story five times: first to Qwilleran, again to Brodie, next to the attorney, then to the prosecutor, and finally to a sympathetic judge at an open court hearing. He spoke with gravity and simplicity. The facts never varied—only the digressions about the cooking of turnips and the quality of Lois's flapjacks. Listeners were spellbound by the man's rambling tale and his ingenuous way of telling it. Onoosh Dolmathakia, the former wife of Victor Greer, made an appearance to corroborate certain details, and Nick Bamba, Aubrey's employer, vouched for his honesty, reliability, and value to the community. No charges were brought against the beekeeper, who was entrusted to the guardianship of his mother.

The "old man" in the case did not appear in court. Gustav Limburger had died, leaving a will in the hands of his Lockmaster attorney. To the surprise and consternation of the locals, his entire estate was bequeathed to a daughter in Germany.

Meanwhile, Wetherby Goode was predicting a severe winter. "We shall have snow, and what will poor robin do then, poor thing?" Merchants reported a run on snow blowers and long johns.

After the first frost nipped the air, Moose County experienced a brief but glorious Indian summer. Polly was preparing to return to the workplace, half-days, and Qwilleran was taking her to Boulder House Inn in Trawnto for a celebratory dinner and overnight.

Trawnto was a quiet lakeside resort with large old summer houses on a bluff. It had been settled in the 1800s by Canadians, ship-wrecked on the rocky shore. They wanted to name their tiny village Toronto, but local officials misunderstood their pronunciation and spelled it T-r-a-w-n-t-o in the county records.

En route to Trawnto on that festive Saturday afternoon, Qwilleran kept glancing at his passenger. "Polly, you look great! Absolutely great!" She was wearing a fuchsia silk blouse with her gray pantsuit, and it gave her face a radiant glow.

"I feel wonderful!" she said. "I'm down to a size fourteen, and I'm in the mood to buy some new clothes. Also, when I return to work, I'm applying to the K Fund for public access computers. I believe we're the only library in the U.S. that still uses a card catalogue exclusively."

"I like card catalogues," he said. "I used to fantasize about being locked up overnight with the card catalogue in the New York Public Library . . . Why don't you also ask the K Fund for some chairs with padded seats?"

Polly said, "I've been reading about Edward Mac-Dowell. He was a very handsome man, with a moustache just like yours. You'd look exactly like him if you'd part your hair in the middle."

"I'll do that," he replied dryly. "I've always wanted to look like a nineteenth-century composer. What else have you been reading?"

"The 'Qwill Pen.' Your column on cheese made me hungry."

"I didn't begin to cover the subject. Do you realize its importance in colloquial speech? *Cheese! What a narrow escape! . . . Cheese it! The cops! . . . Who's the big cheese around here? . . . This is a cheesy hotel!* And there are more that I won't mention."

There was nothing cheesy about the Boulder House Inn. It had been the summer residence of an eccentric quarry-owner, and it was constructed of rough boulders, some as big as bathtubs, piled one on another. Windows were recessed in stone walls two or three feet thick. The floors were giant flagstones, and the staircases were chipped out of rock.

"A house designed for giants," Qwilleran said. "I hope the food is good."

"It's advertised as nouvelle cuisine," Polly said with approval. "I suppose that means light sauces, small portions on large plates, cosseted vegetables, and glamorous fruit desserts."

"Something tells me I should have packed a lunch."

When they checked in, the author of the "Qwill Pen" was greeted as a celebrity, and a hospitable innkeeper conducted them personally to adjoining rooms upstairs.

"I have a four-poster bed!" Polly announced as she unpacked her overnight case.

"I have a refrigerator!" he called back.

"I have a fireplace."

"I have an overstuffed sofa and a chess set."

They spent the afternoon walking on the beach and browsing in shops on the boardwalk, then dressed for dinner and had apéritifs on the stone terrace: dry sherry for her, Squunk water for him.

Although they had talked non-stop during the drive from Pickax, they now lapsed into tranquil silence as they contemplated the turquoise lake, the boundless blue sky with billowing October clouds, and their good fortune in being there together, in good health.

After a while Polly said, "I've missed Koko and Yum Yum."

"They've missed you, too . . . So have I."

"Are you still reading Aristophanes to them?"

"Yes, we're reading *The Frogs*. Their favorite line is *Brekekekex ko-ax ko-ax.*"

"I imagine you read it with amphibian authority," she said.

"Thank you. I did the play in college and still remember some of my lines. The translation we used then was more poetic than the one I'm reading now, but not as humorous. In the comic scene where what's-his-name keeps saying *Lost his smelling salts,* my present translation reads *Lost his bottle of oil,* which somehow seems funnier to me. Don't ask why."

"For the same reason that a plate of sardines is funnier than a slice of bread," she said. "A donkey is funny; a horse is not. Pants are funny; shoes are not."

A large gray cat walked solemnly across the terrace, and Qwilleran said loudly, *"Brekekekex ko-ax ko-ax."*

Other guests looked inquiringly in his direction, but the cat kept walking.

"He doesn't understand frogspeak," Qwilleran said.

"He's hearing-impaired," Polly suggested.

"He's missing a few whiskers."

In the dining room she said she would have an amusing piece of trout. Qwilleran decided on a serious steak.

Then she asked, "Did you ever find out who surrendered Iris Cobb's cookbook?"

"No one has confessed," he replied truthfully but evasively, protecting Madame Fetter's reputation as well as Celia's cover.

"It surprised me that Aubrey Scotten's statement to the court was printed verbatim in the *Something.*"

"Possibly the editors wanted to cool the gossip."

"Why did the bees attack the man? Was it the foul odor?"

"Who knows?" Qwilleran said with a shrug. "Bees are sensitive and intuitive creatures—and even more mysterious than cats."

"Everyone is hoping Aubrey will go back into the honey business."

"He will," Qwilleran said. "I understand his hives have been moved to his mother's farm, and he's found a new swarm of wild honeybees. He'll continue to work at the turkey farm. His mother will feed him well and cut his hair. Aubrey will be all right . . . Too bad Limburger didn't leave him the Bible and the cuckoo clock."

"We were shocked to hear he had a daughter in Germany. What will she do with the hotel?"

"The K Fund is negotiating with the estate for the purchase of the hotel and the house, which will make a good country inn. If the Scottens agree to sell the cabin, the inn property will extend to the river, where the bass-fishing is said to be the best anywhere around."

Accompanying the entrées were tiny brussels sprouts with caraway; spinach and toasted almonds in phyllo pastry; and an herb-flavored soufflé, which Qwilleran pronounced excellent.

"Of course, you know it's turnip," Polly informed him.

"Well, they've done something to it—something underhanded," he said grudgingly. "Do you remember my recent anti-turnip column? I took a lot of flak from readers who are turnip freaks, and someone mailed a large box to me at the office. There was no return address, so the police were notified. There's a way of defusing a bomb with a firehose, you know, so that's what they did. It turned out to be a ten-pound turnip, largest ever grown in Moose County."

The salad course was Bibb lettuce with lemon zest dressing and toasted sesame seeds, garnished with a sliver of Brie.

"Don't eat your cheese," Qwilleran instructed Polly. "It's double-cream. I'll relieve you of it."

"That's so thoughtful of you, dear," she said. "By the way, I saw the video of the cheese party, and the cat-chase is hilarious! What caused Koko's catfit?"

"Your guess is as good as mine." He wanted to tell her about the handgun in the turkey, but there were topics he never discussed with his two best friends. Both Polly and Arch Riker discouraged him from "getting involved" in matters that were police business and not his. There were long hours spent with Polly when Qwilleran had to hold his tongue. Neither could he reveal Koko's uncanny ability to sense wrong-doing and sniff out wrongdoers. The practical librarian looked at him askance, and the cynical publisher suggested he was cracking up.

Over dessert (poached pears stuffed with currants and pistachios and served with cherry coulis), Polly mentioned a subject that emphasized Qwilleran's predicament.

"Lisa Compton is spearheading a program to help battered women," she said. "Apparently there is a great deal of abuse going unreported in Moose County. Remember the wild rumors circulating about the mystery woman? No one dreamed she was a victim, being stalked and threatened by an ex-husband."

Qwilleran huffed into his moustache. Her statement was not true. Koko had sensed the situation. He had tried in his catly way to communicate. He started stalking Yum Yum. He drove her crazy. One might think they were playing games. Cats go through phases; they invent new games and then tire of them. But Koko also developed a sudden interest in *Stalking the Wild Asparagus.* Wild coincidence—or what? Was it a coincidence that Koko lost interest in Euell Gibbons and stopped stalking Yum Yum *after Onoosh revealed her plight in a frantic letter?* Was it a coincidence that Koko howled at the exact moment that Franklin Pickett was shot? Or that he chewed up Lenny's pledge card when the biker was in danger? Or that he campaigned for a ride to the beach on the very afternoon that the mystery woman was trespassing there? And how about the many times Koko pushed *A Taste of Honey* off the bookshelf?

Polly broke into his reverie. "You're pensive, dear."

"I was thinking . . . that these pears could use some chocolate syrup."

"There's a rumor that we're getting a Mediterranean

restaurant. Do you think Pickax is ready for such exotic fare?"

"They'll like it," he predicted, "especially the meatballs in little green kimonos."

After dinner they joined the other guests around a roaring blaze in the stone fireplace and listened to the innkeeper relating the history of the building. During Prohibition it had been headquarters for rum-runners ferrying whiskey from Canada. There were tales of subterranean chambers with sealed doors and Federal agents who mysteriously disappeared. Hollow footsteps were sometimes heard in the night and apparitions hovered outside the windows.

"Pleasant dreams, everyone!" Qwilleran said, standing up. "We're going for a walk in the moonlight."

It was indeed a moonlit night, highlighting the surf that broke on the beach and giving the craggy inn an eerie otherness. Polly was tired, however. It had been an exciting day; she had walked a great deal; she was still in an early-to-bed hospital mode.

They retired to their rooms. Polly left a window open in order to hear the crashing of the surf. Qwilleran, after replacing a 40-watt light bulb with a 70-watt that he always carried in his luggage, sat up reading. It was quiet —unnaturally quiet—in that fortress of massive boulders, until . . . he heard a scream!

He rushed into Polly's room. She was sitting in bed, petrified and speechless. In her bed was a large gray cat.

"Easy, Polly! Easy!" he said soothingly as he grabbed the gray hulk. "It's only Dumbo. He climbed up the side of the building. He was looking for a warm bed." Qwilleran put the cat out on the wide sill and closed the window.

"I was sleeping soundly," Polly said. "It was a terrible

scare—to wake and see that animal in my bed. I'm still shaking."

"Come and sit with me for a while," he said gently. "Curl up on my sofa. Calm down. I'll read to you."

In the breakfast room on Sunday morning, Qwilleran was in a playful mood, and Polly giggled at all his quips. Their waitress had a spectacular hairdo that looked, he muttered to Polly, like a bale of barbed wire. To the young woman he said, with a show of wonder and admiration, "I like your hair! It's different!"

She beamed with pleasure.

"You must have it done by a very good professional."

"No, I do it myself," she said modestly.

"Remarkable! It must take a long time and a great deal of skill and patience."

Polly was suppressing her mirth with difficulty, while kicking him under the table, but the waitress was overwhelmed. She brought extra muffins, extra butter, and extra preserves to their table, as well as an endless supply of coffee.

After another walk on the beach, they checked out. Monday would be Polly's first day at the library after several weeks of medical leave. She wanted to get herself together and switch roles—from convalescent to boss-lady, as the young clerks called her.

On the way home, they stopped at Indian Village. Since apartment leases stipulated no pets, Polly had bought a condominium. It was a two-story unit, and Bootsie would have stairs for exercise and a small screened porch for bird-watching. Under consideration was the possibility of acquiring a companion for him.

As they neared Pickax, both of them enjoying the comfortable silence of a happy couple, Polly startled

Qwilleran by saying, "Qwill, have you been keeping a big secret from me?"

A dozen possibilities flashed through his mind. "What do you mean? Give me a clue."

"Well, there's a woman in Lynette's bridge club who does the bookkeeping for Scottie's Men's Store, and she says you've just been billed for a tailor-made kilt in the Mackintosh tartan."

He gripped the steering wheel and stared stonily ahead. The gossip was true. In a weak moment, when he feared he losing Polly, he had ordered a full Scottish kit to please her—perhaps to speed her recovery. Now she was alive and well, but he winced at the thought of wearing a short pleated "petticoat" with gartered socks and bare knees. "Is this a Congressional investigation?" he asked. "I take the Fifth."

"Oh, Qwill! You're an incorrigible tease!" she said. "Well, anyway, you'll look magnificent in a kilt."

After taking her home and witnessing her emotional reunion with Bootsie (they had been apart for twenty-four hours), Qwilleran drove to the barn, where he was met by two cool, calm, and collected cats. It meant they had breakfasted, and it was too early for dinner pangs. It also meant: no message on the answering machine; no domestic crisis; no gunshot or other incident to report.

"Hi, guys!" he said cheerfully. "How's everything? Did Celia take good care of you?" She had fed them before going to church, according to a note left on the kitchen counter.

Koko acknowledged his greeting with two flicks of the tail, and Yum Yum purred when he asked, "Are you still my little sweetheart?"

After changing into a jumpsuit, Qwilleran settled

down in the library with a mug of coffee and some cheese and crackers.

"Gruyère, anyone?" he asked, expecting a yowl from Koko. When there was no response, he said, "All the more for me! . . . How about some double-cream Brie?" Still there was no reaction. Qwilleran reeled off a list of the world's great cheeses, including goat's-milk feta, but Koko—who had become a cheese gastronome during the Explo—was silent.

What did it mean? He never did anything—hardly anything—without a reason. Abnormal behavior on his part always signified an attempt to communicate information. Now the answers were known; the case was closed; and Qwilleran realized, in retrospect, the meaning of Koko's messages:

The cat had sensed that the evildoer could be identified by a sound like Gruyère, and Brie suggested the unwitting, unwilling accomplice. To a cat's ear Gruyère, Brie, Greer, and Aubrey would be merely sounds, like TREAT or BOOK; to Koko's ear they had significance. If the scientists Down Below ever found out about the psychic cat, they would charter flights to Pickax to test Koko's brain and count his whiskers . . . No way! Qwilleran thought.

Then he slapped his forehead as another possibility occurred to him. "Oh, no!" he said aloud. "Feta . . . Fetter . . . cookbook . . . Iris Cobb . . . meatloaf!" The Siamese had been fond of their former housekeeper, and they missed her special meatloaf, the secret of which . . .

Qwilleran's ruminations were interrupted by a low rumble in Koko's chest, followed by a leap to the bookshelves.

"Okay, we'll have a read. *Brekekekex ko-ax ko-ax!*"

With Koko on the arm of his chair and Yum Yum on his lap, he continued his reading of *The Frogs*.

The dialogue brought back memories. He had played Dionysus in the college production. His mother was living then, and she had attended three nights in a row. He had never forgotten his line: *Who knows if death be life and life be death, and breath be mutton broth, and sleep a sheepskin?* He remembered his costume, too: heavy robes befitting an Olympian god, but they were hot under the lights, and he thought he would drown in his own perspiration. That was a long time ago. Now he was living in a barn and reading *The Frogs* to an audience of two cats.

When he reached his favorite line, he found the translation quite different from the one he had known. He read it seriously, with meaningful pauses: *"Who knows whether living is dying . . . and breathing is eating . . . and sleeping is a wool blanket?"*

"Yow!" said Koko with equal seriousness.

Qwilleran felt a tingle on his upper lip as he guessed the answer to a puzzling question: Why did the bees attack Victor Greer? It was the wool blanket, of course! The old man's heavy woolen blanket from Germany! Did Aubrey realize what he was doing? Did he know the blanket was wool? In the confusion of the situation, did he forget that bees are antagonized by wool? . . . Or did Aubrey purposely take the wool blanket to the cabin? Later, when he found the body, he wept because, as he said, he would not have to shoot Lenny.

"How about that, Koko? Do you have an opinion?"

The cat was sitting in a tall, stately pose on the arm of the chair. He swayed slightly. His blue eyes were large and fathomless.

It was a strange winter in Moose County, 400 miles north of everywhere. First, there was disagreement about the long-range weather forecast. The weatherman at the local radio station predicted a winter of zero temperature, daily snow, minus-sixty windchill, and paralyzing blizzards—in other words: normal. On the other hand, farmers and woodsman who observed the behavior of the fuzzy caterpillars insisted the winter would be mild. Bad news!

No one wanted a mild winter. Merchants had invested in large inventories of snowblowers, antifreeze, snowshoes, and long johns. The farmers themselves needed a heavy snow cover to insure a good summer crop. Dog-sledders and icefishermen stood to lose a whole season of wholesome outdoor sport. As for the First Annual Ice Festival, it was doomed. All that—plus the unthinkable possibility of a green Christmas!

Throughout November, traditionally a month of natural disasters, the weather was disappointingly good, and the natives cursed the fuzzy caterpillars. Then . . . suddenly, in mid-December, temperatures plummeted and a few inches of no-melt snow started to fall every day. In downtown Pickax, the county seat, the Department of Public Works plows threw up the usual eight-foot walls of snow along curbs and around parking lots. Young people did their Christmas shopping on cross-country skis, and sleigh bells could be heard on Main Street. Best of all, the schools closed twice during the month because of blizzard conditions.

The weather was only the first strange happening of the winter, however. In late December, an outbreak of petty larceny dampened the holiday spirit in Pickax. Trivial items began to disappear from cars and public places, prompting the local newspaper to run an editorial:

PLAY SAFE! LOCK UP! BE ALERT!

You leave a video on the seat of your car while paying for self-serve gas. You never see it again.

You forget your gloves in the post office. Minutes later, they're gone.

You hang your sun-glare glasses on a supermarket cart while you select oranges. The glasses disappear.

Who is to blame? Mischievous kids? Gremlins? Your failing memory? The time has come to stop searching for excuses and start playing safe. In Moose County we're foolishly lax about security. We must learn to lock our cars . . . put valuables in the trunk . . . keep an eye on belongings . . . stay alert!

Some say the incidents are minor, and the pilfering is a temporary nuisance like Mosquito Week in spring. If that's what you think, listen to our police chief, Andrew Brodie, who says, "A community that tolerates minor violations leaves the door open for major crimes."

Natives of Moose County were a stubborn, independent breed descended from early pioneers, and it would take more than an editorial in the *Moose County Something* to change their ways. Yet there was one prominent citizen who applauded the police chief's maxim.

Jim Qwilleran was not a native but a transplant from Down Below, as the locals called the metropolitan cities to the south. Surprising circumstances had brought him to Pickax (population 3,000), and he was surprisingly content with small-town life.

Qwilleran was a tall, well-built, middle-aged man with a luxuriant pepper-and-salt moustache and hair graying at the temples. If asked, he would say that he perceived himself as:

A journalist, semi-retired.

A former crime reporter and author of a book on urban crime.

Writer of a twice-weekly column for the *Something*.

Devoted friend of Polly Duncan, head of the Pickax Public Library.

Protector and slave of two Siamese cats.

Fairly agreeable person blessed with many friends.

All of that would be true . . . He would not perceive himself, however, as the richest man in the northeast central United States, but that, too, would be true.

An enormous inheritance, the Klingenschoen fortune, had brought Qwilleran to this remote region. Yet, he was uncomfortable with money—its trappings as well as its responsibilities—and he immediately consigned his billions to philanthropic purposes. For several years, the Klingenschoen Foundation had been managed by a Chicago think tank, with little or no attention from James Mackintosh Qwilleran.

It was not only this generous gesture that caused him to be esteemed in Moose County. Admirers cited his entertaining column, "Straight from the Qwill Pen" . . . his amiable disposition and sense of humor . . . his lack of pretension . . . his sympathetic way of listening . . . and, of course, his magnificent moustache. Its drooping contours, together with his brooding eyes, gave him a look of melancholy that made people wonder about his past. Actually, there was more to that moustache than met the eye.

On the morning of December 23, Qwilleran said good-bye to the Siamese and gave instructions for their deportment in his absence. The more intelligently one talks to cats, he believed, the smarter they become. Their deep blue eyes gazed at him soberly. Did they know what he was saying? Or were they waiting patiently for him to leave so they could start their morning nap?

He was setting out to do his Christmas shopping, but first he had to hand in his copy at the newspaper office: a thousand words on Santa Claus for the "Qwill Pen." It was hardly a newsworthy topic, but he had a columnist's knack of making it sound fresh.

The premises of the *Moose County Something* were always devoid of seasonal decorations, leaving such frivolities to stores and restaurants. Qwilleran was surprised, therefore, to see a small decorated tree on a file cabinet in the publisher's office. Arch Riker, his lifelong friend and fellow journalist, had followed him to Pickax to be publisher and editor-in-chief of the new backwoods paper. A paunchy, ruddy-faced man with thinning hair, he sat in a high-backed executive chair and looked happy. Not only had he realized his dream of running his own newspaper; he had married the plump and congenial woman who wrote the food page.

"Mildred and I are expecting you and Polly to have Christmas dinner with us," he reminded Qwilleran.

"Turkey, I hope," he replied, thinking of leftovers for his housemates. "What's that tree on your file cabinet?"

"It was Wilfred's idea," Riker said almost apologetically. "He made the ornaments with newsprint and gold spray."

Wilfred Sugbury was secretary to the executives—a quiet, hardworking young man who had not only amazed the staff by winning a seventy-mile bike race but was now taking an origami course at the community college. Qwilleran, on his way out, complimented Wilfred on his handiwork.

"I'd be glad to make one for you, Mr. Q," he said.

"It wouldn't last five minutes, Wilfred. The cats would reduce it to confetti. They have no appreciation of art. Thanks just the same."

To fortify himself for the task of gift-shopping, Qwilleran drove to Lois's Luncheonette, a primitive side-street hole-in-the-wall that had been serving comfort food to downtown workers and shoppers for thirty years. Lois Inchpot was an imposing woman who dispensed pancakes and opinions with the authority of a celebrity. Indeed, the city had recently celebrated Lois Inchpot Day, by mayoral proclamation.

When Qwilleran entered, she was banging the old-fashioned cash register and holding forth in a throaty voice: "If we'd had a mild winter, like the caterpillars said, we'd be swamped with bugs next summer! . . . Hi, Mr. Q! Come on in! Sit anywhere that ain't sticky. My customers got bad aim with the syrup bottle."

"How's Lenny?" Qwilleran asked. Her son had been hurt in an explosion.

"That boy of mine!" she said proudly. "Nothin' stops him! He has mornin' classes at the college, and then he's found himself a swell part-time job, managin' the club-house at Indian Village. He gave you as a reference, Mr. Q. Hope you don't mind."

"He's going to be a workaholic like his mother."

"Better'n takin' after his father! . . . Done your Christmas shoppin', Mr. Q?"

"Don't rush me, Lois. It's only the twenty-third."

The first gift he purchased was a bottle of Scotch. He carried it in a brown paper bag under his folded jacket when he climbed the stairs to police headquarters at city hall. He was a frequent visitor, and the sergeant at the desk jerked his head toward the inner office, saying, "He's in." The chief was visible through a glass parti-tion, hunched over the computer that he earnestly hated.

Brodie was a tough cop who resented civilian interfer-ence, and yet he had learned to appreciate the news-man's tips and opinions that sometimes helped crack a case. On the job he had old-fashioned ideas of law and order and a gruff manner to match. Off duty, he was a genial Scot who played the bagpipe and strutted in a kilt at civic functions.

Qwilleran, placing his jacket carefully on a chairseat and sliding in another, said, "I see you got your name in the paper again, Andy. Who's your press agent? Planning to run for mayor? I'll campaign for you."

With a fierce scowl usually reserved for the computer, Brodie shot back, "If I had an overgrown moustache like yours, I'd get my picture in the paper, too. What's on your mind?"

"I want to know if you believe what you said in the paper."

"It's a known fact! Let the hoods urinate in public and—next thing you know—they're spray-painting the courthouse, and after that they're pushing drugs, and then robbing banks, and then killing cops."

"Any suspects in the pilfering?"

The chief leaned back in his chair and folded his arms, "Could be punks from Chipmunk. Could be a roving gang from Lockmaster. Could be the kids that hang around George Breze's dump. We're investigating."

"Do you see any pattern developing? There should be a pattern by now."

"Well, for one thing, there's a pattern in what they don't do. They don't steal Social-Security checks from mailboxes, or rip out car radios, or break into doctors' offices. It's all piddlin' stuff, so far. Another thing: There's no two incidents alike, and locations are scattered. It always happens after dark, too. They avoid shoplifting in stores with bright lights and wide-awake clerks."

Qwilleran said, "I've been thinking it could be a game, like a treasure hunt—perhaps initiation rites for a juvenile cult."

"We've talked to school principals and Dr. Prelligate at the college. They say there's no sign of suspicious activity."

"They'd be the last to know," Qwilleran muttered.

"There's another possibility. I predicted something like this after the financial bust in Sawdust City. The town's had a lot of hardship cases this winter, and it's rough to be hard-up at Christmas time, especially if you've got kids."

"But the organized charities have raised record sums for the Christmas Fund, and the K Foundation is matching their efforts, dollar for dollar."

"I know, but some cases always fall through the cracks, or they panic and try to take things in their own hands." He indulged in a bitter chuckle. "Perhaps they hit on the secret: How to do Christmas shopping without money and without crowds."

Qwilleran said, "If the thefts are scattered, as you say, someone's buying a lot of gas to drive around and swipe trivial items. It must be a group effort."

Brodie threw up his hands. "The whole thing's crazy!"

"Okay, let me add an incident to your list. This is the reason I'm here." Qwilleran paused until he had the man's curiosity aroused. "We all know the Old Stone Church is collecting warm clothing for needy families. There's a drop-off box behind the building. Every Wednesday the volunteers show up for sorting and mending. I told him I'd drop off a bundle Tuesday night—which I did—a plastic bag full of things in good condition: jackets, sweaters, gloves, etc. But when they opened the box the next morning, it wasn't there. They phoned me to see if I'd forgotten."

The chief grunted. "No lock on the box?"

"Who thinks about locks in this neck of the woods? That was the thrust of our editorial! We nagged our readers into buckling up; now we'll nag them into locking up."

Brodie chuckled again. "If you spot a guy walking around town in your rags, follow him and take his picture."

"Sure. And ask for his name and address."

"My old grandmother in Scotland could tail a thief with scissors, a piece of string, and a witch's chant. Too bad she died before I got into law enforcement." Then he grinned. "Why don't you assign your smart cat to the case?" The chief was the only person in the north country who knew about the remarkable talents of Qwilleran's male Siamese. The cat did indeed have gifts that set him apart, and Qwilleran tried to conceal the fact, for various reasons. Yet it had leaked to Brodie from the source Down Below, and now the two men bantered about "that smart cat" whose highly developed senses gave him an edge over most humans.

"Koko doesn't accept assignments," Qwilleran said with a straight face. "He conducts his own investigations. Right now he has a gang of wild rabbits under surveillance." Then he added in a serious tone, "But last night, Andy, he jumped on my bookshelf and knocked down a Russian novel titled *The Thief*. Was that a coincidence, or what?"

"Does he read Russian?" Brodie asked, only half in jest.

"Mine is an English translation."

The chief grunted ambiguously and changed the sub-
I hear you and your smart cat aren't living in the
winter. How come?" There was disappoint-
question. He often visited the converted

apple barn after hours, dropping in for a nightcap and some shoptalk. Qwilleran, though not a drinker himself, stocked the best brands for his guests.

"It's like this, Andy," he explained. "With four stories of wide-open space, it's impossible to heat evenly. The top balcony is like a sauna while the main floor is chilly. The cats used to go to the top level to get warm, and they'd end up half-cooked. They were so groggy from the heat, they couldn't walk straight. So I bought a condo in Indian Village for the cold months. I can rent it to vacationers in summer. It's nowhere near the size of the barn, of course, but it's adequate, and the county snowplows keep the access road open, for the simple reason that so many politicos live out there . . . By the way, I had my condo furnished by your talented daughter."

The chief nodded a grudging acknowledgment of the family compliment. In spite of Fran Brodie's success as an interior designer, her father considered it a frivolous choice of career.

Standing up and presenting the brown paper bag, Qwilleran said, "Here's a wee dram of Christmas cheer, Andy. See you after the holidays."